TOP OF HER GAME

Praise for M. Ullrich

Love at Last Call

Love at Last Call is "a very well written slow-burn romance. Another great book by M. Ullrich."—*LezReviewBooks*

"[I]f you enjoy opposites attract romances—especially ones set in bars—you'll love this book! I'll definitely be looking up the rest of the author's work!"—*Llama Reads Books*

Love at Last Call is "exciting, addictive (I was up all night reading it) and still gave me all the major swoon moments I've come to love from this author. Can I give it more than five stars?"—*Les Rêveur*

"This book was like a well-crafted cocktail—not too sweet, not too bitter, and left me with a warm feeling in my body."—*Love in Panels*

"*Love at Last Call* is M. Ullrich's fifth full-length novel and it's truly excellent. The writing is smooth and engaging, with perfect pacing and a plot that's sure to please fans of contemporary romance. If you're looking for a book to sink into, have some fun, and get away from it all, you'll want to pick this one up."—*Lambda Literary*

Against All Odds

"*Against All Odds* by Kris Bryant, Maggie Cummings, and M. Ullrich is an emotional and captivating story about being able to face a tragedy head-on and move on with your life, learning to appreciate the simple things we take for granted and finding love where you least expect it."—*The Lesbian Review*

Time Will Tell

"I adored the romance in this. I got emotional at times and felt like they fit together very well. They really brought out the best in each other and they had a lot of chemistry. I really did care whether or not they were together in the end…It was a very enjoyable read and definitely one I'd recommend."—*Cats and Paperbacks*

"*Time Will Tell* is not your run of the mill romance. I found it dark, intense, unexpected. It is also beautifully romantic and sexy and tells of a love that is for all time. I really enjoyed it."—*Kitty Kat's Book Review Blog*

"M. Ullrich just keeps knocking them out of the park and I think she's currently the one to watch in lesbian romantic fiction."
—*Les Rêveur*

Fake It till You Make It

"M. Ullrich's books have a uniqueness that we don't always see in this particular genre. Her stories go a bit outside the box and they do it in the best possible way. *Fake It till You Make It* is no exception."—*The Romantic Reader Blog*

"M. Ullrich's *Fake It till You Make It* just clarifies why she is one of my favorite authors. The storyline was tight, the characters brought emotion and made me feel like I was living the story with them, and best of all, I had fun reading every word."—*Les Rêveur*

Life in Death

"M. Ullrich sent me on a emotional roller coaster…But most of all I felt absolute joy knowing that in times of darkness you can still love the one you're meant to be with. It was a story of hope, tragedy, and above all, love."—*Les Rêveur*

Life in Death "is a well written book, the characters have depth and are complex, they become friends and you cannot help but hope that Marty and Suzanne can find a way back to each other. There aren't many books that I know from one read that I will want to read time and time again, but this is one of them."—*Sapphic Reviews*

Fortunate Sum

"M. Ullrich has written one book. That one book is *Fortunate Sum*. For this to be Ullrich's first book, well, that is just stunning. Stunning in the fact that this book is so very good, it was a fantastic read."—*The Romantic Reader Blog*

By the Author

Fortunate Sum

Life in Death

Fake It till You Make It

Time Will Tell

Love at Last Call

Pretending in Paradise

Top of Her Game

Against All Odds
(with Kris Bryant and Maggie Cummings)

The Boss of Her: Office Romance Novellas
(with Julie Cannon and Aurora Rey)

Visit us at www.boldstrokesbooks.com

TOP OF HER GAME

by

M. Ullrich

2019

TOP OF HER GAME
© 2019 BY M. ULLRICH. ALL RIGHTS RESERVED.

ISBN 13: 978-1-63555-500-4

THIS TRADE PAPERBACK ORIGINAL IS PUBLISHED BY
BOLD STROKES BOOKS, INC.
P.O. BOX 249
VALLEY FALLS, NY 12185

FIRST EDITION: OCTOBER 2019

CREDITS
EDITORS: JERRY WHEELER AND RUTH STERNGLANTZ
PRODUCTION DESIGN: STACIA SEAMAN
COVER DESIGN BY TAMMY SEIDICK

Acknowledgments

I always start by thanking Radclyffe and Sandy because without them I wouldn't be here and wouldn't have had the opportunity to share my stories with you all. Everyone at Bold Strokes Books continues to help, support, and encourage in ways that amaze me. My editor, Jerry Wheeler, deserves all the praise in the world. He managed to take a manuscript with many lumps and bumps and walk me (a panicking mess) through smoothing it out. Jerry makes me a better writer with every book.

Thank you to my wonderful friends and found family. Some of you are fellow writers who listen when I need to gripe and give me a slap across the face (via text) when I start to panic. Some of you are not writers, but you still understand when I disappear for months at a time and celebrate with me when I finally get to see sunlight again. I love and cherish each and every one of you; you know who you are.

Maggie, thank you a million times for helping me see the blessing in disguise and getting me to write this book when I did. I love ya, Nush. *shopping cart emoji*

Quick shout-out to Sheila providing me with the word "merriment" when I needed it most. Dare I say that you could be this book's MVP?

Heather, my love, I can never thank you enough. I am truly spoiled. You support me, you exhaust yourself and your creativity when you work on swag or my website, you help me work through my plots, and you're beautiful to boot! I could've never gotten this far without you and your weekend breakfasts.

Women's soccer is a beautiful sport filled with passion, finesse, and fierceness. Many of the players fight for equality and aren't afraid to share their story in hopes of bettering the world. I wish I could shake each player's hand and thank them for all they do, but since I can't, I'll say a thank you here. We can all learn from them and fight to make a change. World Champions, baby!

To every reader: thank you for your support, whether you've read every book of mine or this is your first. I appreciate every single one of you more than I could ever put into words on this page. I hope you enjoy reading this story as much as I enjoyed writing it. (I'm looking at you, Tiffany. Maybe you'll think it's better than okay?)

For Heather,
You make my heart beat faster
than a game that's come down to penalty kicks.

CHAPTER ONE

People who could eat on a nervous stomach were Kenzie Shaw's heroes. Jitters and anxiety killed her appetite. She was supposed to sit at a table of strangers, act like she belonged, and eat a meal like she enjoyed it. *Impossible.* Kenzie took a deep breath and pulled down the visor to check her appearance in the car's mirror. A stack of receipts rained down on her lap. Kenzie tossed them onto the passenger seat and shook her head at her mother's tendency to hoard. She flipped open the mirror and checked that her eye makeup was even, and her wavy red hair was under control. Kenzie frowned. One out of two wasn't bad, she thought as she smoothed her palms over her long thick hair.

She got out of the car and made sure she locked it before walking toward the restaurant. Her first meeting with her new team was happening at Papa Vinnie's, an Italian place. It wasn't quite a chain, but more than a handful of these were scattered throughout the state. A brisk wind whipped through her puffy nylon jacket. February in New Jersey wasn't much different than February in Pennsylvania, but Kenzie wasn't going home to the safety of her childhood bedroom, or a cup of tea and pep talk from her father. Thankfully, Louis Shaw had already given Kenzie enough wise words to carry with her.

She rehearsed her greeting, but her voice was so quiet it got lost in the wind. "Hi, I'm Kenzie Shaw. I'm honored to be playing for the Hurricanes and can't wait to get started." She shook out her hands and stared at the front door. Her nerves were starting to get the best of her. She recalled the words her father repeated to her like a mantra: *I'm an all-star, and your team is better because I'm part of it.*

A man rushed around Kenzie and grabbed the door handle. "Excuse me," he said, turning to her briefly. He did a double take. "Hey, Kenzie Shaw."

Kenzie recognized him from the day of her draft. He looked a little different now, bundled up for cold weather and with a short beard. Her brain short-circuited. "Hi, I'm Kenzie Shaw."

He eyed her strangely. "Yeah, I know." He laughed as he pulled a thick glove off his hand. "Brett McEnroe. We met briefly during the trade, but that day was crazy. I'm not surprised you don't remember me."

Kenzie shook his hand and dreamed of time travel as a way to erase every embarrassing moment from her life. "Right—Brett. I'm sorry. I'm a little nervous to meet everyone."

"Me, too. This is my first year as head coach, and I want everyone to feel comfortable. The team dinner was my idea, actually," he said. "The moment I signed on, I wanted this team to feel like a family. There's something to be said for teams that are close-knit."

"I'm happy to formally meet you, Brett." She let him open the door for her. "Everyone's coming tonight?" She filed through the roster in her head, nineteen women she'd be playing, fighting, and practically living alongside for the next nine months. She knew a few of them, but most faces were new. One face stood out, much more vivid than the rest.

"Yes," Brett said after greeting the hostess.

Kenzie's heart skipped a beat.

"Oh, except Sutton Flores and Tara Best. They're finishing up their national team duty today and will join us for fitness assessments and training tomorrow."

Kenzie's heart tripped over its next beat and sank.

Brett looked around the restaurant and back to Kenzie with a large smile. "Looks like we're the first ones here."

Kenzie had a knack for showing up early, but she really hated herself for it in situations like this. Waiting with Brett made her want to squirm, as did the awkward trickle of teammates coming in around her. Thirty-three minutes later, she was between Meredith and Erin, two defenders who had been with the Jersey Hurricanes for two seasons. They were eating their food with gusto.

"So, Kenzie, you graduated from Penn State last year. How does it feel to win a college championship?" Meredith appeared to be genuinely interested.

Kenzie considered her words carefully while she chewed a small mouthful of pasta. "Invigorating and exhausting," she said with a laugh. "Trying to balance my focus between school and soccer wore me down. I took extra credits every semester so I could graduate in the winter instead of spring. I'm happy to finally be able to focus solely on soccer."

"What did you go to school for?"

Kenzie wiped her mouth and looked around the table. No one else was listening to their conversation, which made her feel a little less under the microscope. "I majored in communications." The silence that followed felt awkward, and she rushed to add, "I'm sure you all know how hard it is to balance everything."

"I didn't go to college," Meredith said. "I joined the league right after high school."

"Meredith is one of the few," Erin said. She took a long sip of her soda. "Her, Chichima, and Isabella all skipped college to go pro. If you've ever watched one of our games, I'm sure you know. Commentators love dwelling on that fact." Erin rolled her eyes.

Kenzie snickered. "I've definitely noticed that."

Erin cleared her throat. "Meredith Langley is down, and the staff has run onto the field to check her for a concussion," she said in her best commentator voice. "The league has really increased their concussion protocol, and did you know Langley didn't go to college?"

Kenzie laughed louder.

Meredith sighed. "Every time."

Brett stood up at the opposite end of the long table, holding his water glass. "Everyone," he said. "Thank you all for indulging me and showing up tonight. I was honored to be your assistant coach last season, and I still can't believe I get to be your head coach this season."

Meredith leaned across Kenzie and said, "Because Tim got fired."

Erin shushed her.

Kenzie's curiosity was piqued, but she kept her focus on Brett.

"I want to go around the table and have everyone introduce themselves. We have seven new players this season, and I want them to feel welcome."

Kenzie started shaking her head. She tried to shake away the memories of middle school and being the new kid in class.

"We're missing two players, but they'll be sure to introduce themselves during training tomorrow."

"I can be Sutton," someone close to Brett said. Kenzie craned her neck to see Taylor Barrell sitting with her hand up. She stood and cleared her throat. "Hey, I'm Sutton Flores, but everyone calls me Flo."

Erin laughed. "*No* one calls her that."

Taylor waved her off. "The only thing I'm better at than soccer is picking up women."

Kenzie swallowed hard, and Erin's laughter grew louder beside her.

Brett put his hand on Taylor's shoulder and encouraged her to sit down. "Thank you, Taylor. Moving on. Kenzie, I saw you first tonight, so let's start with you. Tell us about yourself."

She rubbed her damp palms on her jeans and took a deep breath. Her voice shook the moment she started to speak. "I'm Kenzie Shaw, and I'm a Penn State graduate. I was raised in Pennsylvania, but I was born in New Jersey. Um, and I'm really excited to be here."

Brett looked expectant for a moment before clapping his hands together. "Kenzie was also our first draft pick and crowned Penn State's MVP after taking home the championship trophy last year."

Kenzie's cheeks felt like they were on fire. Everyone's attention was on her, and she only hoped her display of modesty would overpower Brett's unnecessary addition to her short biography. She wanted to be welcomed into the fold, not looked at as a braggart.

Lacey Sheridan leaned across the table and held out her glass for Kenzie to toast with. "I, for one, am very happy to have you back on my team."

Kenzie tapped her glass to Lacey's and smiled. "I must admit, I was happy to be drafted by a team with a few familiar faces." She nodded to the two other women she had played a couple of seasons with. They had great chemistry on the field and got along well off the field, too. She and Chiara Bornemann even held the Penn State record for set piece connections. She smiled at Chiara down the table. "Chiara, think we can still connect like we used to?"

Chiara flashed a brilliant smile. "Me to you to goal. You can count on it."

Kenzie remembered their friendship, and suddenly the idea of playing with so many new people wasn't as frightening. She'd been the rookie before and had no trouble proving herself. She felt silly for her earlier nerves.

"Exactly how much history is between you two?" Erin said.

Kenzie jumped back slightly and looked away from Chiara. "We played together for two seasons. We have a very similar play style even though we're in different positions."

"And how many *positions* did you get her in?"

Kenzie frowned. The question confused her. She had always

played up front as a striker, and Chiara was known as one of the best defenders to come out of Penn State. If Erin had played with Chiara for a few seasons now, why would she ask about Kenzie getting her in other positions…

Recognition dawned.

"Oh. No," she said a little too loudly. "Never anything like that. Our chemistry was strictly professional."

"I feel something between the two of you." Erin ripped a piece of bread in half and wiped marinara sauce off her plate. She took a bite and chewed. "She was looking at you like she's seen you naked," Erin said, pointing the crust in Chiara's direction.

"She has," Kenzie said honestly. "The same way everyone on my team has seen me naked."

Erin eyed her while she finished the last bite. "Fine. I'll drop this. For now."

Kenzie laughed, but she wasn't entirely ready to be picked on. She returned her attention to the introductions, relieved to see more than one or two rookies acting as nervous as she felt.

At the end of dinner, Brett signed the check and thanked everyone for coming. He stood and put his jacket on, then put his hand up to get everyone's attention. "This season will be our best yet, and I'm not saying that as a new coach or as an empty sentiment to get you all fired up."

"That's good, because your delivery was a little flat." Taylor reached over and slapped his shoulder.

"I really mean it. Our roster is the best we've had, and something in my gut is telling me we're going to win it all this year. Kansas City better watch their backs."

Kenzie puffed out her chest. She might have been a rookie, but she was very familiar with the rivalry between New Jersey and Kansas City. If the Hurricanes had never lost to the Smoke in the postseason, it was because they'd done so poorly during the regular season that they'd never made it to the playoffs. She imagined playing a critical part in making that dream come true.

"Our general manager wasn't taking any chances this year. Bob put a lot of thought into his trades—not that he's been flippant with them in the past. But he treated them more like mathematical equations this year. Each and every one of you is an important player in our future success. Now go home and get some rest. The worst day of your lives is tomorrow—fitness testing."

Everyone around Kenzie grumbled, and she shared the sentiment. She knew she'd be run into the ground physically, but she was more concerned about meeting the players who missed their dinner. Kenzie worried her crush on Sutton Flores wouldn't completely disappear by then.

Chapter Two

Sutton stared at her reflection for another minute. The dark circles under her eyes refused to go away no matter how hard she willed them to. Her bronze skin was healthy with color, but her features looked drawn. Maybe traveling back from Utah the day before an early morning fitness test hadn't been a good idea. She was mentally and physically exhausted and hoped she could drum up enough energy for a minimally respectable score on her evaluation. Her phone buzzed from her bathroom vanity. She saw Taylor's name and sighed before opening the text message.

Be there in ten. I will not wait for you.

Sutton typed out her reply quickly. *I'll be ready.*

Taylor's three little dots jumped around. *You say that every time, and we're still always late.*

Sutton put her phone down and continued getting ready. She'd definitely be late if she spent her time arguing with Taylor. She rubbed a small dollop of pomade between her palms before running it through the top of her thick black hair. The sides and back of her head were buzzed close, which made styling a fairly quick process. Getting the rest of her gear together took no time since it was mostly still packed.

She was out the door and climbing into the passenger seat of Taylor's Subaru on time.

"See that?" Sutton said. "Not late." She tossed her bag in the back.

"First time for everything." Taylor pulled away from the curb.

Sutton laughed. "Thanks for driving me. I can't believe how tired I am."

"No problem. How was camp?"

"Great, but I'm happy to be home. I swear the weeks away get longer and longer each time." Sutton watched as the trees passed in a blur. Being on the national team was the highest honor a soccer player could be given, and Sutton was grateful for every opportunity she had. Whether the team was set to play friendly games against other countries or preliminary games leading up to national tournaments, she cherished every chance. But lately, she had grown unexpectedly homesick.

"Sutton?"

"Yeah?"

Taylor frowned at her. "I asked if it had anything to do with Rhea."

"No. Why would it?"

"You two have been together for a while now, longer than any of your other relationships, which makes me think you're pretty serious about her. You must miss her a lot while you're away."

Sutton wondered if Taylor was right. She had been dating Rhea for a year. Most of that time had been happy, but when it wasn't, they were a disaster. Sutton chuckled. "She's actually mad at me right now."

"Why?"

"Because I didn't call her when I got home last night."

Taylor stopped short at a yellow light. "Did you get in late?"

"Not really, but I was tired and just wanted to go to bed. Honestly, I forgot."

Taylor said nothing as she pulled onto the parkway.

"Say it," Sutton said. "I can feel your judgment bubbling up from over here."

Taylor shrugged. "I don't have anything to say. But if I *did* have something to say, it would come from a loving place since I'm your best friend."

Sutton pinched the bridge of her nose. "Out with it, Taylor."

"I just think it's funny how Rhea is the first girl you've dated for longer than a few months or a season, and you do something so stupid to sabotage it."

Sutton shook her head, completely flabbergasted. "I didn't sabotage my relationship. We didn't break up or anything. She's mad at me. That's it."

"Okay."

"Okay." Sutton looked at the traffic surrounding them. "We're going to be late. Why is no one moving?"

"Have you apologized yet?"

Sutton rolled her eyes. "No, but I will. Can we change the subject now? Please?" She pulled out her phone and checked her messages. Rhea hadn't contacted her since sending that scathing text earlier that morning. Sutton knew the situation would require major damage control, but that would have to wait until later. She opened her Instagram to over two hundred new notifications. She scrolled through the comments left on her latest post, a picture of herself with a cup of coffee, and replied to the ones from people she knew.

"Are you nervous for today?"

Sutton looked up from her phone screen. "Why would I be nervous? This isn't my first fitness test or season."

"Because of all the team changes."

"I told you, there's nothing to worry about." Sutton shoved her playfully. "You and I have been on this team for seven years, since day one, and every change has been for the best. I trust Bob, and so should you."

"They let Tim go without any warning or explanation."

"He really didn't do much for the team."

"And our entire front line has changed."

Sutton pulled up the draft details on her phone and started reading. "Our front line was our weakest link last season. I, for one, am excited to meet the new players. We did really well during the draft and with our trades."

"Especially the college draft. We snagged Penn State's MVP."

"Kenzie Shaw," Sutton read aloud. "I remember the championship game." She studied the thumbnail attached to the article. Kenzie smiled brilliantly as she held up a Jersey Hurricanes scarf. Her red hair was wild and nearly hid her features, but her freckled face was still vibrant with happiness. "What's she like?"

"Quiet, kind of shy." Taylor veered off for their exit. "She played with Chiara for two years."

"Chiara is fierce."

"Shit. You were right, we're late anyway." Taylor parked hastily, and Sutton grabbed her bag from the back seat.

They ran together toward the indoor fitness gym, almost tripping over the gravel that led to the doors. As they approached the locker room, the woman opening the door held it for them. Sutton recognized the fiery red hair immediately.

"Thanks, Kenzie," she said as she stepped backward through the door. She watched Kenzie's eyes widen and the handle slip from her grip. Sutton stared at the closing door curiously before following Taylor into the locker room.

The rest of the team greeted Sutton with a round of applause and several shouted hellos. The loudest came from Connie, one of the few original Hurricanes on this season's roster. Sutton raised her hands and soaked up the praise.

Mel, one of the assistant coaches, stepped into the locker room and clapped to get the team's attention. "Welcome back, everyone. You have ten minutes to get dressed. Coach wants you out on the turf as soon as possible." The locker room door opened, and everyone turned to watch the latecomer. Kenzie entered with a sheepish wave. Sutton smiled and couldn't stop herself from waving back, even though Kenzie wasn't looking at her. "Now that *everyone* is actually here," Mel said, "suit up and come out to the gym."

Erin said something to Kenzie, and she appeared to relax a little. She even laughed. Sutton was happy to see her team welcome the rookies warmly. Starting a season with bad blood between teammates was always a recipe for disaster.

"Are you as exhausted as I am?" Tara said, standing beside her in her sports bra and compression shorts.

Sutton nodded. "The older I get, the harder it is for me to bounce back from all this traveling."

"Normally, I'd sleep on the plane, but our flight back from Utah was so bumpy."

"Oh, boo-hoo, your trials with the national team must be tedious," Taylor said with a smirk.

"You should be playing with us," Sutton said.

Taylor snorted and walked away.

Sutton changed into her uniform quickly but took a moment to relish the feel of it. Wearing the red, white, and blue had been an honor, but navy blue and orange felt like home. She glanced over her shoulder and caught Kenzie standing alone in a corner with her back to the room, shaking her hands out at her sides and tapping her left foot. Could've been a ritual or just nerves. Sutton shut her locker and followed her teammates out to the gym.

Brett was waiting for them at the center of the indoor turf field, where they had scattered orange cones and other markers ready to test each player. Sutton felt the first rush of adrenaline surge into her veins. It was showtime.

Two hours later, twenty players lay covered in sweat on the ground, breathing heavily as they gulped down their recovery drinks. Sutton could've fallen asleep on the spot.

"A few quick announcements before I send you all to the showers."

Brett stood in the center of the circle of bodies. "I'm sure you'd like to know who did the best on the beep test."

"I hate that test—don't ever mention it again," Chichima said from where she lay flat on the ground.

"No one loves running back and forth over and over and faster and faster. It's inhumane," Sutton said with a laugh.

Meredith grunted. "I almost puke every time."

Brett held up his clipboard. "I think I speak for us all when I say I'm glad you don't. Anyway, this year's results are interesting because we have a tie. Sutton Flores and Kenzie Shaw."

"Huh," Sutton said. She rolled her head to the side and looked at Kenzie. "I'd high-five you, but I'm pretty sure I'm dead." Kenzie let out a stiff laugh. Out of all the rookies she had met, Kenzie was definitely one of the most peculiar.

"We'll start practice tomorrow as usual, and we'll move it outside as soon as the weather permits. Our final order of business is naming the new captain of our team." Sutton raised her head. "The Jersey Hurricanes suffered a loss when Tanya Baker retired at the end of last season. Now it's time to choose a new leader, the player who will step up and encourage as well as teach. Normally, we ask for player input, but the choice here seemed obvious enough. I'm very confident in naming Sutton as our captain."

The entire team started to cheer emphatically while Sutton sat stunned. She had figured she had a chance at captain, but the announcement still surprised her. She grinned and got to her feet as quickly as her jelly legs would allow, hugging Brett and staff in turn. She jogged around to high-five her teammates.

"Would you like to say a few words to your team, Captain?"

"Yeah," she said, standing beside Brett. "I am beyond honored and can't imagine a better team to lead. You are all fierce and talented, and we have a real shot at being the team to fear this season. Our veterans know how great we can be, and we have acquired some newbies who'll be our secret weapons." Sutton looked directly at Kenzie and smiled. "The Hurricanes are coming in hot this year."

"Hell yeah, we are," Meredith said.

Sutton beamed at her team and couldn't help but echo the sentiment. "Hell yeah, we are."

CHAPTER THREE

Sutton arrived at the field thirty minutes before anyone else was scheduled to be there. She liked to have a moment to herself on the first day of formal practice so she could adjust her headspace and prepare herself for the season.

She walked the perimeter of the indoor field slowly, her hands on her hips and her eyes on the ground. With each step, she named another Hurricanes player and visualized her position on the field. Once she named everyone, she'd start over again and repeat the list until her walk was done. This routine always calmed her down.

She had just finished when she saw the coaching staff file in. Brett was having a serious conversation with his assistant coaches, Mel and Talia. Tyler and Gabby, the athletic trainers, started unpacking gear and placing cones around the field. No one noticed Sutton until she waved.

"Sutton, I should've known you'd be here before the rest of us," Gabby said as she jogged over to meet her in the far corner. She shook her hand. "How are you feeling? Any soreness from your games against Portugal? I saw that foul right before halftime. That had to hurt."

Sutton cringed when she thought of how hard she hit the ground during that game. "Physically, I'm fine, but I'm still a little heartbroken. It's never easy beating my dad's home country like that, and I know he hates it as much as I do."

"I bet every time the US wins, he wishes you had decided to play for Portugal."

"He still teases me about it, but he knows my decision was easy. I may be half Portuguese, but I grew up in America watching players like Hamm, Wambach, and Rampone. I wear the US crest to follow in their footsteps."

"Does your mom rub it in his face?"

"She's supportive and happy for my success, but she doesn't care much for the game." Sutton smiled in spite of the disappointment she always felt when she thought of how little her mom cared about her career.

Gabby shifted from foot to foot. "This may be a little forward of me to ask, and I hope you're okay with it. A friend of mine runs a women's soccer podcast called *WoSo Prime*, and I think your story is one that should be heard."

She laughed outright. "I don't think so."

"I get it. You have a lot on your plate right now." Gabby nodded and started to walk away, but Sutton stopped her.

"It's not that. I just don't feel like my story is all that special. We've heard it all before, a player with connections to two national teams having to choose, like Sydney LeRoux."

"*Your* generation has heard it all before. To this generation coming up, you're their LeRoux, their Wambach and Rampone. Think about it, okay?"

"Okay." Sutton watched Gabby run back to the trainers and help unpack their gear. She laughed to herself. She'd never be a soccer legend, no way, but if her story could influence one young girl to chase her dreams, the decision was a no-brainer.

Practice started promptly, the players running familiar drills and warming up with silly games. Coach Brett split them up into two teams for a quick scrimmage. He had to evaluate the skill of every player and how they played with one another, but Sutton couldn't resist doing the same. Their first-string goalkeeper, Lacey, communicated well with Meredith and Tara. They used very few words but always knew what was being said. On the opposite team, Sutton analyzed the way Kenzie connected with Chiara. Taylor wasn't lying when she'd hinted at their past chemistry. Chiara knew exactly where to place the ball to anticipate Kenzie's speed as she ran toward goal.

Sutton backed up in preparation for another run from Kenzie. Her team was up by one, and the clock ticked away the final minute of the scrimmage. She could see the hungry, competitive look in Kenzie's eyes as she rushed past Sutton's midfielders. Now it was the defenders against Kenzie, the rookie who definitely wanted to prove herself. Sutton smirked as she ran directly at Kenzie.

The move must've startled Kenzie, who looked at Sutton with scared eyes before drawing her right foot back and shooting for the goal. She released a rocket of a shot Sutton couldn't dodge fast enough.

The ball nailed her in the side of the face. She fell to the turf, crumpling like an accordion.

She could hear her team around her and the trainers asking if she was okay. She knew she was probably okay, but she was too afraid to move and find out her face had been permanently disconnected.

"There goes her modeling career," Taylor said from behind her.

"I'm fine," Sutton said into the turf. She rolled on her back but didn't move her hand away from her face. She opened one eye and stared at the fluorescent lighting above her. "I'm okay."

Gabby's face came into view. "How's your vision? Any stars or flashes of light?"

Sutton recognized the evaluation. "I don't have a concussion, Gabby."

"Humor me."

"No flashes and no double vision. I have no pain in my neck or head, just my face. I'm not confused, and I remember the events leading up to the injury. I charged Shaw, she took a shot at the goal, and I intercepted it with my face." Sutton sat up and pulled her hand away slowly. She saw Taylor in the crowd. "How bad is it?"

Taylor gave her a one-shoulder shrug. "I can't call you Two-Face, which is a little disappointing."

Sutton laughed and winced at the pain radiating from her cheekbone. She poked along the tender spot gingerly. She wanted to congratulate Kenzie on owning such a lethal right foot but couldn't find her at first. Sutton leaned to the side and looked between everyone's legs to see Kenzie still standing in the same place she'd taken the shot from. Sutton reached up for a helping hand and let Brett pull her to her feet.

She held Brett's hand for an extra second and swatted his shoulder. "I'm good. Honest."

"You better be."

She walked off to meet Kenzie, who wouldn't even look at her. The sleeves of Kenzie's training shirt were rolled up, showing off her toned arms. One leg of her shorts was hitched up, and her socks were bunched at her ankles, barely holding in her shin guards. Kenzie's arms and legs were deceiving, very thin but packed with power. Sutton took in the prominent curve of Kenzie's backside. She had found the power source.

Sutton extended her hand. "I think it's about time we formally met. I'm Sutton Flores."

Kenzie looked around before taking her hand. "I'm sorry."

"I'm pretty sure your name is Kenzie, not sorry, but I did just get hit in the face pretty hard."

Kenzie laughed nervously and pulled her hand away. "That's what I'm sorry about. I don't know why I took the shot. The last thing I'd want to do is mess up your face." Kenzie closed her eyes and shook her head. When she opened them again, her expression was softer. "Hurt you, I mean. I wouldn't want to hurt you. Or any of my teammates."

Sutton studied Kenzie briefly. "Are you nervous?"

"Yes."

"Don't be." Sutton squeezed Kenzie's shoulder gently. "I may be partial, but you've been drafted to the best team in the league. We're like a family, and we want everyone to be comfortable and play their best."

"I already feel pretty comfortable."

"As your captain, it's my duty to make sure you're completely comfortable, which is why I will tease you about this. Relentlessly."

"Great," Kenzie said with an eye roll but also a smile.

"And I have to give you a nickname, for comfort's sake." She watched Kenzie's eyes widen in terror. They were a true hazel, a color she'd always found attractive, and the warmth highlighted Kenzie's freckles. "Freckles? No, too juvenile," Sutton said, tapping her chin with her forefinger as she came up with the perfect nickname. "Let's get back to the team, Chicken. Time to cool down." She turned and started to jog back to her teammates who were already stretching.

"Why Chicken?"

Sutton stopped and grinned. "Your legs. They're thin but very strong." She could tell Kenzie still didn't fully understand. "Have you ever seen a chicken run?"

Kenzie shook her head.

"Speedy little suckers." She turned and jogged away.

❖

Kenzie watched Sutton leave and waited until no one was looking at her before kicking at the ground. Her first real meeting with Sutton didn't exactly go the way she had dreamed it would. Kenzie had imagined knocking Sutton's socks off with her skills, not almost knocking her out. Literally. And the last thing Kenzie would ever want Sutton to notice about her legs was how they were like a chicken's.

"Great job, Shaw," she said to herself. She scrubbed her face with her hands and let out a long breath. She joined the others once she had shaken off most of her embarrassment. She sat on the ground beside Meredith and started stretching. Meredith leaned in, some smart remark in mind, Kenzie was sure.

"We're never speaking of this," Kenzie said in warning.

Meredith pulled back.

Brett stood at the center and jotted notes on his clipboard. "We look very good for a team who just had their first practice." He tucked his pencil behind his ear. "After last season, I think it's safe to say we're all hungry to take home the championship trophy, and I feel like we have the tools to make it happen."

"We do," Sutton said.

Kenzie took a long sip from her sports drink and looked across the circle to Sutton. She nearly choked when Sutton winked at her. The blue liquid dribbled down her chin and soaked into her shirt. Good thing the team's color was navy blue.

"This weekend will be our preseason team outing and, as usual, our team captain is responsible for picking the activity." Brett turned to Sutton. "Any ideas?"

"I have a few." Sutton rubbed her hands together.

"Remember," Brett said, his tone stern, "the activity should promote team building and communication."

"Then I have only one."

Kenzie didn't know Sutton very well, but something in her gut told her the look in Sutton's eyes was nothing but trouble.

Chapter Four

Kenzie tugged at the sleeves of her camouflage jumpsuit. The cuffs came well past her fingers. She rolled them up before looking at the mandatory padded gloves. Kenzie hated the idea of wearing things strangers had worn multiple times, but it was better than getting a paintball to the bare knuckle.

"Have you ever been paintballing?" Sherri Maddox asked from behind her.

She had grown a little closer to Sherri over the past week of training. They were both forwards and played with a similar style, but where Kenzie relied on her speed, Sherri relied heavily on her agility.

"No, and I never wanted to."

Sherri smiled, her rosy complexion highlighting her plump cheeks. "What a relief. All the other girls seem very excited. I'm not."

"We should stick together, then." Kenzie felt nervous extending this kind of invite, a suggestion of a friendship. Even after a week of practicing and joking around, Kenzie still didn't know how she fit in. "Pick a corner to hide in?"

"That's the best idea I've heard all day. One thing, though."

"What?"

"If we see Sutton, we shoot her multiple times."

"What if we're on her team?"

Sherri raised her eyebrows and shrugged.

Kenzie laughed and decided she liked Sherri. "Deal." She extended her hand, surprised by the vigor behind Sherri's handshake. She pulled on her gloves before putting her mask on. She'd never willingly choose an activity that required safety masks.

Kenzie and Sherri walked together to the center of the paintball course with the rest of their team. Sutton stood out, as she always did, with her blinding smile and air of merriment. Her mask was atop her head, and she kept poking at Taylor's butt with the barrel of her gun. The more annoyed Taylor got, the more Sutton would poke her.

Kenzie would normally be turned off by childish antics, but something about Sutton's relationship with Taylor warmed her heart instead. She blamed being an only child and never having a sibling. Kenzie jumped at a sudden sound, then noticed a large red splat on Sutton's left foot.

"You're a dick," Sutton said loudly.

"I told you to stop poking me."

Two instructors, a young man and woman, chose that moment to call out for the group's attention. Kenzie kept her eyes on the woman the entire time as they went through the many rules of paintballing. She had the most beautiful bone structure, and she caught Kenzie staring. Kenzie turned her attention back to Sutton, who was now trying to wipe her foot on Taylor's leg.

"Evens on one team, odds on the other," Sutton said, quickly taking command of the activity after the staff had finished their introduction.

The Hurricanes split according to their player numbers. To Kenzie's dismay, she was on the same team as Sutton and Sherri. Revenge shots would have to wait.

Taylor stretched her limbs dramatically. "Don't worry, I'll make your feet match, Flores."

Erin stepped in front of Sutton. "Not if I have anything to say about it."

"Oh, snap." Ariana high-fived Erin.

Sutton squared her shoulders. "Let's get to it."

Kenzie spent the first twenty minutes running in circles just to avoid being shot. She didn't believe she'd hide well enough, so she relied heavily on her quick feet. She ran from one obstacle to the next, only checking over her shoulder from time to time to make sure no one was on her tail. Thirty minutes in, she decided she really hated paintball. Her heart was pounding, and she was genuinely afraid. Who thought being chased and shot at was fun?

Heavy footsteps headed her way. Kenzie ducked behind a barrel and held her breath. She waited for the footsteps to stop before peeking around the corner and seeing a pair of legs less than a foot in front of her face. Doing the first thing she could think of, she shot round after round into the person's kneecaps.

"Ow, ow, ow." Sutton lifted her mask, limping in circles before falling down next to Kenzie. "Son of a bitch, they weren't kidding when they said this shit hurts."

Kenzie's jaw dropped the moment she realized what she had done. She threw down her gun and stood up, instantly feeling a sharp pain between her shoulder blades. Kenzie fell down over Sutton with a yelp.

Sutton laughed heartily under her. "I have never seen karma work that quickly before."

Instinctually, Kenzie grabbed on to Sutton and started to squeeze as she fought through the pain. "I am so sorry. Why the hell would you propose this? Why did you want us to hurt each other?" She knew she was whining. She didn't care.

"Are you really that hurt?"

Kenzie knew she was overreacting, but for all the abuse she could handle on the field, pain like this was damn near intolerable. She nodded.

"Okay, then." Sutton eased Kenzie aside, readjusted her mask, and got up. She grabbed one of Kenzie's wrists and urged her to her feet. Kenzie hesitated, considering what happened the last time she stood up. "Come on, Chicken, I'll get you to safety," Sutton said, her words muffled slightly but no less clear. Kenzie was pulled to her feet and quickly lifted over Sutton's shoulder. Sutton began rushing through the obstacles, shouting. "Everyone out of the way, I've got an injured one here."

Kenzie bounced and bobbled along the way, her attention focused mostly on Sutton's strength. "You can put me down." Her words bounced along with her body.

"Not until we're back at home base." Sutton made it to the safe zone and lowered Kenzie to her feet. She stood to her full height and removed her mask. She grinned broadly and motioned for Kenzie to remove hers.

Kenzie took off her mask, but she knew she wasn't smiling.

"Are you okay?" Sutton grabbed her shoulders and turned her around. "Ouch. Right in the middle."

"You don't have to tell me," Kenzie said as she rolled her shoulders. The pain had begun to subside. She grimaced. "How are your knees?"

"They'll be bruised for sure, but I'll survive. I have to ask you something."

Kenzie swallowed hard. "What?"

"You don't plan on taking me out during our games, do you? Tell me now if you do, so I know to keep an eye out for you."

Kenzie let out a long easy breath. She even laughed. "No, Captain, you have nothing to worry about." Kenzie scanned Sutton's face. She still couldn't believe looking at Sutton Flores almost every day was her new reality. "I promise."

"Good," Sutton said, running her fingers through her hair. The long strands on top had started to fall into her face. "The last thing I need is our hottest rookie playing against me."

Kenzie opened and closed her mouth several times and not a sound came out. What was she supposed to say to that? Sutton must've enjoyed her speechless moment because the corner of her mouth twitched. Not that Kenzie was staring at her mouth.

"Oh, great." Taylor's voice cut into the moment. "Now I have to sit here with you." She pushed Sutton's shoulder and took a seat on the bench. Taylor looked around and counted everyone in the safe zone. "Odds are winning."

Sutton looked out at the field. "For now," she said.

Kenzie followed her line of sight and saw Erin tucked into a corner, covered completely by fake moss and wooden obstacles, which allowed her to take out player after player while remaining undetected. Kenzie raised her hand to high-five Sutton and received one right away. She finally started to believe she could be her normal self around Sutton.

After too much time on the paintball field, Kenzie walked into her house in need of a shower. A long, very hot shower. "Mom, I'm home." She walked into the kitchen for a glass of water and heard her mother's footsteps behind her.

"What happened to you?"

"We went paintballing for our outing."

"Oh, my," her mom said, pulling paint out of Kenzie's hair.

"It washes out. I made sure to ask before I agreed to play."

"Whose terrible idea was that?"

"Sutton's."

"As in Sutton Flores?"

Kenzie swallowed hard. She was going to have to share this tidbit of information with her mother eventually, she just would've preferred later rather than sooner. "Yes. She's my team captain."

"*Your* Sutton is on the same team?"

Kenzie gripped her glass of water more tightly. "Please don't call her *my* Sutton."

"Well, you used to."

"She was my favorite player, and now she's my teammate. So we can forget about all that. You would know this if you followed anything soccer related."

"I'm only interested when you're playing in the game or watching and yelling at the screen."

"I'm going to take a shower." Kenzie marched off, still holding her glass, and ran up the stairs as quickly as she could without spilling. She put her glass on her nightstand and gathered clean sweats. She stopped at a linen closet on her way to the bathroom for a towel and jumped when she turned to find her mother standing behind her.

"I think it's weird you didn't tell me this before. Like, say, when you were drafted to the Hurricanes and moved in with me so you wouldn't be placed in an apartment."

"It didn't seem important," Kenzie said with very little conviction. Of course it was important, but she didn't want to admit how important to anyone. Not even herself.

"Kenzie, you fawned over her for years. Being on the same team as Sutton is like me being on the same team as John Stamos."

Kenzie couldn't connect those dots even if she tried. "Sutton and John Stamos are not the same." Except maybe their dreamy eyes, perfect hair, and killer smiles. She shook those comparative images away.

"A celebrity crush is a celebrity crush. Make sure you condition after getting all of this out."

She ducked away when her mom reached for her hair again. "I don't have a crush on Sutton."

"Anymore," her mom said quietly.

"Mom, please stop. I'm getting in the shower."

"I'm not stopping you."

Kenzie took a calming breath. She should be used to her mother's immaturity by now, but sometimes it still shocked her. "I'm getting Chinese for dinner once I'm done in the shower. If you'd like something, I'll order it."

"I'll look at the menu."

Kenzie watched her mother trot down the stairs. She rolled the annoyance from her shoulders and walked into the bathroom, closed the door, and started the water. She was worried the paint pellets would leave marks, but thankfully, she hadn't gotten shot a lot. She thought of Sutton's knees and winced, wondering if Sutton really would bruise. She'd hate to mar her beautiful skin.

"I don't have a crush," she repeated to her reflection, "anymore."

She stared at her unruly red hair and worried expression in the foggy mirror. Once she finally stepped under the hot stream of water, she groaned in satisfaction. Feeling the rivulets of water course over the dips of her muscles, Kenzie ran her fingertips down her abdomen and in between her thighs. She clamped her eyes shut before opening them wide again. Sutton was her captain, the teammate she needed to respect more than anyone else. She couldn't touch herself and think of Sutton. "Anymore," she said aloud. The one word echoed in the steam-filled shower.

CHAPTER FIVE

Sutton knew her first-game jitters were completely normal, but being a first-time captain added an unexpected layer of nerves. None of their preseason games could prepare her fully for this day. The coach had just finished saying his piece and Brett was motivational enough, but Sutton had her own small speech to give once they went out on the field, and she had no idea what to say. Sure, she had rehearsed different ways to get her team hyped, but reality was no match for her imagination.

The Hurricanes were facing the Portland Chargers, a team they always had a hard time beating. Portland was also her girlfriend's home team. Sutton was no stranger to facing off against the woman she was dating, but considering she and Rhea still hadn't fully smoothed out the hiccup when she'd come home, Sutton felt uneasy. She didn't like bringing distractions on the field and hoped that wouldn't be the case. Instead of stressing about things she couldn't control, Sutton watched Kenzie.

Kenzie methodically laced up her boots and shifted her shin guards from side to side. She tied and untied the drawstring hidden inside her shorts and adjusted her jersey. Her long-sleeved base layer hid her thin arms.

"Earth to Sutton."

"What's up?" she said to Chiara as Kenzie adjusted the tight bun at the top of her head.

"I was talking to you forever. Where'd you go? Don't tell me you're nervous because I'll be even more nervous."

Sutton laughed. She squeezed Chiara's shoulder. "I'm no more nervous than I usually am right before games. I'm more excited than anything."

Chiara nodded, her long braid following her every move. "I'm happy to be back."

"So am I."

Brett signaled for them to line up and get ready to go on the field. She pulled on her thin gloves and a headband to keep her ears warm. Everyone was a little more bundled up than usual, except their goalkeeper, Lacey, who was lucky enough to have thick gloves on at all times. She zipped up her team jacket and started for the locker room door.

Sutton always loved the moment when they stepped out of the locker room, but on cold days like this she worried there wouldn't be anyone in the stands. "What's it like out there?" she said to Brett.

"It's not sold out, but you know how loyal our fans are." He patted Sutton on the back and opened the door for them.

Sutton marched out with her head high, her chest filled with pride for the nineteen women walking behind her. The captain's armband she wore on her left bicep felt tight suddenly, reminding her of her new role.

Game introductions passed in a blur and before Sutton knew what was happening, she was shaking her opponent's hand. In her peripheral vision, she saw Rhea stretching her hamstrings. For the next ninety minutes, they were opponents. She ran up and gathered her team in a huddle.

"This is the moment we've been waiting for. Let's start this season on a high note, okay?" Everyone nodded. "We are the team to beat this season because we have the goods and the heart. Each and every one of you is the greatest in my eyes—now let's show everyone else what we got. We're starting with a three-four-three. Push forward." She put her hand in the center of the circle. "Hurricanes on three."

"One, two, three, Hurricanes!" The team shouted and dispersed on the field. Sutton looked up and said a silent thank-you to the higher power that granted her this opportunity.

She took her place on the field and listened to Lacey as she barked out orders to her defensive line. Once the whistle blew, any outside thought would leave Sutton's mind. Her relationship faded into the background. She'd be focused on the ball and the way her own players were moving.

Portland's offense went to work quickly and kept possession of the ball for the first ten minutes. Sutton ran a steady pace for the entire time, chasing their number one striker to keep her from getting too close to the goal. She went down for a few hard tackles but managed to strip the ball from the player's feet every time. The grass bit her cold thighs when she slid across it. She knew she'd be sore later, but for now she was numb. She noticed a shift in the Chargers' offense.

"Cover the left side," she called out to Meredith, one of her other starting defenders. "All the way to the line."

Sutton read the other team's play easily and was able to prevent their forward from sneaking past Meredith. The Chargers had come close several times, but Sutton could communicate quickly using very few words. As the clock neared halftime, Sutton saw a small commotion on the sideline. The Chargers were already subbing out one of their players, an odd move early in the game, but Sutton knew who it was and why. Trish Braka was known for her lethal strike and her compatibility with Rhea. Together, they'd assisted each other more than any two players combined. Even though Trish could only play so many minutes thanks to multiple surgeries through the years, Sutton would still have her work cut out for her if she wanted the game to remain scoreless.

Sutton ran harder and faster than she ever had, her thighs burning from exertion. She chased Trish, careful not to foul her but staying close enough to make her teammates think twice before passing to her. When the halftime whistle blew, Sutton wanted to collapse on the grass.

"You're all doing great," Brett said the moment the whole team was in the locker room. Sutton fell into her seat and took a few long pulls from a water bottle. "We just need to push a little harder, closer to the box. You're up, Shaw," Brett said loudly to Kenzie. "Anita, you're out for the second half. How's your ankle?"

Anita gave him a thumbs-up.

"Sutton, keep the back line as tight as it has been. If we press aggressively with our front line, I think we'll have our first win of the season. Just make sure we keep an eye on Braka."

"I'll take care of her," Sutton said. She readjusted her shin guards and got to her feet. "Let's do this."

The Hurricanes took the field with a renewed fire. Sutton took possession from Trish every time she had the ball and ran her ragged until the minute she was taken out of the game. Sutton collided with a Chargers player, feeling the impact in her chest as she looked behind and saw the other player still on the ground holding her elbow. Sutton took the opportunity for a small huddle.

She called over Taylor and Chiara. "Listen, I'm going to pass to either of you every time I get the ball. No one else. We have twenty-two minutes to make something happen. I'm not going to waste time passing with a defender. So, wherever you are, know the ball is coming for you if I have it."

Taylor slapped her shoulder. "I got it."

The whistle blew. Sutton dribbled the ball up to the midfield line and passed it off to Taylor who immediately sent it to Chiara, positioned in the far corner of the field. Sutton hung back a bit and watched the play unfold.

Chiara used her right foot and launched the ball into scoring position. Sutton kept her eye on the Chargers' goalkeeper as she bounced from foot to foot in preparation for an attempt at goal. Chiara's placement was precise and perfect, and Kenzie received the ball smoothly. A flock of Chargers surrounded her.

Kenzie shifted the ball from the right to the left before slotting between Rhea's legs and right to Chiara. Chiara pulled back and sent the ball flying directly to the upper right corner of the goal. The net made a beautiful swooshing sound as the ball made contact.

The crowd jumped to their feet and screamed. Even with the group's small size, the cheers echoed in the stadium. Sutton rushed to celebrate with her teammates. Chiara ran in circles with her arms spread out before hugging Kenzie tight. Everyone jumped on them, creating a pile of players. Sutton fought her way through, held Chiara's face in her hands, and kissed her forehead. She then wrapped her arms around Kenzie and lifted her off the ground. Kenzie wrapped her legs around Sutton, and she spun them a few times before putting her down. She gripped Kenzie's shoulders and shook her.

"Welcome to the team, Chicken." She wanted to remember Kenzie's brilliant smile forever.

The whistle blew, signaling for game play to resume. The rest of the game flew by in a flurry of one team chasing the other. Sutton was determined to hold on to the win, and she did. She was a very proud captain as she stood in the locker room and watched her team cheer for themselves. She couldn't wait to go out and celebrate.

CHAPTER SIX

Nothing felt as great as celebrating a win. Sutton bopped to the music filling the bar and nursed her Jack and Coke. She felt amazing, and positive about the road ahead. The way her team had come together on the field showed great potential, and that was all a captain could ask for after only one game. She heard Taylor laugh at something Meredith had said, and she leaned in to hear more.

"I think Sutton scared the referee when she challenged the foul."

"It was a bullshit call," Sutton said. She had to speak up to be heard over the noise filling the bar. "Unless there's a new rule where players can be called for *being* tripped."

"You were practically foaming at the mouth."

"I'm the captain now. I have to stand up for my team." Sutton held up her glass to propose a toast. "You all are the absolute best, and I can't wait to win the championship this season."

"To us." Meredith touched her glass to Sutton's.

"Hey, Shaw!" Sutton shouted down the bar to catch Kenzie's attention and beckoned her over. Kenzie approached slowly and Sutton took the opportunity to look her up and down. Kenzie wore tight jeans and a sweater that looked incredibly warm and soft. The light blue complemented her skin tone perfectly. She tapped Kenzie's glass. "What are you having? I'd like to buy you a drink to celebrate your first game."

"Brett beat you to it. He insisted my first cap should be recognized by the coach." Kenzie held up her empty glass.

"Then let me buy you another. It's only right for the coach *and* captain to treat you."

Kenzie licked her lips. Her eyes were a little heavy lidded, but they were clear and bright. "Rain check? I don't like to drink much during the season." Kenzie cringed. "Not that I drink a lot anyway, but the dehydration messes with me when I train, and I don't feel good."

Sutton could feel herself going soft for Kenzie the same way she always did for charming pretty girls. "Why do I have a feeling you'll be one of Captain's favorite players?" She shifted to the side and invited Kenzie to lean against the bar with her.

Kenzie spun the ice in her glass around with a straw. "I'm just trying to be responsible."

"A turn-on for team captains, I assure you."

Kenzie's eyes seemed dark in the low lighting. She wore her hair up, and her stud earrings sparkled. Sutton wanted a snapshot of the moment.

Sutton started when someone wrapped their arms around her from behind. She turned to find Rhea smiling at her. "Hey, you," she said stiffly. She bent to give Rhea a peck on the cheek, but Rhea locked their lips in a serious kiss. Sutton fell into the softness immediately. Perhaps she did miss Rhea after all. When she pulled back, Rhea was looking at her with pure adoration.

"I hate that we lost, but I love watching you play." Rhea ran her hands inside Sutton's open flannel and caressed her sides over her T-shirt. Rhea was petite for a soccer player, barely breaking five foot three with tiny features to match. She was more cute than beautiful, but an undeniably attractive package. Rhea adjusted her long black ponytail and reached for Sutton's glass. She finished the drink off in one long swallow. "Gotta catch up." She showed the empty glass to Kenzie.

"Rhea, this is Kenzie Shaw. One of the Hurricanes' rookies this season."

Rhea shook Kenzie's hand politely. "Nice to meet you, although I think we were already introduced when I stripped the ball from you."

"Pretty sure our formal introduction was when I nutmegged you just before assisting with our winning goal," Kenzie said, her eyes never leaving the ice in her glass.

Sutton couldn't speak, but even if she wanted to say something, this was a lose-lose situation.

Rhea pointed at Kenzie and shook her finger. "I think I really like you."

Sutton let out a breath. She put her arms around Rhea's waist and held her close. She had missed the feeling of holding someone. She and Rhea hadn't been able to see one another before Sutton had to leave for national team camp, and the separation weighed heavily on them. Or maybe it just weighed on Sutton.

Sutton leaned in to kiss Rhea's temple and whisper in her ear. "I missed you." Rhea slipped her hands under Sutton's T-shirt and scratched her lower back. Sutton shivered. Any worry she had about Rhea making a scene over her forgotten phone call had flown out the window.

Out of the corner of her eye, Sutton saw Kenzie walking away. She had the sudden urge to call her back and keep her near, but her brain told her Rhea should be her priority. She framed Rhea's face and pulled her in to a sweet kiss.

"Get a room, you two," Taylor said.

Sutton rolled her eyes. "I think that's a pretty good idea, actually. What do you think?"

"I think it's a great idea, baby."

Sutton had to close her eyes and steady herself when Rhea reached into the back of her pants to scratch her bare asscheek. When she opened her eyes, she spotted Kenzie watching them. The pulsing between her legs intensified.

"Good night, everyone. We're heading out," Sutton said, avoiding Kenzie while she made her rounds quickly and left with Rhea.

❖

Kenzie continued chewing on her straw long after Sutton and Rhea were gone. She hadn't spoken to anyone or moved from the table in the corner. An odd mood had washed over her the moment Rhea walked in and staked her claim on Sutton. She felt smaller, less important, more like the rookie she was.

As she watched Sutton touch and kiss Rhea, Kenzie felt a spark of jealousy. But how could she be jealous? Sutton was her captain and barely qualified as an acquaintance on a personal level. Sure, they'd shared a few moments together that felt a little more than casual, but that didn't mean anything. Did it?

Kenzie smiled around the straw and laughed at how silly she was being. Her celebrity crush was just macking on her sexy girlfriend, and she was wasting her time trying to figure out why it bothered her. The answer was simple and ridiculous. Kenzie wanted it to be her. She finally let her empty glass go and pulled on her jacket. Time for her to leave.

Chiara stepped in front of Kenzie. "Where do you think you're going?"

"I was just heading out. First game jitters really tire me out."

"Are you driving?"

"Yeah. I'm fine, really." Kenzie could feel Chiara's analytical gaze sweep over her.

"I'd feel better if you stayed a little longer." She liked the way Chiara put things simply. She smiled and nodded. Chiara had always been incredibly sweet to her, even back in college when most young women were trying to figure out who they were and how they fit in on and off the field. "Fine, but only if you play me in foosball."

"You didn't learn a thing in college, did you?"

"I learned a lot then, but even more after you graduated."

"Okay, bring it, Shaw." Chiara looped her arm through Kenzie's and led her to the worn foosball table.

Kenzie took some time getting back into her foosball groove, but Chiara started to sweat when she did. They played three games, and Kenzie walked away the champion. She had to admit laughing and joking around for another hour beat sitting at home in her bedroom, overthinking about Sutton Flores.

She walked out of the bar with Chiara, giggling as she headed to her car, Chiara at her side. "This is me." Kenzie stuffed her hands into her pockets and shivered.

"I'm really glad we're teammates again, Kenzie. I missed this," Chiara said with a small poke to Kenzie's stomach.

Kenzie grew nervous. She kept thinking about what Erin said. "I missed this, too. You know, Erin thought we had a thing back in college." Kenzie laughed as if it was the funniest concept on earth.

Chiara's laugh matched Kenzie's. "If only she knew how badly I wish that was true."

Kenzie's laughter died. "Wait. What?"

Chiara looked at her skeptically. "Are you serious?"

"Seriously confused."

"I had it bad for you back then. You were hot and funny, and we killed it on the field together, but I knew you never felt the same, so I kept it to myself."

"Chiara, I'm sorry. I had no idea."

"You have nothing to apologize for. You never seemed interested, and you always had a boyfriend. I'm just glad I wasn't too obvious. The last thing I'd want is to make you uncomfortable."

Kenzie was seeing Chiara in a new light, with her inviting dark skin and thick brown hair. She was gorgeous and so exquisitely feminine, but not Kenzie's type. Maybe if she had been, a few other issues in Kenzie's life would be easier.

"I'm sorry, because you're a catch," Kenzie said.

Chiara dusted off her shoulder. "Your loss now because I'm very much taken."

"Oh? What's her name?"

Chiara smiled goofily. "*His* name is Sam."

Kenzie could see how happy she was. "I hope to meet him someday soon."

"He'll make it to a few games. He always does."

Kenzie opened her arms and hugged her tightly. "I'm so happy for you."

"What about you?" Chiara said as she drew back from Kenzie. "Any of those boyfriends stick around?"

"The boyfriends…poor guys." It felt like a lifetime ago, but it was only a few years in her past. "They were helping me figure a few things out."

"You're saying I *did* have a shot."

Kenzie laughed. "A better shot than they did, that's for sure."

Chiara gave Kenzie another quick hug before breaking out into a dramatic shiver. "Drive safe, and I'll see you at practice."

She waved as Chiara went back inside. She got into her car, started it, and blasted the heat. She held herself tightly and bounced to create warmth. She was shocked Chiara once had feelings for her, and she couldn't get the thought out of her head. She supposed anything was possible. She thought about the look she'd shared with Sutton earlier, and she snorted.

"No way," she said to herself. She put the car in drive and looked in the rearview mirror. She caught her eye in the reflection. "You'd win the lottery first." She pulled out of her spot and drove home without another word to herself.

CHAPTER SEVEN

L osing at Uno three times in a row was an insult. Sutton threw her cards down and laid her head back against the bus seat. She wanted to accuse Taylor of cheating or Kristy of being an Uno shark, but she hadn't been paying attention closely enough to win. A thought in the back of her mind wouldn't leave her alone, but it'd somehow elude her every time she tried to focus on it. How could she work through a problem if she didn't know what it was? She watched Taylor shuffle the deck of Uno cards, soothed by their blur.

Taylor extended the deck to Sutton. "Want a chance to redeem yourself?"

She held up her hands. "I can only handle so many losses." She looked over her shoulder to see what the rest of the team was up to. She spotted Kenzie in one of the last rows, sitting by herself with headphones on. Her head was down, and she was closed off to the world. "Has she been sitting alone this whole time?"

"Who?" Kristy said.

"Shaw."

"Yeah. I think so."

Sutton decided it was her duty as captain to make sure every player felt included. "I'm going to check on her."

"You do have a knack for making rookies feel welcome," Taylor said.

She held on to the seats to steady herself as she went to the back of the bus. Everyone was engrossed in their bus activities and didn't even glance at her. When she got to Kenzie's row, she realized Kenzie had been reading. The book was thick with a small font. She stood in the aisle, not wanting to startle Kenzie, until she finally stopped reading.

Kenzie pulled off her headphones and smiled up at her.

"Is this seat taken?" Sutton said, pointing to the seat next to Kenzie.

"Of course not." Kenzie moved her legs to let Sutton pass.

Sutton sat and waited a minute before speaking. She didn't want to intrude, but she also couldn't bear the thought of Kenzie feeling alone. She pointed to the book on Kenzie's lap. "What're you reading?"

Kenzie eyed her suspiciously.

"What's that look for?"

"I'm trying to decide whether or not you'll laugh at me," Kenzie said.

Sutton held up her right hand and covered her heart with her left. "I promise I won't."

Kenzie closed the book and showed Sutton the cover. "The third Harry Potter book."

"Very cool."

Kenzie's eyes brightened. "Have you read it?"

Sutton shook her head. "No, I haven't."

Kenzie's excitement disappeared and silence stretched on between them. It turned awkward.

"I'll let you get back to reading, then. I didn't mean to interrupt."

Kenzie held the book to her chest. "You didn't, not really. I've read this so many times at this point, I just like to travel with it. Like a security blanket."

"Do you not like traveling?"

"It's not my favorite thing. I get restless pretty easily, so I like to have something for my hands and mind to do." Kenzie put her headphones away. When she sat back up, she flipped her long hair over her shoulder.

Sutton caught the scent of her shampoo and a subtle perfume. She felt a pleasant tightness in her chest she couldn't ignore no matter how hard she tried. "You smell very nice."

"It's my shampoo." Kenzie grabbed a strand of her hair and brought it under her nose and across her face. "It's a lavender calming shampoo. I'll take all the help I can get with this crazy hair."

"You have great hair," Sutton said quietly, wanting the compliment to be exclusively between the two of them. "It suits you, and you wear it well."

Kenzie tucked the strand she was playing with behind her ear and said a coy thank-you.

For the rest of the bus ride to New York, Sutton watched Kenzie out of the corner of her eye, only interrupting her reading from time to time to say something about the upcoming game.

Once the bus arrived at the home arena of the New York Lightning, everyone stood and stretched their limbs. The drive wasn't a long one, but it was enough to make them antsy. The excitement of their second game didn't help. Sutton stood after Kenzie got her stuff together and shuffled into the aisle. Before Sutton could step forward, Kenzie turned around to say something, bumping into Sutton and knocking her back into the seats. Sutton erupted in laughter while Kenzie looked horrified and covered her mouth. Kenzie didn't move when Sutton stood up again, which left Sutton very little space. Her front was pressed against Kenzie's side and she was still smiling.

"Come on," she said, standing behind Kenzie and placing her hands on her waist. "I'll guide you to make sure you don't knock anyone else over." They walked slowly down the bus aisle, Sutton pulling Kenzie back or swaying her to the side just to make her laugh. They were giggling when they stepped off the bus, standing close to one another. A crowd had gathered. Hurricane fans cheered for Sutton and a few even shouted Kenzie's name. Their phones were out, and they asked for pictures and autographs. Sutton noticed a strange look on Kenzie's face. She stepped away from Sutton and started toward the players' entrance.

Sutton noticed how quickly she walked, like she couldn't put space between them fast enough. She wondered if she had done something wrong. She put on a smile and waved to the fans as she walked toward the building. She caught a quick glimpse of a young girl no older than six, wearing her jersey. Sutton ran up to the crowd of people standing against a metal barrier and leaned in to give that little girl a high five. The expression on her face lit Sutton's heart up like a Christmas tree.

She heard a trainer calling her name—duty called—but she checked on Kenzie as soon as she could.

"You seemed a little freaked out back there." Sutton dropped her gear in front of her locker.

"I'm still not quite used to the fans—people wanting to meet me. So strange."

"They're great. Fans on the road are very special. It's hard being a fan of the away team, and it's rare to have your favorite player in town."

"I bet you always draw a crowd."

She held her index finger and thumb apart. "A small one, but you'll start to as well. Come on." Sutton held out her hand. "Trust me?"

Kenzie nodded hesitantly and took her hand. Sutton checked with the staff and got the okay to step out for a minute.

She led Kenzie back to the crowd, which was still large and standing in wait. She dropped Kenzie's hand and waved. The fans erupted in a fresh round of cheers and applause. She encouraged Kenzie to wave, then took her phone out, pulled Kenzie against her, and they posed for a selfie with the fans in the background.

Once they were back in the locker room, Sutton showed Kenzie the picture. "All these people show up for us, and they're what make every game a great experience."

Kenzie smiled at the picture, but Sutton wasn't paying attention to the picture when Kenzie looked back at her.

"We do have the best fans."

Sutton nodded. "We definitely do."

CHAPTER EIGHT

Sutton pulled off her boots and threw them into her locker. She hated losing, but she really hated losing early in the season. They'd never had a problem breaking through the Lightning's defensive line before, but this game was a joke. She took off the captain's armband and started to wind it up, but she thought better of throwing it. The band and her role still deserved respect. She grumbled to herself and took a seat.

"Okay everyone," Brett said as he stepped into the locker room. "I know we're all disappointed."

"I'm fucking pissed," Sutton said loudly.

"Me *fucking* too." Kristy started unlacing her cleats angrily, whipping the laces around.

"This was a tough loss, but I'd rather it happens now instead of fifteen games later when we're fighting for a playoff position. We have a lot to learn from today's game, and I'll have a detailed list at practice. See you on the bus in thirty minutes." Brett didn't cast a glance over his shoulder as he left.

Kristy looked at Sutton oddly. "I'm used to being yelled at when we lose."

"Maybe Brett isn't a yeller," Sutton said. "We shouldn't have lost today."

Lacey pulled off her gloves and dropped them into her bag. "You can say that again." Her tone was heavy with disappointment and guilt. Goalkeepers always took losses personally because a ball shouldn't get past them. Ever.

"Okay, listen up." Sutton stood tall despite her wilted spirit. She had a responsibility to lead and encourage this team. "We lost ourselves during the second half. We got sloppy and slow, and I don't know why.

I saw you all trying, and I know I was, too." She scanned the faces staring back at her, but Kenzie's head was down. "I noticed how our strikers were pushing and trying to outsmart the defense. I saw how the midfielders scrambled to create opportunities, and I know the defense worked hard to be everywhere at once. We lost and that's on us, but it doesn't mean we failed."

Taylor raised her hand. "But a loss is a failure."

"Only if you let it be, and I refuse to. We're a great team. Brett will have notes for us, and we're going to be better because of this game. If you don't believe that, your negativity will be more detrimental to this team's success than today's loss." Sutton saw a few of her teammates nod, but Kenzie continued to stare at her feet. "Who's a force of nature?" Her question was met with silence. She let out a bark of fake laughter. "I'm sorry, maybe you didn't hear your captain. I asked, who is a force of nature?"

"We are," the whole team said with little enthusiasm.

"And why are we a force of nature?"

"Because we're Hurricanes." This time, their response was more forceful.

"That's right and let's not forget it." Sutton clapped her hands and went about stripping her uniform and heading to the showers. She didn't see Kenzie again in the locker room.

When she climbed the steps to the bus, she spotted Kenzie in the same seat as earlier with her headphones on and hood up. All the leave-me-alone signals were loud and clear, so Sutton sat in her usual spot beside Taylor.

The drive back to New Jersey was quiet. Only a slight murmur of voices could be heard over the bus engine. Sutton couldn't stop checking over her shoulder from time to time, just to see what Kenzie was up to. Every athlete dealt with a loss differently, but Sutton would have been lying if she said she didn't prefer the vocal approach. Chiara was sitting by herself, so Sutton switched seats and joined her.

"Hey, Cap," Chiara said before looking back to her phone. She was playing a *Match 3* game.

"How are you doing?"

"About as well as everyone else. I'm pissed and disappointed but looking ahead to the next game." She locked her phone and faced Sutton. "How are you taking our first loss? Your speech was pretty good."

"Could've been better."

"Yeah, but I'm sure you weren't expecting to give a post-loss motivational speech so soon."

"Very true." Sutton looked back again as she tried to wrangle her thoughts. "Can I ask you something?"

"Sure."

"It's about Shaw."

"Oh." Chiara shifted uncomfortably, a move that intrigued Sutton. She wanted to know more about Kenzie, but she respected Kenzie's right to a private life, and it'd be wrong for her to abuse her friendship to find out more about Kenzie.

"You two played together for a while, right?"

"Two seasons in college."

"Did she always take losses like this?"

"Like what?" Chiara turned to look at Kenzie and shrugged.

"Quiet, isolated, I don't know." Sutton felt silly now for asking. "Never mind. I'm sorry."

"That's just Shaw," Chiara said simply, like Sutton should already know this. "She always sat alone on bus trips and always kept to herself after losing a game. Our team was thick as thieves, joking around with each other constantly, but we knew Shaw would fly solo when we traveled. It's like she gets into her own little zone."

Sutton nodded, feeling slightly better to know this wasn't new behavior.

"If I can be completely honest," Chiara said, "I was shocked to see you sitting with her earlier."

Sutton made a face. "You don't think I messed with her juju, do you?"

Chiara laughed outright, a sound that sounded odd in the quiet melancholy surrounding them. "No. I've never known Kenzie to be the superstitious type."

Sutton pulled off her team snapback and ran her fingers through her hair. She placed the hat back on her head at an angle and decided to ask one more question. "How good were you two together? When you played, I mean." Sutton wanted to slap herself.

"*Very* good. Kenzie was rookie of the year, and in that season, she held the record for hat tricks. I was the assist for most of them. We just have this incredible chemistry on the field, and I hope Brett gives her more minutes soon because I want to show off."

"We got to see a little bit of it during the first game."

"Sutton, believe me when I tell you that was nothing."

The sparkle in Chiara's eye both excited Sutton and made her a little jealous. She was unsure where the latter came from. She slapped Chiara's thigh. "Can't wait."

Sutton returned to her seat, casting one last glance at the back of the bus. This time, Kenzie's eyes locked on hers. Sutton wanted to join her, make her smile or at least feel a little better about her first loss with the team, but she didn't feel like she was welcome even as captain. Instead, she went to her own seat and laid her head back. Once they got home, she'd know how to handle the quiet players.

By the time the bus pulled up to the Hurricanes' headquarters, Sutton was emotionally and physically drained. She said a quick good-bye to her team and dragged her feet as she walked back to her Jeep. The cold, dark night highlighted her discomfort. She couldn't wait to get home and under her covers. She sat in the driver's seat and stared out into the darkness, waiting for the energy to start the car. Her phone buzzed in her jacket pocket.

Pulling the phone out of her pocket took all the energy she'd reserved for driving. She was confused when she saw Kenzie's name on her screen. They had each other's numbers because of the team contact list, but they had never texted.

Don't let this loss lead you to believe you're not a good captain.

Sutton smiled even as the bright light of the screen hurt her eyes.

This is Kenzie, by the way.

Sutton started to respond but another message interrupted her typing.

Kenzie Shaw.

Sutton took a breath and let it out through her nose. She couldn't fight the smile on her face as she typed a reply. *Thanks for saying that.* Sutton sent the message, but she didn't like how cold it read. She typed up another response. *And thank you for clarifying. I have you saved in my phone as Chicken.*

Sutton waited for a response, but after five minutes, she started her car and drove out of the parking lot. She was almost halfway home when her phone buzzed. She waited until she hit a red light to check her message.

Are you kidding?

Sutton let out a small laugh. *At the moment, yes. But I'm changing it as soon as I get home.*

Drive safe.

The light turned green, and Sutton tucked her phone back into her pocket. She thought about Kenzie and her impromptu message as she drove the last ten minutes to her house. Kenzie didn't have to message her at all, even to make her feel better as the team captain. She thought about their earlier conversations on the bus and was very happy to think they had started to forge a real friendship. As soon as she pulled into her long driveway, she took out her phone. Sutton played around in her contacts for a second before opening her messages again.

Changed it. Thanks again for the nice message, Chicken.

I can't believe that's the nickname that's going to stick.

Believe it, baby. Sutton stopped typing immediately and erased the last word before sending her message. She chuckled when Kenzie sent only an eye roll emoji back. *What are your plans for our off day tomorrow?* Sutton second-guessed herself but sent the text anyway with a shrug. It was a friendly question.

Dancing dots appeared and disappeared, and Sutton held her breath as she waited for Kenzie to say anything. At this point, she would've taken another emoji.

Laundry. That's it. Kinda sad, right?

Not sad at all. We all need clean clothes, and I, for one, am thankful you wash yours. I've had some stinky teammates in the past.

Gross!

Sutton laughed to herself. She really enjoyed getting Kenzie to react. *Can you do your laundry later in the day?*

Why?

My lease will be up soon, and I have to car shop. Want to come along and test drive a bunch of cars I may or may not want?

Are you sure?

Sutton stared at her phone. She was confused by the question. *Of course I am. Text me your address, and I'll pick you up around ten.*

Okay.

Sutton had a new spring in her step as she got out of her Jeep and walked up to her front door. Her house was chilly and silent. She flipped on a few lights as she bumped the thermostat up to seventy. She sent Rhea a quick good-night message, but she ignored Rhea's reply. She was just too tired to get involved in what was likely to be a lengthy conversation.

Sutton knew deep down she wasn't lying. She was tired, but tired of *what* wasn't a question she was ready to analyze.

Chapter Nine

"Change of plans," Kenzie said as she held the door open for Sutton and ushered her into her house. "I forgot I had a thing today, and I didn't get a chance to message you." Kenzie watched Sutton take in the modest home. She felt mildly embarrassed by the worn carpet and dated wallpaper.

"Is everything okay?" Sutton asked.

"Yeah, I just forgot I was supposed to help my mom dye eggs for the church's Easter egg hunt. Looks like you'll be car shopping solo. I'm sorry."

Sutton started to undo her jacket and let it fall from her shoulders. "I love dyeing Easter eggs."

"Kenzie? Who's at the door?"

Kenzie turned to the sound of her mother's voice then back to Sutton, sheer panic pulsing through her. She tried to pull Sutton's jacket up, but Sutton fought back. "You don't want to dye eggs with us."

"I do, actually."

"But your lease is almost up."

"I have a couple months, and I was thinking about keeping my Jeep anyway."

Kenzie closed her eyes and pressed her fingertips to her forehead. This was her reality. She took a deep breath before shouting an answer to her mother. "I invited someone over to help us. She's a…" Kenzie looked up at Sutton, completely at a loss. "Teammate," she said weakly.

"Is that all I am to you?" Sutton smirked, and Kenzie needed a deep breath to calm her heart.

"The more hands the merrier," her mom said as she walked into the great room. She was wiping her hands and had yet to look up. "I have dozens of eggs to dye and no desire to do it." She smiled at Kenzie and then to Sutton. She stopped in her tracks. "I know you."

Sutton extended her hand. "Sutton Flores. It's so nice to meet you Miss…Mrs.…"

"Just call me Liz." She shook Sutton's hand and wouldn't let go. "After seeing your picture everywhere and watching you on TV, I feel like I already know you."

"Let's get to those eggs," Kenzie said. She pulled Sutton away from her mother and led her to the kitchen. "Excuse the mess and everything," Kenzie said while looking around at the disarray and open cabinet doors. "Are you hungry? I have some snacks around here or I can cook you something."

"I'm fine for now. Liz, are you a soccer fan?"

Liz looked genuinely ashamed. "Not really, but Kenzie always put on the games. Every time they showed you, she'd spew your stats."

Kenzie groaned. "Oh my God."

"I swear my little girl was in love with you."

Sutton turned to Kenzie with raised eyebrows. "Is that so?"

Kenzie wanted to die on the spot. She opened the refrigerator and stuck her head inside, hoping the air would cool her heated face. "Please, Mom. Eggs."

"They're all on the bottom shelf, honey." Her mom rushed over and shooed her out of the way. She pulled six cartons of eggs from the refrigerator and stacked them on her small kitchen table. "They're all already hard-boiled. Or at least most of them."

Kenzie picked up one of the cartons. "What do you mean?"

"You try boiling seventy-two eggs without losing track once or twice."

"I can't believe the church still uses actual eggs. That's why they make plastic ones." Kenzie tapped the top of an egg. Her mother always managed to make a small project into a daylong ordeal.

"They prefer the old-time charm or something like that. I could've gotten twice as many fake eggs for a third of the price."

"I know a trick," Sutton said. She took the carton from Kenzie. "You take an egg and spin it on a flat surface."

Both Kenzie and her mom watched as Sutton spun the white egg around and around.

Sutton pointed to the egg. "This one's been boiled." Kenzie looked at her skeptically. "If it stops after one or two spins, then it's raw."

Kenzie took a different egg out of the carton and held it in her hand. The shell was cold in her palm. She tossed it up and caught it before placing it on the table and spinning it. The egg spun several times.

"Where did you learn that trick?" Kenzie said, staring up into Sutton's soft brown eyes.

Sutton's smile was small and warm. "Google."

"And it works?"

Sutton shrugged. "Hasn't failed me yet."

They shared a smile.

"Smart and beautiful," her mom said, breaking the unusual moment. "Now let's see if she's artistic, too."

They looked at the pile of dye boxes her mom had put on the table. "Did you save any for the kids in town?" Kenzie said.

"Shush, and let's get started." Her mom rolled up her sleeves, and she and Sutton followed suit.

After setting up over a dozen cups of dye, the three of them set out on an Easter egg dyeing marathon. More than a few times, Kenzie cursed at her dye for splashing back on her shirt and chastised Sutton for laughing. Her mother made more excuses than anyone thought possible to leave the room. She and Sutton were down to a dozen left before they started to talk about things other than Easter.

"I'm sorry you got roped into chores on your off day," Kenzie said as she blotted her teal egg on a paper towel.

"You're kidding, right? I'm having a blast. I can't remember the last time I dyed eggs, let alone for such a good reason." Sutton picked up one of the plastic cups and swirled it, staring at her egg as it danced in the cyclone. She looked mesmerized.

And Kenzie felt mesmerized. She cleared her throat. "Thank you, Sutton, I really mean it. I would've been here all night."

The childlike wonder was gone from Sutton's eyes, and something new and unnamable crossed her features. She smiled stiffly and pointed at the egg in Kenzie's hands. "And all of your eggs would've been some shade of blue."

"What?" Every egg she had done was some kind of blue or accented heavily with blue details. "Huh."

"Favorite color?"

"Not really." Kenzie started to laugh, and when she looked back to Sutton, she realized that Sutton's very soft-looking sweater was blue.

She hadn't subliminally chosen blue dyes to match Sutton, right? "I guess I'm just in a blue mood," she said, feeling a bit dumb immediately after.

"I'm meeting Taylor and a few of the girls for dinner. You should come with—it'll help with that blue mood."

"No, I…I should probably stay here and help clean up."

Her mom reentered the room. Impeccable timing as always. "Nonsense. You go have fun with your team. I can take care of this," she said, instant regret visible on her face.

"I can stay and clean."

Sutton placed her hand on Kenzie's arm. "Please come." Kenzie looked down at Sutton's hand and then back up to her eyes. Sutton pulled back. "Only if you want to."

Kenzie knew she should take a breath soon, but the genuine sparkle in Sutton's eye and the touch that still lingered held her captive. Once she finally breathed, she managed a small nod along with it.

"Only three raw so far. That's not so bad," her mom said triumphantly.

Sutton's laughter cut the tension, and they continued to dye eggs in silence. Once they were done, Kenzie changed from her splattered shirt and into a black shirt more appropriate for a bar. She grabbed their coats and tried her best to pry her mother from Sutton before she could embarrass her any more.

"Let's go," Kenzie said, tossing Sutton her jacket and guiding her toward the door. "Taylor's waiting. Can't be late."

"Thanks for letting me be a part of your Easter prep, Liz."

"Thanks for the hard work, Sutton. I hope to see you again soon. I know my daughter wouldn't mind if you came over more often."

Kenzie clamped her jaws shut. "You were doing so good," she said between clenched teeth.

"I'll definitely be back." Sutton smiled smugly.

She rolled her eyes. "I'll be back later, Mom."

Kenzie rushed to the car to avoid the chill…and Sutton. Part of her wanted to run right back into the house and up to her room where she could dive into a pile of blankets, she was so embarrassed. She was grateful Sutton was driving because she knew she didn't have to look at her. But she could feel Sutton glancing over as she drove. She chose to ignore it and watch the passing scenery instead. They'd had a nice afternoon together, and the last thing she wanted to do was make things between them weirder than they already were.

"So…" Sutton started.

Kenzie could feel the tension roll between them with just that one word. "The game against Dallas should be interesting. Their offense has been unstoppable so far. I hope you're ready for that."

"We're really not going to talk about what happened back there?"

"I don't know what you mean."

"Okay, if that's how you want to handle this, I'll follow your lead." Sutton adjusted her grip on the steering wheel. "You seem embarrassed, and I figured you wouldn't be if we talked about it."

"You're right, because if we talk about it, I will die on the spot and never feel embarrassment again."

Sutton laughed.

Kenzie shot Sutton a lethal glare. "Don't laugh at me."

"I'm not laughing at you. I'm laughing at how dramatic you're being."

"Fine. I had a crush on you. It was a silly, small crush, and really I just admired how well you played."

"Really?"

"Really."

"You turned on all my games?"

"I turned on all the *team's* games."

"And my gameplay is all you noticed about me?"

"Please don't tease me." Kenzie covered her face with her hands. "I knew my mom was going to do this to me. She doesn't know the difference between appropriate and inappropriate." She dropped her hands. "Is there any way I can convince you to forget this ever happened?" Her patience started to wane when Sutton didn't answer right away.

Sutton shifted in the driver's seat and stayed quiet. She took a few turns. "I don't ever want you to feel uncomfortable around me. If you want me to pretend I never heard about an adorable crush you had on me, I can do that." She pulled in to the parking lot of the restaurant and parked in the first available spot.

Kenzie recognized Taylor's and Erin's cars in the same row as them. She unbuckled her seat belt, placed her hand on Sutton's, and thanked her. "My mother will live to see another day."

Sutton covered Kenzie's hand with hers. Her palm was soft and warm. "I'd hate for Liz to meet her end because of me."

Kenzie smiled easily and felt truly relaxed for the first time all afternoon. She reluctantly pulled her hand back. "I'm sorry for how I'm reacting. I just hate the icky feeling of being embarrassed."

"I get it."

"Do you? I find it hard to believe you embarrass easily."

"I don't, but that doesn't mean I don't get embarrassed."

"Tell me the last time you were embarrassed."

"Will it make you feel better?"

Kenzie nodded.

"I had a little tightness in my hamstring for a few games last season, which led to me spending extra time doing stretches and getting stretched. After practice one day, I was in the middle of getting stretched, and I farted in the trainer's face."

Kenzie didn't react immediately. The information had to sink in before she broke out into a broad grin and laughter. "No, you didn't."

"I did," Sutton said, dropping her head and shaking it. "It snuck out."

"Oh my God."

Sutton tilted her head. "I bet that killed any bit of a crush that still lingered."

"You say the *C* word one more time, and I'm killing my mother. Her life is in your hands."

"After I just confided in you? I didn't even tell Taylor that story."

Kenzie's heart skipped a beat, but she kept her expression hard.

Sutton chuckled "Okay, okay. Let's get inside before I press my luck." She unbuckled her seat belt and got out of the car.

Kenzie followed suit and caught up to walk beside Sutton. The evening was crisp but refreshing. "I should warn you, if you keep teasing, I'll pay that trainer to tell people."

"Can't. The trainer died that day."

Kenzie's loud laughter echoed into the night as they walked together to meet their friends.

Chapter Ten

Sutton stretched her left triceps and then her right. She was standing in the corner of the gym waiting for instructions from Brett. The team was on the road, and their home for the next two days would be in Dallas. Sutton missed her house, but she loved the dry heat.

"We're going to start today with an hour in the gym, and then we'll hit the field." Brett scribbled on his clipboard as he spoke.

Taylor leaned in to Sutton. "This is punishment for losing."

"I have more notes on last week's game. Dallas won't know what hit them." Brett's smile seemed normal, if not a little evil, when he left the gym.

"He's definitely going to punish us," Sutton said, searching for Kenzie. She found her stretching against the opposite wall near the free weights. Sutton decided that starting out with cardio was getting old.

"I'm going to work with some weights for a bit." Sutton strode across the gym and stopped at a bench not too far from Kenzie. She dropped her towel and grabbed two ten pound dumbbells. She let them hang at her sides and felt them pull at her shoulders, but half of Sutton's attention was on Kenzie. Sutton could tell by the set of Kenzie's eyebrows and her small smile that whatever she was chatting about with Sherri was amusing. She had seen that look many times when they got to spend the day together, especially when they sat at the bar and traded stories of their toughest games.

Kenzie had seemed to really click with Sherri and Erin, and Sutton felt a bit excluded. She started her lunges. With each extension, she allowed herself to think a little bit more about her feelings. She wanted to be loved by all, but she also knew she couldn't be everyone's best friend. She thought she and Kenzie had made some progress after their day together, but a disconnect still lingered between them.

Taylor's sudden voice made her jump. "Starting with weights, huh? We've been training together for years, Flores. You seem to forget that."

"I never forget that, Taylor." Sutton let out a rough breath when she finished her set. "Pick up some weights before Tyler comes over and makes you do burpees again."

"I've been dying a little each day since they named him head athletic trainer." Taylor made a show of picking up weights and mirroring Sutton's lunges. "First you show up at the bar with a plus-one, and now you're starting with weights. You never start with weights."

"I also don't like losing the second game of the season. Sometimes, I need to switch things up."

"Training routines or girlfriends?"

Sutton dropped her weights on the rack loudly and turned her back to Kenzie, walling off Taylor's comments. "You don't know what you're talking about, and can you please lower your voice?"

"I know your rookie-of-the-year reputation is still alive for a reason, but Rhea really loves you and still wants to be with you."

"That's great, but what about what I want?"

"Do you even know what you want?" Taylor stared Sutton down for an intense moment before stepping back. "I'm hitting the elliptical."

Sutton huffed. "Fuck." She picked up her towel and marched to a bike. She needed to stick to her routine. She needed to stick with her girlfriend. She needed to stick a knife in whatever it was she felt for Kenzie because her bad habit of falling for rookies needed to end now. She climbed on the bike and started pedaling. She didn't care about time or goals, just about getting her heart beating fast enough to be a distraction.

But the only real distraction was Kenzie working with resistance bands across from her. Kenzie's body was long and lean and rippled in the most pleasant places. Sutton shook her head and felt sweat trickle down her temple. Beautiful women were always a temptation. She pedaled and pedaled.

Kenzie was more than beautiful, and that was a big problem. She was funny, thoughtful, and shy, which added to her charm. Sutton struggled to forget Kenzie's crush. *Past crush*, Sutton reminded herself.

She would be lying if she said learning that little tidbit didn't make her feel good. She actually felt great. Sutton slowed her pedaling as a realization hit her. This was all about the crush. She was definitely attracted to Kenzie, but Kenzie's former crush made this feel different.

She'd let it go to her head and inflate her ego. If her breathing wasn't so ragged, she'd laugh at herself.

By the time the team was outside on the field, Sutton had started to calm down and decided to partner with Taylor for a quick round of piggybacks. "I'm sorry," she said while carrying Taylor from one line to the other. "I overreacted. I appreciate your friendship and how you call me out on my bullshit."

"Apology accepted, and I'm taking this as you admitting to your bullshit."

Sutton laughed as she dropped Taylor and switched positions. Riding on Taylor's back allowed her to speak directly into her ear. "Kenzie used to have a crush on me, and I let that get to my head. But there's really nothing going on there. You know I wouldn't cheat on Rhea."

"I know, but you could be better to her, too." Taylor dropped Sutton.

Sutton shielded the sun from her eyes and looked at Taylor. Brett was in the distance helping set up cones for a drill. "I don't think she's the one," she said, finally admitting it aloud.

"Then you need to stop stringing her along." Taylor took a ball from a trainer.

Sutton took a ball from Gabby as well, juggling it with her feet. "That's the thing. We're great when we're together, but I don't really miss her when we're apart." She let the ball fall to the ground and watched it bounce. "That made me sound like an asshole."

"Split up. We're working on elevator passes," Brett said. He followed the order with a blow of his whistle.

"You're not an asshole, but you will be if you don't figure this out soon." Taylor slapped Sutton's shoulder and ran off to get into formation.

Sutton sighed. Easier said than done.

❖

As Sutton paced her hotel room later that night, she tried to focus on her relationship and her feelings for Rhea. What did Sutton *really* want? Every time she would gain even a hint of clarity, she'd remember a special moment with Rhea. Like the specialty cake she'd ordered for Sutton's birthday or the cute notes she'd leave around Sutton's house. She stood still. Maybe she was too busy focusing on a million things other than how great Rhea was and missed her chance to fall in love. Sutton blew out a long breath and decided she had done enough thinking for one night. She unpacked her laptop and pulled up Netflix. Some downtime with her favorite show would do wonders for her scattered mind.

A knock at the door caused her to jump. Sherri had left their room twenty minutes earlier to meet up with some of the girls for ice cream. She wouldn't be back so soon. Sutton couldn't figure out who it could be. Without a glance through the peephole, she swung the door open and smiled instantly at her guest.

"What brings you to my neck of the woods, Shaw?"

Kenzie fidgeted with the hem of her team T-shirt. "I was actually looking for Sherri."

Sutton tried not to be offended. "She left a little while ago to get ice cream. You could probably catch up with her if you wanted."

"No, that's okay…" Kenzie toed the carpet. Her shoulders hung, and her eyes were slightly sad.

"Is everything okay?" Sutton said.

Kenzie hesitated, opening and closing her mouth a few times before forming words. "Do you ever not want to be alone, but not because you're lonely?"

Sutton had a million answers to give Kenzie, but she chose to seize the opportunity before her instead. "As a matter of fact, I'd love some company. I was just about to turn on some *Wynonna Earp*." She stepped aside and welcomed Kenzie into her room.

"Is that a movie or a show?"

Sutton turned to her slowly. "You've never heard of *Wynonna Earp*?" She raised her eyebrow as Kenzie shook her head. "Buckle up, Chicken, you're in for a wild ride." Sutton didn't mean to sound so suggestive, but her night had just taken an exciting and unexpected turn.

They laughed and talked all night. Sutton answered Kenzie's many, many questions enthusiastically and watched Kenzie intently as she reacted to the show. After Kenzie left, Sutton realized she'd totally forgotten about Rhea and hated how that proved what she already knew. And what she was trying so desperately to deny.

CHAPTER ELEVEN

Two games on the road usually wore a team out, but the Hurricanes now had two more wins on their record. Even though they were heading to the Orlando airport early the next morning, that didn't stop a few players from heading out to celebrate their return to the winner's circle.

Kenzie sipped at the Michelob Ultra Sutton had insisted on buying her, stating she still owed her for her first game. She stared as Sutton addressed the players in front of her. She knew her admiration was probably obvious and she didn't care.

"I am so proud of each of you. We took down Dallas last week like they were a junior team, and you'd think we were all psychics with the way we read the Tropics' plays today." She held up her drink. "To keeping the momentum."

Kenzie couldn't restrain her smile as she raised her bottle and tapped Sutton's glass. She took a drink of her beer and swayed to the music playing in the bar. The high of winning and the small buzz from the alcohol had her feeling delightfully loose. She guffawed when Sutton kept hitting the bottom of Taylor's glass, making it impossible for her to drink without spilling.

"Hey, Chicken." Sutton turned to Kenzie and started to mimic her relaxed dance moves.

Kenzie wanted to give her a stern look but found it impossible to break her jolly mood. "I hate that nickname, but I feel so good tonight that I'm gonna let it slide."

"You look good."

She didn't think she heard Sutton correctly. "Excuse me?" Kenzie placed her hand on Sutton's shoulder as she leaned in closer.

"You look like you're feeling good."

Kenzie giggled. "There's very little in this world that feels better than winning two games in a row."

Sutton bit down on the thin straw from her drink. "I can think of one or two things that feel better."

Kenzie felt each word as a pulse between her legs. "Better than winning an Olympic gold medal?"

Sutton put the straw back into her drink and stirred it a few times. "Okay, that one's pretty hard to top."

"And I bet you thought you could top anyone—um, anything." Kenzie looked at the beer in her hand like it had just betrayed her. Sutton was clearly trying to fight back laughter. She decided to change the subject. "How do you think we'll do without our national team players?"

"The time off will be good for your mentality going into the game. But you'll win, regardless. I know it. Our team is loaded with talent. I actually hate to leave for camp and miss one of our games."

"No one hates being called up to the national team."

"I don't hate that I'm called up, but I hate leaving my league team. This team is my home, you know? I want to fight for a win with you guys every game. I don't want to miss a minute."

Kenzie tried to hide her adoration. Sutton was loyal to a fault and so incredibly good-looking. Even as they stood in a strange bar after washing up in a locker room, Sutton's hair was sculpted back, and her face was bright. She wore a simple T-shirt and tight dark jeans. Sutton looked incredible and perfect, and Kenzie really needed to get over it.

"New Jersey is lucky to have you."

"That sentiment goes both ways, Shaw." Sutton touched her glass to Kenzie's bottle again. "I actually remember when there were talks of drafting you. Every team wanted you."

"I'm happy the Hurricanes drafted me. I still feel like I'm home. I know some players have a hard time making the adjustment to league play after college."

"I watched some of your college games."

"Why?"

"For one, I always watch the championships."

"Oh."

"I didn't think you looked like a soccer player."

Kenzie laughed. "No? Why's that?"

Sutton placed her drink on the bar. "You're really beautiful and your frame is so"—she motioned to Kenzie's body—"delicate."

Kenzie focused on the possible insult instead of the compliment. She felt way more comfortable tackling that. "Are you calling me weak?"

Sutton's eyes widened. "No."

"Frail?"

"No," Sutton said, shaking her head frantically.

"Then what do you mean?"

"You're not as muscular or thick as other players."

Against every instinct, Kenzie looked down at Sutton's chest and thighs. "There's nothing wrong with that."

"No, there's not. There's actually a lot right with it." Sutton started to fidget, and Kenzie took great pride in knowing she'd managed to fluster her for once. Kenzie waited for more of an explanation, because she couldn't let this go so easily. "You're feminine and strong. You have a very nice body, especially your—" Sutton frowned suddenly and reached into her back pocket. She pulled out her phone and answered it. "Hey." Sutton raised her index finger to Kenzie and walked away.

"Especially my what?" Kenzie called out to Sutton's back.

"Kenzie, drink this." Sherri tried to hand her a shot.

"No, thank you. I'm done after this."

"Okay." Sherri shrugged and downed the shot herself. "Where'd Sutton go?"

"She took a phone call." Kenzie didn't want to think about Sutton anymore. "How's your night going?"

"Great, but I'm ready to head home. I haven't seen my boyfriend in a couple weeks, and we'll finally get a few days together over our short break."

"Dating another athlete is hard, especially if your seasons are at the same time."

"Are you speaking from experience?" Sherri's eyes were a little glazed over, but she seemed genuinely interested.

"I am, yes."

"What are your plans for our break?"

Kenzie hesitated with her answer. She didn't want to feel like a loser because she wasn't traveling like some of her teammates or hunkering down with a significant other. "I'm heading back home to Pennsylvania for most of it. Just giving myself a little time to relax and recover."

"Not spending the time with anyone special?"

Kenzie was happy the bar was loud enough to hide her groan.

"No. I've been single for a while. My last couple of relationships ended because we just couldn't make time. I'm hoping that gets a little easier now that I'm out of school." Kenzie could see the wheels turning in Sherri's head. "Just ask it."

"Are we talking about guys or girls here?"

"I've dated both, but I'm driving down the one-way lady highway now." Kenzie scrunched her nose at her own description.

"Cool. Oh hey, Sutton's back." Sherri raised her hand for a high five, which Sutton readily gave.

"Everything okay?" Kenzie said and pointed to Sutton's phone.

Sutton looked at the device in her hand. "Yeah, that was just Rhea." Kenzie's spirit fell. "She wanted to talk since I'm leaving for camp, and it's always a little harder to get in touch with me then. I'm gonna head out so we can FaceTime. You all have a good night." Sutton put a twenty on the bar and walked out.

Kenzie felt her good attitude leave right along with Sutton. She sighed and put her beer on the bar. She sat on the stool and tried to revive just a little bit of the good feeling she'd had earlier.

Sherri sat beside her. "A soccer player walked into a bar, and the bartender said, why the long face?"

Kenzie grimaced. "That was terrible, you know that, right?"

Sherri smiled broadly. "You bet I do. But really, what's up? I felt the chill roll off you just now."

Kenzie slumped slightly. "You don't want to hear about my silly problems."

"Yes, I do. We're teammates and friends. We have to watch out for one another." Sherri pushed her shoulder into Kenzie.

"Fine. There's a girl—"

"I knew it. I can sniff out girl problems from a mile away."

"I like this girl, a lot, I think, but she's with someone else." Kenzie felt gross just saying the words aloud.

"Tricky. Does she like you back?"

"I don't think she does, even if I imagine it sometimes."

"Then what's the point? It seems like you should leave well enough alone."

The blunt, obvious truth cut into Kenzie. Sherri was right. Even if being drawn into Sutton's gravity felt incredible, it was wrong. Kenzie needed to get over whatever feelings she had for Sutton and learn to look at her like her teammate and captain. Maybe she'd be able to see her as a friend one day, too.

"Thank you, Sherri. You said exactly what I needed to hear." She opened her arms and hugged Sherri. She needed the comfort more than anything. "You're a good friend."

Sherri grabbed Kenzie's beer from the bar and held it up. "Hell yeah, I am." She downed the rest of it.

Kenzie simply shook her head. She continued dancing in place for a bit, just allowing herself to think and act beyond soccer. She liked moving her muscles to a rhythm instead of with exertion for a change. Taylor and Constance approached her a few minutes later with drinks in hand and giddy smiles plastered on their faces. Everyone was having a great time together, even with Sutton gone. Kenzie was a part of a team, a group of women she had come to genuinely like and enjoy spending time with. Her happiness and success with the Hurricanes had very little to do with Sutton, and Kenzie was going to focus on that.

She decided she'd spend her upcoming break cleansing her mind—and, hopefully, her heart—of Sutton. She'd center herself with quality time with her dad, and she'd probably forget all about Sutton and Rhea after being home. Yes, time apart was exactly what she needed.

CHAPTER TWELVE

Kenzie felt refreshed and more focused than ever after spending three days at home with her dad. They talked endlessly about her life with the Hurricanes, playing for a professional league, and the friends she'd made. She told her dad about her reunion with Chiara and how she'd found new friendships with Meredith and Sherri. She tried her best to leave thoughts of Sutton behind, but when she opened her dresser and found her Flores jersey sitting atop the rest of her shirts, she cringed and moved it to the top shelf of her closet instead. When she drove away from her father's house, she decided any feelings she had for Sutton were folded up neatly and left behind in Pennsylvania as well.

She didn't have Sutton to distract her, so she trained hard for the next week. With each bead of sweat that fell from her face during exercises and every time she fired off a shot at goal, Kenzie felt more like herself than she had in months. Today was the first game without their national team members.

"Hey, Kenzie," Brett said, holding the locker room door open for her. "Are you ready for this?"

Kenzie squared her shoulders and walked in. "Ready to win? You bet."

Brett smiled. "That's what I like to hear. Now, go get ready because you're starting."

Kenzie knew she had proven herself during their first four games, but that didn't make this announcement any less exciting or surprising. Kenzie was getting her very first start with her league team. She channeled the urge to jump up and down into an enthusiastic grin. She nodded at Brett. "Thank you."

He waved her off. "You've earned this, Shaw."

Kenzie tried her best to be subtle, but she skipped toward her locker. The bliss she felt must've been obvious because Sherri laughed at her.

"I take it you saw the starting eleven?"

"Brett just told me." Kenzie hung up her coat and took off her sweater and sneakers. She pulled at the button of her jeans and stopped, her hands trembling slightly. "What if I fuck it up?"

Sherri placed her hand on Kenzie's shoulder. "You won't. You're a great player, and as long as you bring that to the field, we're good."

"You're right." Kenzie shook out her arms and jumped in place. She punched Sherri's shoulder. "Thanks, buddy."

Kenzie got ready and started stretching in the locker room. You could never be too loose. She focused on the pull of her muscles instead of her nerves, but she thought about Sutton as the team prepared to leave the locker room. Taylor stood in as captain. Even though Kenzie knew Taylor could rally the team, she could really use a signature Flores pep talk.

Chiara lined up behind Kenzie and grabbed her shoulders, shaking her. "We *finally* get to show them what we can do, and not just in the last quarter of the game."

Kenzie squeezed Chiara's hands. "We're going to destroy Portland." With such supportive teammates, maybe she didn't need that pep talk after all.

The Hurricanes stepped out of the locker room and warmed up. Kenzie glanced over at the away team while they got ready to take the picture of their starting lineup, noticing Rhea's frown. Kenzie wondered if that was just her regular game face, but when Rhea caught Kenzie looking at her, her expression grew more serious and she turned away. Kenzie wasn't going to let Rhea intimidate her. She was about to start her first game, and she believed in her team and their ability to beat the Portland Chargers for the second time that season. She posed for her team's picture and then moved directly into a huddle.

Taylor clapped her hands rapidly, her giddiness palpable. "I haven't been this excited for a game since…" She looked around at everyone's faces. "Okay, fine, I'm always this excited for our games, but this one really got me going. Remember, Portland's offense is fast, but we're faster. Hurricanes on three," Taylor said, putting her hand into the center of the huddle. The whole team joined in and called out their name.

Kenzie took her position on the field. Portland won the coin toss, so they started with the ball. She took stock of everyone's whereabouts. The best defense for an offensive player was knowing where attacks could come from. She noticed Rhea watching her, but she chalked it up to Rhea knowing her opponent and moved on. The referee raised the whistle to her lips, and Kenzie took a deep breath. The cheering crowd disappeared, and Kenzie focused on the ball as the whistle blew.

She accomplished very little in the first half of the game except chasing the ball from one Portland player to another. Every time she'd gain possession, Rhea would be there to push her off the ball. Her first break came during the three extra minutes tacked on to the first forty-five.

She stripped the ball from one of Portland's defenders right after they received a pass from their goalkeeper. They didn't know Kenzie was already behind them, and she was grateful for her natural-born speed. She could see Chiara flying up the opposite end of the field toward the box. She knew she could push forward and take the shot herself or pass it off to Chiara. With another look and a quick calculation of the angle she'd have to shoot from, she made a split-second decision, aimed a cross pass to Chiara, and hoped Chiara had enough space to make the most of the opportunity.

Kenzie stopped running the moment the ball left her foot. She watched it soar through the air and knew her aim was right on target. Chiara's first touch was smooth, and she received the pass with little effort. Chiara fired her shot with accuracy, but the Chargers' goalkeeper read the play and caught the ball in her hands. Kenzie kicked at the grass beneath her feet. The whistle blew, signaling the end of the first half.

The locker room was buzzing during halftime. They knew they'd had a strong first half and were hungry to get back out there. Brett announced one substitution, but Kenzie felt relieved he wasn't taking her out of the game, and she'd have another chance to make up for the earlier missed goal. She took the water bottle Sherri handed her. "I know I could make it to the goal if Rhea would just focus on someone else for a minute." She took a few gulps of water. "It's like her sole purpose is keeping me off the ball."

"She's a good player," Sherri said, taking the bottle back from Kenzie and walking away.

Kenzie frowned. "Never said she wasn't."

When Kenzie stood on the field again, a new wave of determination hit her. This game was hers, and she was going to own it. The Hurricanes started with the ball, pushing forward the moment the whistle blew.

She was able to get herself into scoring position immediately, but the Chargers kept possession and she was unable to make a connection. The next chance Kenzie had with the ball, Rhea bumped her with a shoulder check, more forcefully than necessary. Kenzie fought to keep her balance and chased after Rhea immediately. Kenzie was not about to lose possession to the same player multiple times in one game. She charged forward and met Taylor in front of Rhea, who was unable to keep control of the ball with two players on her.

Taylor passed the ball upfield and Kenzie caught up to it, cutting to the center of the field. Rhea charged her from behind just as she started to slow her speed and count the players around her. Kenzie stumbled for a second before regaining the ball. She passed it smoothly between Rhea's feet, cheers erupting in the stadium. The crowd always went wild when a player nutmegged someone, and it was always embarrassing for the victim. Kenzie smiled and slotted the ball behind her. Chiara picked it up, and Kenzie made a run for the goal.

Chiara's pass was perfect, dropping the ball in front of Kenzie with a small bounce that put it on a platter for her. She took her shot and watched as the ball soared with impressive speed past the keeper into the back of the net. Kenzie fell to her knees and raised her hands in the air. Her teammates rushed her and started to pile on top of her. Everyone was cheering and congratulating her.

She relished a few seconds of celebration, and then she returned to her starting position. As she readied herself to resume play, the announcer called out her name and goal time. She grinned but snapped back into the moment when the whistle blew.

The Chargers were obviously more determined than ever to score, but the Hurricanes wouldn't give up their lead without a fight. They spent thirty minutes playing an aggressive game of keep-away. With nine minutes left on the clock, Kenzie saw a potential play to Chiara, but Rhea tackled her before she could make her move, sliding directly into her feet. Kenzie hit the ground with a loud yelp. Her chest hurt as she tried to breathe after having the wind knocked out of her. She was lucky she hadn't slammed her head into the ground.

Rhea pushed Kenzie off, leaning closer as she stood up. "There's more where that came from if you don't leave Sutton alone."

Kenzie stared up at her. The stadium lighting made her squint and she continued to breathe hard. She wiped grass from her forehead and got to her knees.

Taylor rushed over and pulled Kenzie to her feet. "What did she say to you?"

Kenzie was going to tell her, but she shook her head instead. "Nothing. Let's close this out." She patted the captain's band on Taylor's arm and moved back into position.

The desire to go for a revenge tackle was great. Kenzie took a deep breath to calm herself and jogged over for the free kick. She wanted to take it, but that's not what they had practiced as a team. They were still in Chargers territory, so they had a good chance for another goal opportunity. She waited patiently as Taylor ran down the clock by slowly getting ready to take the kick. The Chargers grew obviously anxious, and their captain yelled at the referee to do something about the time being wasted. Taylor raised her hand, signaling she was about to take the kick, and started toward the ball.

Kenzie ran directly to where the ball landed in a group of Chargers. She felt fearless as she used her body to gain space for herself. She grabbed the ball with her cleats and pulled it behind her. When she spun around, she saw Rhea coming at her. Kenzie ran to the left and passed the ball off to Isabella Dias, one of their best passers.

Kenzie dashed off to the far goalpost and waited to see what kind of magic her team could make happen, but they lost control and the ball went out of bounds. She ran her palms over her face, along her slicked-back hair. She whipped her long ponytail and ran back up the field. The clock signaled two minutes left, and she knew they'd spend that time keeping the ball from the other team.

Both teams played at full speed for the remaining minutes, and when the final whistle blew, Kenzie collapsed on the field. She lay on her back, breathing hard and laughing. They won, and they won because of the goal she scored. She got to her feet to shake hands with the staff and opposing team. Rhea didn't look at her when they shook hands, and that was fine by her.

"Chicken."

Kenzie turned at the familiar nickname and the unforgettable voice calling to her.

Sutton ran to her and pulled her into a hug, then lifted her off the ground and spun her in circles. "Congratulations on your first goal."

Kenzie looked up at her in confusion. "You're here."

"We got in a little while ago, and I came right to the game. You were amazing." Sutton reached out to grab her arm and Kenzie dodged the touch.

"I have to cool off." Kenzie walked to the far side of their group and grabbed a water bottle. She sat on the cold grass and tried not to watch Sutton walk over to Rhea. But she watched them anyway.

Sutton's whole demeanor changed when she started talking to Rhea. Her body was rigid, and she pressed her lips together into a thin line. Rhea looked just as guarded. They didn't touch one another, and the space between them was wider than it should have been. Sutton motioned back to her team and became more animated as she spoke. Rhea put her hand up and walked away. Sutton turned and looked directly at Kenzie. Suddenly under a shadow, Kenzie looked up to see Sherri standing over her.

"I'm sorry," Sherri said, "but Rhea's been my friend for years, and it's kinda girl-code to tell your friend when someone's after their girlfriend."

Kenzie gawked. "I'm not after her girlfriend."

Sherri gave her a disbelieving look. "Look, I'm apologizing because I didn't know she'd be that aggressive with you."

Kenzie choked out a laugh. "Sure, great." She stood and rolled her shoulders. The night chill started to bite at her damp skin. "Please go tell your bestie I received her message loud and clear." She stepped around Sherri and was faced with Sutton again. Kenzie felt trapped. She needed space from Sherri, but she couldn't go near Sutton. She started toward the bench.

She should've been celebrating, but instead she was losing a new friend and fighting what her heart wanted. No matter how hard she tried to ignore her feelings, they all came flooding back. What was the point of denying how she felt when she was already being punished for it?

Chapter Thirteen

Sutton knew whatever had happened at the game changed things with Kenzie, and she was trying to ignore why. She was mad at Rhea for acting like a child, and she was sad because Kenzie wouldn't talk to her. They spent the day training with the team and Kenzie didn't cast her a single glance. When they went through drills, Kenzie would follow instructions and then move on. Not one joke or playful moment. She didn't even see Kenzie leave. Sutton missed her.

Sutton packed up her gear so slowly she was the last one out. She was grateful she hadn't carpooled with Taylor because she needed the time to herself to think. She needed to fix things with Kenzie, but she didn't know where to start without knowing exactly what had happened in the first place. All Sutton really knew was she needed get back that lightness Kenzie put in her chest.

She threw her bag over her shoulder and walked out the door. She heard a strange sound coming from the field and discovered it wasn't empty. Kenzie stood in front of the far goal.

Sutton walked onto the field but stayed close to the sidelines. She didn't want to be spotted just yet. She watched Kenzie move around the ball, using fancy, fast footwork that impressed Sutton. Kenzie kicked the ball, and it curled right into the net. She jogged up and grabbed the ball, turning back to do it all over again. But she stopped walking and dropped the ball the moment she saw Sutton watching her.

"Hey." Sutton twisted the strap to her bag. "What are you doing out here all alone?"

"I need to improve my footwork. I shouldn't have lost the ball as many times as I did the other day." Kenzie's hands were on her hips, and she looked down at the ball.

"You looked great to me."

"I need to be better."

Sutton didn't understand why Kenzie looked angry. "Are you okay?"

Kenzie nodded.

"You don't seem okay."

"Just frustrated with how I played."

Sutton knew a wall when she saw one. Kenzie wouldn't say anymore. "Let me help you."

"You don't have to. I'm sure you have better things to do."

Sutton set her bag down and pulled out her soccer shoes. She changed out of her sneakers and pulled another ball from the bagful Kenzie had by the benches. "I didn't have any plans, and I'd really like to help my teammate."

Kenzie's shoulders sagged when she finally looked Sutton in the eye. "Fine. One on one, that's where my problem is. My feet aren't fast enough."

"Your feet are very fast and precise. You need to focus on your goal instead of the other players. Here," she said, dropping a ball at Kenzie's feet, "come at me."

They played against each other for almost a half hour, and Kenzie couldn't break free of Sutton's defenses. Sutton kicked the ball away from Kenzie's feet with ease. "You're not listening to what I'm telling you."

Kenzie growled in frustration. "I am listening." She wiped the sweat from her eyes and pointed to Sutton's feet. "You're tricking me. I don't know how, but you are. I've been playing soccer since I was five. This shouldn't be so hard."

Sutton dropped another ball between them. She shook her head and shot Kenzie a humored look. "I'm not tricking you. I'm just predicting what you're going to do."

"Because you're my teammate. You know all my secrets—other teams don't." Kenzie flipped the ball onto her toe and started a simple volley from foot to foot.

Sutton rushed forward and caught the ball midair. "I doubt I know all your secrets."

Kenzie stepped back and kept her eyes on the ball. "You tell me to focus on the goal and not your feet, but your feet keep getting in the way." The way Kenzie's forehead creased in frustration was attractive and Sutton felt a fraction of the lightness she missed return to her.

"You're an unbelievably skilled player. I love watching you play," Sutton said, the words feeling more like a confession than a compliment. Kenzie blinked rapidly. "You do?" she said in a breathy tone. Her plump lips thinned out as she smiled, but they were still sinfully full and captivating. "When do you watch me?"

"Every practice and every game. If you have a foot of open space, you're unstoppable, but if your opponent closes in, you fumble the ball a bit. It has nothing to do with your skill. It's almost like you get nervous."

Kenzie's face fell. She looked genuinely disappointed and Sutton wondered if she was looking for more compliments or more honesty.

"Take the ball down to midfield. Charge back like the opposing team left you with an open lane, and I'm the only one standing between you and the goal. Charge at me and score."

Kenzie picked up the ball. "What makes this exercise any different from every game?"

"You're not usually going against the best defender in the game."

"Were you born this cocky or is it something you developed over time?"

Sutton laughed loudly. "Go," she said with a nod downfield. "I'll be here waiting for you."

"Great." Kenzie started to jog away from her.

Sutton watched Kenzie's hips sway. "That's far enough, Chicken."

Kenzie turned. "What did I say about calling me that?" Her shout echoed down the field.

"I can't help it when you sprint like that." Sutton shot her an open-mouthed grin.

"Ready?"

"Ready."

Kenzie dropped the ball and took off. She dribbled it flawlessly. Handling the ball was obviously second nature to her. She drifted to the right and Sutton watched her carefully. Sutton squared up as Kenzie got closer. Kenzie cut the ball back to the left and shifted her gaze to Sutton's feet.

"Focus on the goal," Sutton said.

Kenzie picked her head up just enough to look at the goal, but then she went right back to the ground. After looking back and forth too many times, Kenzie lost her focus completely and collided with Sutton. They tumbled to the ground together.

Sutton groaned, one leg thrown across Kenzie's. "Shit," she said as she moved from her side to her back. "I didn't expect you to tackle me." Her back was sore, but nothing felt out of place or seriously injured.

"I'm sorry." Kenzie rubbed her shoulder, then reached down and grabbed Sutton's leg. "Are you okay?"

"Yeah, I'm fine." She placed her hand on Kenzie's and gave it a squeeze. "You really pack a punch with that body of yours, Chicken."

"Please stop calling me that."

Sutton rolled back on her side and propped herself up on her elbow. She stared down at Kenzie. Kenzie's hazel eyes were impossible to read but her smirk revealed so much. "If you really hate it, I'll stop. The last thing I ever want to do is upset you or make you uncomfortable." Her imagination started to stray as her other senses came to life in the wake of the impact. Kenzie's body felt firm beneath her leg, and she watched Kenzie's chest rise and fall with her breathing. The setting sunlight highlighted the kaleidoscope of colors in Kenzie's eyes. With little to no effort, she could lean over and kiss Kenzie. Instead, she jumped to her feet and extended a hand. She lifted Kenzie to her feet like she weighed nothing.

Kenzie laughed.

"What's so funny?"

"Nothing, it's just…" Kenzie tilted her head slightly. "I knocked you down and you still helped me up. You should've left me down there to think about what I've done."

Sutton started laughing, too. "Nah. You wouldn't be able to get the grass off my back from down there."

"I did make a little bit of a mess out of you," Kenzie said. She reached out to fix Sutton's hair.

"You have no idea." Sutton's whisper was delicate. She felt like she had to force the words out. She guided Kenzie's hand to her face and sucked in a breath. Kenzie's palm fit perfectly against her cheek, as if she was always meant to hold Sutton's face in her hands. Their eyes locked and time stood still. Sutton watched Kenzie's face carefully, making sure she felt their connection, too.

"Tell me," Kenzie said, demanding and not begging.

"I can't explain it, but I'm drawn to you. I feel…"

"Connected." Kenzie ran the pad of her thumb to the corner of Sutton's mouth as Sutton nodded. "I thought I had made it all up in my head."

Sutton closed her eyes to the divine touch. "You didn't." When she looked at Kenzie, she couldn't focus on anything but her lips. She wanted to be devoured by that mouth. She stepped closer and reveled in the feel of Kenzie's body against hers, feeding off the intimate touch. When she looked back into Kenzie's eyes, she noticed something new flicker in their depths. Kenzie smiled sadly and withdrew her hand. She stepped away from Sutton without another word.

"Wait," she said, reaching for Kenzie.

"I can't, Sutton, not like this." Kenzie walked to the bench and packed her bag.

Sutton didn't move until Kenzie threw her gear over her shoulder and started to leave. "Kenzie," Sutton said in a tone so desperate she surprised herself.

Kenzie turned to Sutton. "You need to talk to Rhea. She knows there's something here."

"How? We've just admitted it to each other."

Kenzie scratched the back of her neck. "Sherri and I were talking a while back, and I admitted to liking someone who was unavailable. She put two and two together and told Rhea."

Sutton sighed. "They're pretty good friends."

"I know that now."

Sutton stood with her hands on her hips. She just wanted some things in life to be easier, like being able to pursue the girl she liked. But she was the one in a relationship past its expiration date, not Kenzie. "I'm sorry."

Kenzie smiled. "You have nothing to be sorry for."

She resisted the urge to move closer to Kenzie. She licked her lips and matched Kenzie's smile with one of her own. "Say it again before you go."

Kenzie shook her head and asked, "Say what?"

"That you like me."

Kenzie giggled. "Call your girlfriend, then we can talk about it." Kenzie spun on her heel and left the field.

Sutton watched her go. As the distance between them grew larger, the clearer Sutton's life became. She had to do the one thing she had been avoiding for months. Rhea wasn't going to take their breakup well, especially after the latest developments, thanks to Sherri's big mouth. Breakups were hard, but as she watched Kenzie disappear in the distance, she knew the pain would be worth it.

CHAPTER FOURTEEN

The next three weeks wore on Sutton more heavily than any recent period of time she could remember. The Hurricanes hadn't been at their best, having a loss, a win, and now a draw over the course of that time. The tie was just as bad as a loss. Sutton was frustrated with her team, but mostly with herself. She and Kenzie had suffered an obvious disconnect since the almost-kiss on the field, but Sutton couldn't bear to break up with Rhea over the phone and this weird in-between was eating away at her. She even avoided Taylor because she knew she'd realize something was up. Sutton felt alone and aggravated, and that bled into her game.

She left immediately following the Hurricanes' tie with Kansas City. She could usually put anything on the back burner before a game, but seeing Kenzie was a constant reminder. When Brett had torn them apart during halftime, Kenzie requested to be taken out of the game because she wasn't helping the team. Brett told her that if she felt responsible for the mess they were in, she could stick around to clean it up.

Sutton lost herself to the never-ending Portland night sky. The brick stoop was cold beneath her and the chill bit at her skin through her jeans. She counted the cars as they passed by, trying not to overthink what she was about to do. She didn't love Rhea, but she respected her and cared about her—which was why she'd jumped on the first flight to Portland after her early game. Now she sat on Rhea's doorstep with nothing to do but think. Think about how she should've ended things months ago. Think about how she knew her heart would eventually belong to Kenzie after the very first time they met. Think about where she'd like to take Kenzie on their first date.

Rhea pulled in to the driveway, and all Sutton could think about then was how badly she didn't want to hurt her. Rhea got out of the car and smiled.

"This is unexpected," Rhea said. She grabbed her bag out of the back seat and shut the car door. The sound echoed in the quiet neighborhood. "We have the place to ourselves for a while." She walked up to Sutton and placed her hand on her knee. "I've missed you."

Sutton could feel her eyes start to tear up. She shook her head and bent forward so she could rest her forehead against the back of Rhea's hand. She greedily soaked up the warmth before sitting up again. "I came here to talk." She didn't want to dance or lead Rhea on any more than she already had.

Rhea pulled her hand away and stepped back. Anger flared in her eyes. "Come upstairs." She stepped around Sutton and opened the door. They walked silently up to her shared apartment. Rhea threw her keys on the small kitchen table and placed her bag on the floor. When she turned back to Sutton, she already had tears in her eyes. "Just say it."

"I'm sorry."

"I don't want your apology, Sutton, I want a reason. I want the truth."

Sutton took a deep breath. She leaned with her back against the counter and crossed her arms over her chest. The words were there, but she struggled to get them out. "I've been unfair to you. I don't feel the same way you feel, and I haven't for a while."

"Let me guess, you haven't felt the same since the beginning of the season."

"No—"

"Since a gorgeous rookie stepped on the field to entertain you."

"What? No, Rhea, it's not like that."

"I know you. I know how you operate and what gets you off."

Sutton fought against her rising anger. Rhea had the right to be mad, not her. "You do know me, and you must've noticed I haven't really been in this since the off-season." Sutton watched Rhea pace. She wanted to reach out and touch her, to calm her and try to get her to understand. But Sutton knew better. "I came here because I care about you and didn't want to do this over the phone."

Rhea stopped and turned so quickly her ponytail whipped across her shoulders. "Tell me it has nothing to do with Kenzie Shaw, and I'll believe you. I'll accept your apology, and I'll believe we just didn't work out."

Sutton looked Rhea in the eye. She worked her jaw multiple times and opened her mouth to lie, but the truth came spilling out. "I'm not doing this for Kenzie or because of Kenzie, but I am doing this *now* because of my feelings for her."

"I knew it," Rhea said with a shake of her head, wiping a stray tear away. "Sherri was right. I can't wait to tell her. What exactly did Kenzie do for you that you were so quick to drop me?"

Sutton clenched her fists to keep her patience under control. "She didn't do anything. I've felt like this for a while. Instead of putting myself in a position where I'd cheat, I came here to talk."

"I bet she makes you feel like a superstar. Is that it? She looks at you with those big doe eyes and you eat it up like the self-centered asshole you are."

"I don't love you," Sutton snapped. "I haven't loved you, and I don't know that I ever did. I came here out of respect, but I'm starting to question even that right now." Sutton pulled out her phone and ordered a car service to come get her. She'd rather sit in the airport for hours than endure any more name-calling. She understood Rhea was hurt, but she needed to maintain a little self-worth. "I'll see you at our next game against each other." She was shocked to see tears streaming down Rhea's face. She stepped in and took Rhea in her arms. "I really am sorry," she said quietly into her ear.

"So am I." Rhea pushed Sutton away, breaking their embrace. "I'm sorry I wasn't enough."

Sutton used the pads of her thumbs to wipe away Rhea's tears. "You were always enough—I just wasn't right for you." She held still when Rhea stood tall and kissed her. Sutton kissed her back as sadness filled her heart. She stepped back.

"You can just ship anything I left at your house," Rhea said, wiping tears from her face.

"We'll see each other eventually."

"No. We may be able to be friends one day, but for now, for a while, I don't even want to look at you."

Sutton's heart stung. She nodded solemnly. "I understand."

"I hate how much I love you, and I've hated it since day one because I knew you were going to break my heart."

"I didn't know. I never thought I'd be the one to end us. Despite popular belief, I'm not always looking for someone else." Sutton started for the door.

"Is that really true?" Rhea's question held no malice. "I hope it is, because Kenzie doesn't deserve to feel this way."

Sutton arched her eyebrow. "But she deserved your beatdown on the field?" She shook her head when Rhea shrugged. "I'll see you around, Rhea." Sutton opened the door and stepped in the hallway. She cast a glance back to Rhea before closing the door on over a year of her life. She took the steps slowly and walked right to the car waiting for her. She felt lighter. Rhea could go on to be happy now, and maybe she was ready to find her own happiness.

She had to wait hours for a return flight, so she busied herself with an airport dinner and a nap in an uncomfortable lounge chair. She could've used her status to score more comfortable accommodations, but the discomfort was her penance.

CHAPTER FIFTEEN

For the first time in a long time, Sutton was nervous. Deep down, shaking in her boots nervous. She took every back road she could, hoping the extra minutes would quell her nerves. She knew she had no rational reason to be scared. She wasn't stuck in an odd gray area with Kenzie. Their feelings were obvious, but Sutton couldn't bring herself to drive the rest of the way to Kenzie's house.

Every what-if she could think of popped into her head and festered in her imagination. What if Kenzie wasn't home, and her mom answered the door? What if Kenzie'd had enough time to talk herself out of what was growing between them? What if Kenzie never really wanted her after all?

Once she was in front of Kenzie's house and saw the car in the driveway, she resorted to an old-fashioned pep talk. "You're not going to announce you're single, and you're definitely not going to act like you just came here for that reason." She checked her appearance in the rearview mirror. Her hair was in place, which gave her a small boost of confidence. She grabbed her phone and typed out a quick message to Kenzie.

Are you home?

Sutton sat and waited for a response. She bounced her leg up and down and turned off the radio because it added to her jitters. She continuously checked it but still jumped when it buzzed in her hand.

Yes?

Sutton smiled. She could hear Kenzie's confused tone in her head. *Are you home alone?* She hesitated for a second before hitting send. She stared out the windshield at the blossoming trees as they swayed in the breeze.

Yeah. Mom's at work.

Sutton jumped into action. She hopped out of her Jeep and started up the winding walkway to Kenzie's front door. She wouldn't give herself any time to think, or she might talk herself out of what she was about to do. She knocked and took a deep breath. Her neck felt tight. Before she could stretch it, the door swung open.

Kenzie stared at her quizzically. "What are you doing here?"

"I wanted to, um…" Sutton's mind reeled with every way she could finish that sentence. *Tell you something? See you? Kiss you?* She coughed nervously. "I just got back from Portland and wanted to stop by." She looked at the concrete step she stood on and then out to the front yard. She had never felt so awkward in her life.

"You were in Portland?" Kenzie stood with her arms crossed, in an old sweatshirt and yoga pants, looking every bit as confused and apprehensive as Sutton felt.

"Yeah. I went yesterday and got in really early this morning. Listen, can I come in? I feel a little like what I'm going to say will be broadcasted," she said with a sweep of her arm toward the neighborhood. "You know?"

Kenzie stepped to the side. "Okay. Sure."

Sutton froze once she was few feet into the house.

"Are you okay?" Kenzie said. "You're acting weird."

"I'm a little nervous." Sutton ran her hand over the back of her head. "I went to see Rhea."

"Wow. A trip across the country to see your girlfriend for a night." Kenzie's shoulders fell slightly. She turned and walked toward the kitchen. "Would you like something to drink or eat? I have some roasted veggies."

"I had to go see her."

Kenzie stopped walking but didn't turn around. "Why are you telling me this?" Her voice sounded small and sad.

Sutton decided to blurt it out. "She's not my girlfriend anymore. That's why I went to Portland with no warning and for less than a day. Rhea and I had been together for over a year. I couldn't break up with her over the phone."

Kenzie turned slowly. "And you came right here?"

"I tried to sleep for a few hours, but I couldn't wait to see you."

"Why?"

Now she was more confused than nervous. "Because I wanted to talk, like you said we could."

Kenzie pressed her hand to her forehead. "I didn't think this would actually happen."

"Wait," Sutton said as her heart sank. "I thought we were on the same page. I thought you wanted this." She motioned between them.

"I do, Sutton. I want this so much I'm convinced I'm imagining it."

"It's real."

"No one flies thousands of miles to break up with someone just to be with me."

"Someone just did." Sutton cautiously stepped closer, studying the way Kenzie fidgeted and avoided looking at her. "Talk to me. What's going on in that lovely mind of yours?"

"It's too soon. You shouldn't go from one girl to another. You should take time to be alone and think about this. If you still want it down the road, then fine. We should talk and take the chance."

"I'm not going from one girl to another." Sutton reached out for Kenzie's hand, dismayed but not surprised when Kenzie stepped back. "It's been you and only you for a while. The only difference now is the obstacle between us is gone."

Kenzie remained silent.

Sutton sighed with frustration. "This is not how I imagined this going."

"What did you imagine? Me hearing you're single now and throwing myself at you?"

"Well, no. I mean, not exactly like that, but not as poorly as this."

"Tell me how you thought this would play out." Kenzie sounded earnest but not upset or aggressive.

"I thought I'd come here, and we'd talk a little, you'd be happy to see me and tell me about what's been going on with you. We'd laugh and relax, but there'd still be a tension between us because we almost kissed, and I know we've both been thinking about that moment since it happened. Then, when I got up the nerve, I'd tell you where I went and why. You'd have a bunch of questions like how Rhea took it and what I said, or if she knew it was for you."

"Those are questions I would ask," Kenzie said, fidgeting with her hands.

"And once you've turned over my every answer in your head at least a dozen times, you'd ask what it meant for us. Because you'd need me to say it."

"Say what?"

"That I want to be with you."

Kenzie ran her hands through her hair and pulled it up, securing it with an elastic from her wrist. Her face was flushed in the most attractive way.

"And then after I tell you how badly I want to be with you, I thought I'd finally, *finally*, get to kiss you."

"That sounds lovely," Kenzie said with a nod. "Almost like a fairy tale."

Sutton could feel her hesitation. "But…?"

"But it's unrealistic. I think we need time."

Sutton dropped her head in surrender. She wasn't going to beg or treat Kenzie like her feelings were any less important than her own. "Okay. I understand."

"You do?"

Sutton bobbed her head from side to side. "Barely, but what I definitely understand is you're asking me for something I can very easily give you." She closed the distance between them and hugged Kenzie tightly, wanting Kenzie to feel every ounce of safety and security she was offering. "I'll be here when you're ready," she whispered into Kenzie's ear.

She gave herself one last moment to relish Kenzie's warmth and scent before she stepped away reluctantly.

"What about you?" Kenzie said. "How will I know when you're ready?"

Sutton smiled softly, barely a curl of the corner of her mouth. "I was ready the moment you opened the door." Before she could stop herself, Sutton leaned forward and kissed Kenzie's forehead. "I'll see you at practice tomorrow."

She walked out the door. She couldn't be around Kenzie for another minute before her resolve would falter. Kenzie hadn't rejected her, but why did it feel that way? Her heart was hammering by the time she reached her Jeep. She put her hand on the door handle but didn't open it. She pressed her head against the window and let the cool glass calm her.

"Sutton!"

Sutton spun around to see Kenzie running toward her. She fell into Sutton's arms and kissed her then, a sexy, simple meeting of lips. They discovered how well they fit together. Sutton dropped her hands to Kenzie's waist and gripped her tightly. She separated briefly to take a breath before matching Kenzie's enthusiasm head-on.

Kenzie pulled back suddenly and looked startled. "I'm sorry."

"For what?"

"I should've asked if that was okay." Kenzie toyed with the metal buttons of Sutton's jean jacket.

"You knew it was okay. That's why you did it." She felt Kenzie start to step away, and she tightened her grip. "Would it be okay if I kissed you again?"

Kenzie's eyes lit up, and any worry on her face melted away. "Please."

Sutton leaned in slowly this time, feeling the warmth of Kenzie's skin and the softness of her mouth as they barely brushed each other. She ran her hands up Kenzie's arms and concentrated on the plush feel of her shirt. She wanted to immerse herself in every detail, to overwhelm her senses. She breathed Kenzie's perfume and tasted the peppermint on her tongue.

"Kiss me already," Kenzie said, tugging on Sutton's jacket.

Sutton laughed. "There's no way I'm going to rush this." She brushed her nose against Kenzie's. "You feel so good." She brought her hands up to the back of Kenzie's neck and played with the soft skin and baby-fine hairs there. She ran her fingertips along the side of Kenzie's neck before tracing the slight curve where her neck met her shoulder. Kenzie's jaw tensed as Sutton grazed it with her thumbs.

Sutton finally kissed Kenzie fully. She felt and heard Kenzie's answering moan. Sutton opened her mouth just enough to peek her tongue out and taste the bow of Kenzie's upper lip. Kenzie surged forward and tried to gain the upper hand, but Sutton expertly controlled the pace. She slid her tongue between Kenzie's lips with a slow, torturous, and sinfully delightful motion. She knew this moment was meant to happen as soon as Kenzie welcomed her with her own velvety tongue.

The first day they met.

When Kenzie hit her with a ball.

When Sutton sat beside her on the bus.

Every single moment between them had led to this kiss.

Sutton pulled their hips together and opened her mouth wider. She couldn't get over the intoxicating dance they were doing. Everything about Kenzie felt delicate and feminine, and Sutton grew wetter with every touch. By the way Kenzie shifted to pull Sutton's thigh between her legs, Sutton knew the feeling was mutual. Sutton ended the kiss and rested her forehead against Kenzie's. Their breathing was labored.

"We could go inside or back to my place, if you'd like."

Kenzie stilled. "As tempting as that is, and believe me when I say I'm tempted, it's also a little fast."

"I should say good-bye, then." Sutton gave Kenzie's pouty lips a peck. "Because I want to do this right." She gave her another chaste kiss. She hoped for a green light from Kenzie to take it further, but one never came.

Kenzie's eyes were still closed. "You should definitely go."

"I want to take you out."

Kenzie opened her eyes and her face broke into a wide grin. "Okay. I like the sound of that. What were you thinking? Dinner tonight or maybe a movie?"

"Atlantic City this weekend."

Kenzie looked shocked.

"And breakfast before practice tomorrow."

"You're taking me to Atlantic City?"

"Yes. There're a few shows I'm interested in and so many restaurants we won't know what to pick, but I think it'd be nice to get away for a little bit. We can leave as soon as we get back from our game on Friday and stay until Sunday. I leave for camp next week, so I'd like some real time with you before then."

"Stay over?"

"Yes."

"In the same room?"

Sutton couldn't help but chuckle as she pulled Kenzie in for another kiss. She was so dang cute. "In the same room with no expectations. I'll even book a double. I just want to get away with you." Sutton brought her palm to Kenzie's cheek and Kenzie reached up to hold it in place. Sutton stared at her contented expression. "God, you're beautiful."

"I'm a wreck, but I'll pull myself together for the weekend."

"Every way I've ever seen you, you've been perfect."

Kenzie poked Sutton's stomach. "Save the lines for this weekend when you wine and dine me." She stood tall and kissed Sutton. "You better go before I start listing reasons for you to stay."

"I'd love to hear those reasons."

Kenzie held Sutton at arm's length and winked. "I bet you would. Good-bye, Sutton," she said before turning and going back to her house.

"Good-bye, Chicken." Sutton laughed when Kenzie's stride faltered.

Chapter Sixteen

During the week leading up to their next game, she and Sutton went on like a date wasn't planned in their near future. They trained and talked and shared more than a few laughs. Sutton even invited her out to meet Taylor and a few other friends for a drink, but Kenzie politely declined. She wasn't sure how to be around Sutton when she was with her friends now. She wanted to either touch Sutton or run away from her. There was no in-between for Kenzie.

Kenzie stopped to sign as many autographs as she could after the Hurricanes' game against the Dallas Heat. The away team wasn't always expected to sign autographs, but they'd had a great game. Kenzie stood out as the star of the show after scoring two goals in the first half and a third in the last ten minutes. Celebrating her first hat trick of the season with cheering fans distracted her from the boulder of nervousness weighing in her gut. After the team returned home, Sutton was taking her away on a trip for just the two of them. She tried her best to not dwell on what could happen, or what was expected to happen.

She was grateful Sutton drove because she knew she couldn't concentrate on the road and the millions of thoughts in her head. From time to time, Sutton would rest her free hand on Kenzie's thigh while she drove. She'd tap Kenzie's leg as she told a story or squeeze her knee when Kenzie would make her laugh. All the touching worried and excited her, and those warring feelings exhausted her. By the time they arrived at the hotel, Kenzie couldn't stop yawning.

"I'm sorry, I promise I won't sleep the whole time."

Sutton broke out into her own wide yawn. "Tonight *is* for sleeping. I can't believe how much harder these games get with each passing year." Sutton stepped aside and let Kenzie enter the resort first.

"Rampone played until she was forty, so I don't want to hear you complain."

"Good point." Sutton led them to the front desk and checked in. Sutton had kept her promise and reserved a room with two beds. Kenzie remained quiet as Sutton collected the keys and walked them through the main floor of the casino. She loved the chatter and sounds from the slot machines. She knew she'd have to come back to play when she had a few extra dollars in her pocket.

Sutton insisted they pick up sandwiches from a twenty-four hour deli on the ground floor before finally heading up to the room. After a picnic on one of the beds, they changed into soft and worn pajamas. When Kenzie emerged from the bathroom she saw Sutton stretched across a bed with her head propped in her hand. Her eyes were heavy and smile soft.

"I'm very excited to be here with you, but I think it's time for bed," Sutton said, letting her head fall on a pillow. Kenzie's nerves reignited and she started to pace. Sutton sat up. "You okay, Chicken?"

She took a deep breath and clasped her hands together. "I should've told you about this before…well, before everything."

Sutton looked much more awake as she sat on the edge of the bed and planted her feet on the floor. "Should've told me what?"

Kenzie wrung her hands and then cracked her knuckles. "Sex is a really big thing for me and I haven't had it in a long time."

"What's a long time? If you don't mind me asking."

Kenzie knew she could trust her, but she was still embarrassed. "Over two years now."

"Wow," Sutton said, sitting back on her elbows. "That's a long time. No one special?"

Kenzie glanced at Sutton's team T-shirt, stretched so attractively across her breasts it momentarily scattered Kenzie's thoughts.

"Kenzie?"

"What?"

"I asked if you couldn't find someone special enough."

"Something like that."

Sutton patted the mattress beside her. "Come here." She waited for Kenzie to sit beside her before lying back. "Lie with me."

Kenzie lay back and stared at the ceiling, her arm pressed against Sutton's. She heard Sutton move, her face only inches away. She looked at her full lips and knew how sweet and soft they were. Their last stolen kiss felt like forever ago.

"You can talk to me, Kenzie. Always." Sutton took her hand and laced their fingers together.

Kenzie turned back to the ceiling and closed her eyes. "I never really thought about my sexuality because I was always surrounded by straight people," she said quickly, trying to race through her story. "But when I got to college and met the rest of my team…"

"Lesbians everywhere?"

Kenzie laughed. "Lesbians everywhere."

Sutton brought Kenzie's hand to her lips and kissed her knuckle.

"I had a few boyfriends in high school but nothing serious, and then I started to question things once I saw so many women happily together. But even though I felt comfortable around gay women, I didn't accept that I could be one of them. How do you just wake up gay, you know?" She looked at Sutton just in time to catch her nodding. "I spent my freshman and sophomore years dating guy after guy and trying to prove to myself I just hadn't met the right man. God, I can't believe I just admitted that." She rolled on her side and buried her face in Sutton's neck.

"Your story is more common than you think." Sutton kissed her head.

"Once I finally admitted to myself how my lack of feelings for men had everything to do with me and very little to do with them, I started dating women. Everything made sense then, and it was like I had to make up for lost time." Kenzie pulled back and placed her index finger against Sutton's chin. "I got tired of sex not meaning anything, and I promised myself I'd wait."

"May I ask you a question?"

Kenzie's heart felt like it seized, and her ears started to buzz. She knew what question was coming because it always did. *How many people have you slept with?* She took a deep breath and faked her calm. "Of course. You can ask me anything."

"What were you like as a child?"

Kenzie stared past Sutton at the wall, silent and confused as she turned the question over and over in her head. She busted out laughing. "I'm sorry." She covered her mouth, smothering unrelenting belly laughs that caused her to cramp and cry. "I'm really sorry, but I wasn't expecting that question next and I just lost it. I think I'm overtired." She wiped the tears away.

"What question were you expecting? No. Wait. Tell me what you were like as a kid in case this is your way of avoiding the question."

"You're very suspicious of me," she said, shifting up the mattress to prop herself against the pillows. "Can we get under the covers first? I'm getting cold."

Sutton stood and pulled back the covers. She waited for Kenzie to get comfortable before climbing into bed beside her. Kenzie had to admit, the move was simple and sexy and one she could easily get used to. Sutton gathered the covers up around them, and they faced one another. "Better?"

Kenzie nodded.

"Good. Now tell me."

"I was wild, and no one would've guessed I was an only child because I was constantly following other kids around in the neighborhood. What I lacked in brothers and sisters, I made up for in friends."

"That's hard to picture."

"What? Me having friends?"

"No," Sutton said, kissing the tip of Kenzie's nose. "That you were so social. You're so quiet and to yourself now."

"High school and college change people. So does a divorce."

"How old were you when they divorced?"

"Sixteen."

"You took it pretty hard?"

"Not the divorce, no, but I hated how hurt my dad was."

"What about your mom?"

Kenzie started to wish Sutton had stuck to talking about sex. "She, uh, wasn't the best mom when I was younger. She was never really meant to be a parent—too immature and selfish. We just started talking again last year."

"How's that going?"

"Okay, I guess. She's apologized, so that's something." Kenzie shifted.

"You don't like talking about this, do you?"

Kenzie chuckled. "No, and I think it's time you told me a little about you. Stuff I didn't learn from interviews."

"Not to sound like a dick, but my parents are pretty great. My dad is one hundred percent Portuguese, and it shows. He's very intense about anything he loves, and he only loves three things." Sutton pulled her hands out from under the covers to count on her fingers. "His wife, his kids, and *futbol*," Sutton said with an accent.

"So it does run in the family."

"He tried to get my older brothers into the game. David enjoyed playing and was very good, but he really wanted to be in the kitchen with my mom, not on the field. But Gabriel was interested in going pro."

"Is Gabriel as good as you?"

Sutton shot her an incredulous look. "Is anyone?" Her smile was bright and cocky, and Kenzie could feel her pulse between her legs. "He actually played better."

"Played? Past tense?"

"He's six years older than I am. I was just trying to make a name for myself as a freshman in high school when he had major league teams scouting him in college. All of my dad's attention went to Gabriel. They trained together every day, and when he was away for a game, my dad would talk to him to make sure he was following his regimen closely. My dad was looking for his dream career through Gabriel," Sutton said wistfully. "But then he was caught doping, got kicked off the team, and not one pro team has come looking for him since."

"Oh no." Kenzie placed her hand on Sutton's shoulder. "I'm sorry."

"I'm not. He made a stupid choice and got punished for it." Sutton's voice was colder than it had been all night. "Then my dad turned his attention to his second best, and the rest is history."

"He must be very proud of you, though."

"He is, but it's clear I'm not Gabriel."

"I, for one, am very glad you're not." She brushed her fingertips across Sutton's cheek, the dimness highlighting the intense color of Sutton's eyes. She never imagined she'd get to see this beauty up close.

"What question did you think I was going to ask you?"

Kenzie no longer felt afraid or embarrassed. "I thought you were going to ask me how many people I've slept with."

"I never even considered it because it's none of my business."

Kenzie surged forward and kissed Sutton, fueled by her pent-up nerves and desire. When she pulled back, Sutton smirked.

"I couldn't help myself," Kenzie said.

"I hope you never try to."

Kenzie felt like she needed to explain herself. "I've always been safe, and I got myself checked—"

Sutton placed her finger over Kenzie's lips. "I appreciate you telling me that, and I've been checked, too. But if I have learned anything about you over the past few months, it's that you'd never intentionally do something to put another person at risk. I trust you, Kenzie, and you don't have to rehash your past for my benefit. I'm here with you now, and that's all that matters to me."

Kenzie kissed Sutton softly before burrowing her face into her neck. Holding Sutton was dizzying, and she knew she had to say something. But she also knew she had to tread carefully when it came to her heart and Sutton. "This feels nice."

"It really does."

Chapter Seventeen

Waking up next to Kenzie wasn't quite what Sutton expected. Kenzie's body was warm all over, bordering on overheated, and yet she was still wrapped up in the majority of their shared blanket. Sutton's uncovered left leg was freezing, but she wasn't about to move. Kenzie had burrowed into the covers so deeply, only a mass of red hair peeked out from the top, and her backside nestled perfectly into Sutton's front. Sutton searched beneath the blanket for her. She just wanted to hold her a little tighter before they'd get up and start their day.

She snuggled closer and wrapped her arm around Kenzie's waist. Kenzie turned and cuddled into Sutton. Sutton held her, her focus shifting between the feel of Kenzie's body and making sure to keep her hands in safe places. She wanted nothing more than to show Kenzie respect, so she'd let Kenzie control the pace. Sleeping together did not entitle Sutton to anything more than sharing Kenzie's space, and she knew that.

"Mornin'," Kenzie said, muffled by the blanket and Sutton's shirt.

"Good morning." Sutton pulled the covers away just enough to sneak her leg beneath and get a good grip on Kenzie before she rolled onto her back. She loved the weight of Kenzie atop her. Sutton clasped her hands together on Kenzie's lower back. "Did you sleep well?"

Kenzie stretched her body like a cat, molding herself even tighter against Sutton. Her leg fell between Sutton's. "Very good," she said, lifting her head and pushing her wild hair from her face. She looked at Sutton with a lazy smile and puffy eyes. "I'm really comfortable right now, but I have to pee."

Sutton's heart fluttered. Kenzie was equal parts cute and sexy in the morning. "I do, too, but I don't want to let go of you."

"Five minutes to relieve ourselves and freshen up."

"Deal." Sutton flipped Kenzie over to the empty side of the bed and dashed to the bathroom. She shut the door and laughed loudly as Kenzie whined on the other side. "You were too slow, Chicken."

"I thought you called me Chicken because I'm fast."

She could hear the pout in Kenzie's voice, so she rushed through her morning routine. She swung the door open a minute later and invited Kenzie into the bathroom with a sweep of her arm. "All yours," she said, winking.

They wound up back in bed exactly five minutes later, trying their best to recreate their earlier position, but they couldn't seem to get it right. Kenzie huffed and sat up, straddling Sutton's hips.

"I can't get comfortable again."

Sutton felt Kenzie's legs squeezing her sides and the weight of her settled on her mound. Everything within Sutton urged her to touch, to grip, to encourage Kenzie to move her hips, but she smiled instead and settled her hands on Kenzie's bare thighs.

"This is pretty comfortable for me," Sutton said. She moved her thumbs back and forth, indulging in the feel of Kenzie's soft skin. She stared up at Kenzie and felt a shift between them. She had to look away from the intensity of Kenzie's stare. She watched her thumbs move back and forth, dancing delicately over light freckles. "Is there anyplace you don't have freckles?"

Kenzie laughed and placed her hands over Sutton's. "I suppose this is where I invite you to find out?"

"No, that's not what I meant. Not at all," Sutton said, flustered. "I'm curious."

Kenzie visibly softened. She gripped Sutton's hands. "They're light on my thighs but start to get darker on my knees. You've seen my shoulders and chest—they're covered." Kenzie brought Sutton's hands up to her hips. Sutton swallowed hard. "The ones on my face get darker every year."

"That explains the SPF seventy," Sutton said with a smirk.

"I've become less sensitive to the sun over the years, but this complexion will never handle the rays with grace. I have a lot of freckles on my lower back, but barely any on my belly." Kenzie brought Sutton's hands around to her lower back and then up and under her shirt.

Sutton sucked in a breath, struggling to keep her composure. Her fingers twitched and her palms itched to touch more and feel everything. "I think you're trying to kill me."

"How's that?" Kenzie looked every bit the temptress she was playing.

"Sitting there, being so close, and looking like that." Sutton drummed her fingertips on Kenzie's skin.

Kenzie blinked slowly. "Looking like what?"

"Like you."

Kenzie tugged Sutton into a seated position by her shirt. She kissed her briefly but firmly. "I still don't see the threat to your life."

Sutton wrapped her arms around Kenzie and shifted her so their bodies were flush. She traced Kenzie's chin with the tip of her nose, the delicate touch bordering on a tickle. "You're forcing me to think naughty things, but I want to be respectful."

"You're very sweet, but not a very good listener," Kenzie said while running her fingers through Sutton's hair. "I said I take *sex* very seriously, and last time I checked there were a lot of other things two people can do in bed. Or anywhere, for that matter."

Sutton nearly purred when Kenzie ran her short nails along the back of her head. "But I don't want to sleep anymore."

"Ha-ha. Very funny." Kenzie pressed her breasts into Sutton.

Sutton enjoyed their relaxed, playful mood too much to give up easily. "What kind of things are you talking about, then?"

"Kissing," Kenzie said, pecking Sutton's lips, "and maybe some touching."

"Maybe?" She ran her hands up the bare plane of Kenzie's back. Kenzie started to move her hips in response.

"Definitely."

Sutton kissed the side of Kenzie's neck. She took a deep breath and basked in the scent she had grown to depend on over the past few months. She nuzzled below Kenzie's ear and felt Kenzie shake in her arms with a giggle. She nipped at the angle of Kenzie's jaw. "You feel so good," she said quietly into Kenzie's ear.

Kenzie ground herself into Sutton's lap. She touched Sutton's face and neck before gripping her shoulders tightly. She kissed her hard, wasting no time.

Sutton settled back and pulled Kenzie down on top of her. She kissed and nipped at Kenzie's lips, never wanting to disconnect from her. She felt Kenzie grinding against her thigh and needed some friction of her own. She flipped their positions and stretched out over Kenzie.

"This is much better," Kenzie said, spreading her legs for Sutton. She took the invitation and pumped her hips forward, licking at

Kenzie's parted lips as she moaned. She cradled Kenzie's face with her right hand before caressing her throat and coming to rest at the center of her chest. She kissed her slowly as she circled her hips into the apex of Kenzie's thighs. Sutton moved her hand slowly down Kenzie's sternum to the hem of her plain T-shirt.

Kenzie yanked her shirt up and covered her bare breast with Sutton's hand. Sutton froze. "It's okay, Sutton. I'll let you know if you're doing anything I'm not comfortable with. And I'll definitely tell you when you're doing something I really like."

"Promise?" Sutton started to move again, making circles with her hips and gently gliding her palm along the stiff peak of Kenzie's nipple.

Kenzie nodded. "That's good, very good."

Sutton shifted around and brought one of Kenzie's legs between hers. She started to grind her center against Kenzie's thigh as Kenzie searched for pleasure against her. She pulled her hand away from Kenzie's breast and licked her lips. Kenzie's nipples were small and pink, dark enough to contrast her pale skin. A spattering of freckles spread out between her small breasts but faded the lower Sutton's gaze went. Kenzie's belly was nearly blank, save for a small scar on the lower right side of her abdomen.

Sutton kissed above Kenzie's heart and then a little more to the right. She could hear the change in Kenzie's breathing as she got closer to her nipple. She licked the tip before taking the peak between her lips. Kenzie's breasts were very small and delicious. Sutton sucked on the skin and bit down, earning a loud keen from Kenzie.

"I can't believe this is happening," Kenzie said between breathy moans.

Sutton smiled against Kenzie's breast. She sat up quickly and pulled her shirt over her head, exposing her naked torso. She tensed her stomach ever so slightly, just enough for her abdominal V to pop. She would've felt embarrassed for such a move if Kenzie didn't look like she was about to eat her alive. Sutton leaned forward and grabbed Kenzie's hands. She mimicked Kenzie's earlier movements and moved her hands to where she wanted them. She put them on her bare skin, right above the waistband of her classic white boxer shorts.

"Do you believe it now?" She watched as Kenzie's lips moved, but no sound came out. She looked beautifully demolished. Her hair was a mess across the pillow, her shirt was bunched up, and the skin of her chest was blotchy red. Sutton moved on top of Kenzie again, slowly dragging her breasts across Kenzie's bare skin.

Kenzie reached her hands into the back of Sutton's boxers and squeezed her ass. She brought her lips within a whisper of Sutton's. "Make me come."

Sutton pulled back slightly and looked down at Kenzie quizzically. "I thought…"

"Like this," Kenzie said, guiding Sutton to continue circling more firmly against her.

Sutton planted her elbow on one side of Kenzie while her free hand roamed every inch of the body Sutton had dreamed of over the past months. She wasn't sure how Kenzie felt, but she knew it wouldn't take much to bring herself to orgasm.

Kenzie scratched up her back and pinched both of her nipples. Sutton's hips stuttered for a moment before redoubling their efforts. Kenzie's breathing was labored, and Sutton's heart started to pound with the telltale force of an impending orgasm.

Kenzie threw her head back and screamed Sutton's name, the sound pushing Sutton into her own climax immediately. Sutton buried her face in the crook of Kenzie's neck and grunted as she controlled the speed of her hips and the waves of pleasure pulsing around her clit.

She shifted off to Kenzie's side but kept her hand on Kenzie's bare abdomen. "I can't remember the last time I came so fast," Sutton said. Her limbs felt heavy, but her body buzzed, and for the first time in a while, her heart felt completely open and light.

"See? There's a lot of things we can do."

"I didn't expect any of those things to end like *that*."

Kenzie looked adorable when she shrugged shyly.

Sutton smiled softly and kissed Kenzie's cheek. She traced a circle around her belly button, and the scar on Kenzie's abdomen caught her eye again. She touched it gently.

"Appendicitis. Got me good in tenth grade. I almost died."

Sutton said a silent thank-you for Kenzie still being around. She placed her hand over the scar protectively, kissing around the shiny skin first, then pressing her lips directly to it for several seconds. She continued to kiss down to the band of Kenzie's shorts, tugging at the elastic slightly and running the tip of her tongue along the indentations left in Kenzie's skin.

"Shit," Kenzie said, hissing the word and lacing her fingers into Sutton's hair. She hesitated for a moment. At first, she started to push Sutton down before pulling her back up. She kissed her deeply, like she was tasting her for the first time. "I don't want to leave this bed."

Sutton grinned. "I'm sorry, but we have to start our day." She kissed Kenzie lightly and then hopped out of the bed. "I'm going to take a shower. Order room service for breakfast if you'd like, or we can go out. You decide." Sutton started for the bathroom, but she could feel Kenzie's eyes on her the whole time. She turned back right before entering the bathroom.

Kenzie was on her side, watching her. "You're incredibly sexy."

"Back at ya." She didn't bother closing the bathroom door when she started the shower. She wouldn't be mad if Kenzie decided to join her. No, she wouldn't be mad at all.

CHAPTER EIGHTEEN

Kenzie basked in her after-meal glow and watched Sutton across the small table. The dim lighting of the five-star restaurant did wonders for her defined cheekbones and dark eyes. She wore a simple black shirt, buttoned all the way with a silver collar bar to accent the look. Kenzie wished for a million more opportunities to get dressed up because, as good as Sutton looked in uniform and athletic clothes, a more refined style definitely suited her. Even the way she accessorized, with a thin black metal cuff bracelet on her right wrist and a large watch on her left, proved Sutton knew how to dress. Kenzie couldn't stop looking at her.

"I'm so full. I think I'm going to pop a button," Sutton said, rubbing her stomach.

"You're the one who insisted on an appetizer, three sides, and dessert."

"Athletes are known for their big appetites."

"They're also known for eating healthy." She pushed aside her dessert plate with only a smear of chocolate sauce left behind.

Their server approached with the same grin he had worn throughout the entire meal. "I'll leave this for when you're ready."

Sutton reached for the check before he had the chance to set it between them. She slipped her credit card under the cover and nodded as he stepped away. "I won't tell Brett about this cheat day if you won't."

"I don't plan on telling anyone about this," Kenzie said, holding up her drink.

"Because you think they'll make fun of you for drinking a mint julep?" She signed the receipt and thanked their server.

Kenzie looked at Sutton over the rim of her glass. "I'm not

ashamed, because it's delicious." She felt a warm buzz throughout her body, but she wondered how much of that feeling was from the alcohol and how much was from Sutton.

They had spent the morning and afternoon walking the boardwalk and beach, cuddling close when the early spring breeze got too chilly. They stopped in several different casinos to compare and judge them on their interior design, talking like they knew what made a casino successful. They made sure to drop a few dollars into slot machines here and there. Sutton even insisted on buying Kenzie an over-the-top Atlantic City sweatshirt as a souvenir.

"Are you okay?"

Kenzie hadn't realized how badly she had zoned out. "I'm fine, great, actually. I was just thinking about how wonderful today has been."

Sutton leaned forward and placed her hand in the center of the table, palm up.

Kenzie looked around before placing her hand in Sutton's. "What's next on the agenda?"

"A comedy show in twenty minutes."

Kenzie traced the length of Sutton's middle finger and had to press her thighs together. Sutton made her body pulse with little to no action, but she couldn't be all that surprised. She had always thought Sutton was sex appeal personified. "Is the comedian funny?"

"I have no idea, but I certainly hope so. The only reason I got tickets is because I love your laugh."

"Shut up."

Sutton frowned. "Okay."

"I'm sorry," Kenzie said. She covered her mouth briefly and shook her head. "You're so sweet and smooth, and gorgeous to boot. You're perfect, and it's hard for me to understand how I'm here with you right now." Sutton smiled but remained silent. "I just ruined the mood, didn't I?"

"Far from it." Sutton brought Kenzie's hand to her lips. "I was drawn to you because I found you interesting. Do you remember the first time we saw each other?"

She did, of course, but she played dumb. "No, I don't."

Sutton hitched an eyebrow. "You held the locker room door for me and Taylor, and then shut it when I said your name. That's a first impression I'll never forget."

"I was shocked you knew who I was."

"And you're always so quiet and to yourself, but not in a cold way. You're warm and funny and absolutely stunning."

Kenzie pulled her hand back and fussed with the ends of her hair. "Don't tell me you have a fetish for redheads."

Sutton laughed. "No, but I do have a thing for charming, mysterious women."

"Mysterious? Me?"

Sutton nodded.

"Hardly," Kenzie said, highly amused by such a thing. "I'm the opposite of interesting, which is why I'm usually quiet."

"Let's agree to disagree and get out of here. What do you say?"

Kenzie smiled, relieved to be off the spot. "Let's go." She placed her napkin on the table and grabbed her purse. "I hope you realize our next dinner is on me."

"I'll hold you to it," Sutton said. She led Kenzie out of the restaurant with a hand on the center of her back.

Kenzie wore a navy blue lace dress with long sleeves and a hemline that fell slightly below midthigh. The back scooped low enough for Sutton to touch her bare skin with little to no effort, which she took full advantage of. Kenzie was entirely focused on the feel of Sutton's hand.

"Excuse me," a gentleman called out.

Kenzie's back felt cold when Sutton took her hand away. She turned to see a few people approaching them. Her heart rate increased while Sutton engaged them immediately.

"I'm sorry to interrupt your night, but we were dining a few tables away, and when I saw you, I knew I'd have to ask for an autograph. My daughter is a huge fan of yours," he said, clearly a little nervous. "But I wasn't about to interrupt your meal."

Sutton's smile was charming and genuine. "I can't begin to tell you how much I appreciate that." She took the pen and paper from him and started to write.

Kenzie's heart slowed down, but as she observed Sutton talking about the man's daughter and her interest in soccer, it warmed considerably. She quickly took his phone to snap a few pictures of them together for evidence, as he called it. Kenzie stepped away when she was done, wanting to give them a moment to themselves.

After a round of thanks and well wishes, she and Sutton were alone again. "You love the attention," she said once they started to walk again.

"I like thinking about how excited that kid is going to be, but I have a sneaking suspicion a lot of that was for him."

"What makes you say that?"

"He knew our stats and mentioned our upcoming game. And he said you're the best rookie the league has seen in years. Which is completely true."

Kenzie stopped walking. "Wait, he knew who I was?"

"Yeah. He was going to ask for a picture with both of us, but he didn't want to take up any more of our time. I wish everyone was that respectful."

"Do you think he knew we were on a date?"

"He may have assumed. Do you not want people knowing we're dating?"

Kenzie continued walking, not entirely sure what direction to go, but she trusted Sutton to guide her. "I don't know. I'm barely comfortable with the idea myself."

"Whoa, whoa, whoa," Sutton said, grabbing Kenzie's wrist to get her to stop. "You're not comfortable with the idea of dating me?"

"Well, no."

"Why not?"

"Because," Kenzie said. She crossed her arms over her chest. They stood in the center of the busy casino floor. Bells and voices rang out around them. "You're *Sutton Flores*. This is all a little crazy. You're just so—"

Sutton held up her hand. "Do not call me perfect again."

"But you are."

"I'm not, but the more you say it, the more I wonder if you're here for the right reasons."

Kenzie stepped back. "What's that supposed to mean?"

"Are you here because you like me or because I'm *Sutton Flores*?"

Kenzie was momentarily offended, but the more she thought about it, the more she understood. Her ire dissipated the moment she noticed the way Sutton's eyes shone. She looped her arm into Sutton's and pulled her into a small alcove by the elevators.

"I really, really like you. Probably more than I should at this point, but I say you're perfect because of the person you are to me, not because of any of this." Kenzie waved her hands around them. "We could've gone to the movies and had Chipotle for dinner for all I care. I call you perfect because you didn't hesitate to dye Easter eggs with me, and you didn't run when my mom was being…my mom." Kenzie laughed with Sutton. "And you're patient with me while never judging me for my past. Those are big things in my book."

Sutton framed Kenzie's face and kissed her firmly. "I really, really like you, too."

She wrapped her arms around Sutton's waist and held her close. She didn't want the moment to end, but they were on a date. "We should get to the show."

Sutton held Kenzie's hand the entire way to the theater and opened the door for her. "Hopefully the comedian won't heckle us for being late," she whispered the moment they were seated.

Kenzie shot her a panicked look.

"I'm kidding." Sutton winked.

The comedian was funny, if a little vulgar for Kenzie's tastes, but she laughed a lot throughout his set. Every now and then she'd look over and catch Sutton watching her. Sutton's eyes sparkled in a new way. Kenzie reached under their small table and rested her hand on Sutton's thigh. Flashes of their earlier activities flooded her thoughts, and she dug her fingertips into Sutton's leg. She looked at Sutton, whose stare conveyed the same not-so-innocent thoughts. They were the first ones to leave after the comedian's bow.

Kenzie fought with her inner voice as they rode the elevator back up to their room. The night was still young by Atlantic City standards, but their bodies were used to an early and vigorous routine, so they'd agreed to retire early. Kenzie stood far enough from Sutton for space to think, but the reflective doors did little to help her concentration. She stared at Sutton, her body on fire for the feel of her skin. She walked out first when the doors opened, keeping her distance. Once she got to their room, she waited for Sutton to unlock the door.

Sutton stepped up behind her and pressed herself against Kenzie's back. She reached around her and opened the door. "If I didn't know any better, I'd say you're trying to avoid me," Sutton said as Kenzie rushed into the room.

"I'm just trying to keep my wits about me."

"Good to know I'm not the only one who's affected here."

"Definitely not the only one." Kenzie pulled off her heels and turned to find Sutton standing right behind her. Their kiss was hurried and greedy. As much as Kenzie wanted to get lost in their desire, she slowed their pace to gentle caresses and delicate kisses. She pulled back and smiled coyly. "Will you unzip me?" she said, pulling her hair to the side and turning around.

"But you look so good in this dress." Sutton's protest wasn't very convincing as she pulled Kenzie's zipper lower and lower. She touched every inch of skin along the way.

Kenzie shivered. "I want to get comfortable and lie in bed with you for a while before we have to get back to normal life tomorrow. Who knows the next time we'll just get to relax together, especially with you leaving for camp next week."

Sutton nuzzled the back of Kenzie's neck. "For the first time in a long time, I wish I hadn't been called up. I'm going to miss you."

Kenzie knew she would miss Sutton, too, but she was too scared to admit how much. Instead, she offered Sutton a small, sad smile before stepping away to change.

They fell asleep within minutes of getting under the covers. Sutton held her tightly as she rested her head on Sutton's chest. She thought of their day and their evening, and how good they were together. She pushed away nagging thoughts of their earlier disagreement and wouldn't allow herself to focus on how or when they'd tell anyone. None of that mattered now. All that mattered was the sound of Sutton's heartbeat, a lullaby Kenzie knew she'd want to hear for many nights to come.

Chapter Nineteen

Training resumed Monday as if nothing had changed. No one on the team was any wiser, and the coaching staff had no clue two of their players were dating. Sutton bet they wouldn't care. She watched Kenzie on the field, conjuring vivid memories of how her bare skin looked when she flexed her muscles. She was distracted, but she didn't think it was obvious. She waited for the perfect moment to bring Kenzie a water bottle.

"When we're done, head straight for the showers."

Kenzie eyed her curiously. "Okay, but I usually shower at home."

"I know." Sutton took the water bottle back and drank as she winked then ran off.

The team worked through a few more drills and Sutton kept knocking the ball away from Taylor every chance she could, just to get a rise out of her. She couldn't help it. She was in a great mood—the sun was warm, her team was performing at its best, and she was with Kenzie, who was positively vibrant in the sunshine and in Sutton's heart.

Brett blew his whistle and told everyone to head to the locker room. Sutton shot Kenzie a look and started on her way toward the shower room. She waited impatiently and reached out the moment the door opened. She locked her lips on Kenzie's and backed her into a secluded corner of the room. It had been too long since she'd last kissed her.

"I really like watching you play, and I really, really like kissing you," Sutton said as she pinned Kenzie against the locker room wall, holding her hands above her head.

"The team is just outside." Kenzie's voice was weak.

"Do you want me to stop?" Sutton slid her right hand down the side of Kenzie's neck and along the outer curve of her breast, coming to rest on her upper thigh. She leaned against Kenzie's chest. Sutton parted her lips just as she was about to kiss her. She smirked when she felt Kenzie's breath puff against her sensitive skin.

Kenzie pulled her hands free and twisted them into the bottom of Sutton's training shirt. "No."

Sutton kissed her roughly. She wasted no time tasting Kenzie's plump wet lips and entering her mouth with her tongue. She felt Kenzie's hands everywhere at once, dainty running up her back and immensely strong gripping her shoulders. She bit back a moan when Kenzie wove her fingers into her hair and tugged.

The shower room door opened, and they jumped apart. Sutton pointed in one direction and signaled to Kenzie that she'd go in the opposite. She fixed her hair while watching Kenzie walk away. She turned to round the corner but Taylor blocked her way.

"What are you doing back here?"

"I was going to shower."

"You don't have a towel."

Sutton looked down at her empty hands and feigned surprise. "I knew I was forgetting something." She stepped around Taylor and let out a sigh of relief.

"Don't, for a second, think I don't know what you're up to."

Sutton stopped with her hand on the door handle. "What are you talking about?"

"I don't know if I'm more insulted by you playing dumb or by you thinking you're subtle." Taylor let out a humorless laugh. "I saw Kenzie come back here with you, and you posted a lot of pictures from your trip to AC. She wasn't in any of them, but it doesn't take an FBI agent to put two and two together. She put up plenty of her own pictures."

Sutton couldn't explain her reluctance to share her new relationship with Taylor, but she followed her gut instinct and played her cards close to the vest. "We wanted to get away for a little bit. There's nothing wrong with that."

"The timing is suspect, since you just flew across the country to break up with your girlfriend." Taylor's face remained stiff when Sutton looked at her in surprise. "Word travels fast around here, you know that."

"Rhea and I have been done for a while. I just took your advice and stopped dragging it on." Sutton crossed her arms and stood defiantly. "Was that wrong?"

"No, but the sudden urgency is telling." Taylor scratched at the back of her head, her short blond hair wet with sweat. "I really hope you know what you're doing," she said, stepping around Sutton and reaching for the door. "Let's get changed."

"Wait," Sutton said with a hand on Taylor's shoulder. "Why are you being so weird? I'm used to you butting in and voicing your opinions on my love life, but this doesn't sound like you. Do you have a thing for Kenzie?"

"What? No."

Sutton let her body sag in relief. "Okay, good."

"I'm worried about the team. It's one thing when you date women on other teams, but what happens when this relationship goes south? You think it won't affect how we work together on the field, because you wear these blinders every time you fall in love."

"I do not," Sutton said, offended that her professionalism was being questioned. She fought to keep her voice even. "The team will be fine because my personal life has nothing to do with what happens on the field."

"You really believe that?"

"What Kenzie and I have is different."

Taylor snorted. "It's always *different*. Face it, Sutton, you love the idea of being in love. Your relationships never work out because you bail the second they shift from the honeymoon phase into real life. And Kenzie? She's probably another fangirl checking you off on her bucket list."

"Don't talk about Kenzie like that." Sutton's anger flared, and she stepped closer to Taylor. "You're crossing a line."

Taylor smiled sadly. "No, I'm not—I'm making you face the truth. You need to do what's best for your team, *Captain*." She stepped around Sutton and left the room as three teammates walked in and started the showers.

Sutton stood in place, trying her best to collect her scattered feelings and thoughts. She still believed Kenzie was different, but she had to wonder how much of what Taylor said was true. Sutton couldn't breathe in the steam from the showers. She just wanted to get out of there. When she got back to the locker room, both Taylor and Kenzie were gone. She grabbed her phone from her bag and saw a message from Kenzie.

Sorry I left without saying good-bye. I promised my mom I'd be

home for dinner. She's having her boyfriend over and wanted me there.
Sutton smiled at the string of eye roll emoji that followed.

Let me know when you're done?

You're more than welcome to join. Please? Please save me? We both know my mom would love it if you were there.

Sutton felt her chest loosen slightly. *I can't, I'm sorry. I have a few things to do.*

Kenzie's first response was a sad face, but she quickly added, *Fine. I'll forgive you this time because you're so cute.*

Sutton frowned at those familiar jittery butterflies in her stomach. Now she second-guessed her feelings when just twenty minutes ago she felt invincible because of them. She tossed her phone into her bag and changed her shoes in a hurry. A few teammates asked if she wanted to grab something to eat, but she needed to get out of there and be alone. She needed to figure out what she was doing.

❖

"Are you sure you don't want to come to the movies with us?"

"I'm sure, Mom. I'm tired from training today," Kenzie said from the bottom of the stairs. "It was nice seeing you again, Michael."

"You, too, Kenz." Michael shook her hand.

She thought the nickname was weird, but he was nice enough. "Have a good time." She waved good-bye as they shut the door.

She sighed happily and basked in having some quiet time for herself. A knock at the door broke her reverie. If she had a dime for every time her mother forgot her keys…

Kenzie swung the door open and forgot the sarcastic comment sitting on the tip of her tongue. She smiled at Sutton and pulled her inside. But as happy as she was to see her, she quickly grew concerned the more she looked at Sutton. She was still in her training gear, down to her socks and shin guards, and her hair was a mess. Her features were drawn and worry lines creased her forehead.

"What's wrong?" She looked into Sutton's sad, tired eyes.

Sutton opened her mouth but closed it quickly and shook her head.

"Talk to me," Kenzie said.

"Can we just sit for a little while? I needed to be with you."

"Of course," Kenzie said, taking Sutton's hand and leading her upstairs. She stopped just outside her bedroom door. "Do you want to get cleaned up first? You can shower, and I have some clean sweats that'll fit you."

"That sounds great," Sutton said, clearing her throat.

She analyzed Sutton's face, wishing she could dive into her brain to see what was going on in there, but she grabbed her a towel from a nearby linen closet and led her to the bathroom instead. She showed Sutton her favorite body washes—she was passionate about body washes and had an abundance of them—and promised a clean outfit when she got out.

"I'll be out in five minutes."

"Take your time."

"I can't take long showers anymore," Sutton said with an empty tone. "The game has trained me to be quick. Anytime I'm in there for too long, I get anxious."

Kenzie touched Sutton's face gently, fearing she was unwelcome. She breathed easily when Sutton closed her eyes and submitted to her touch. "I'll be right down the hall when you're done." She stepped backward out of the bathroom and closed the door, waiting until the water started. Kenzie swallowed hard, finally acknowledging the worry in her gut. Whatever was going on with Sutton scared her.

She rushed back to her room and started straightening up. Her gear was all over the place, and her dirty clothes were strewn across her bed. She packed her hamper and then ran to her closet in search of the sweatpants she'd promised. It took her longer than expected, but she held up the large Penn State pants in triumph.

"Are you trying to turn me into a Penn State fan?"

She jumped and spun around at Sutton's sudden voice. "Just trying to make you comfortable, that's all." She tossed the pants to Sutton. "No ulterior motives, promise." They stared at each other as seconds ticked by, Kenzie getting lost in the appeal of Sutton glistening in a towel. "A shirt," Kenzie said, snapping back into the moment.

"Don't worry about it. I'm sure I can find one." Sutton walked over to Kenzie's dresser and gripped the handles to the top drawer. Kenzie couldn't move fast enough to distract Sutton before the drawer was fully open. She pushed Sutton's hands out of the way and closed the drawer with a loud slam.

Sutton smirked. "Is that your panty drawer? Or better yet, your *toy* drawer?"

"No—I mean, yes. To both. You'll find a shirt in the bottom drawer."

"You're a terrible liar."

Kenzie sighed and dropped her head. "I know."

"I'm okay with you not telling me, but I am very curious."

She still saw some of that earlier sadness clouding Sutton's eyes. She would do anything to wash that away, including opening the drawer. "I keep my team shirts in here," she said, mortified. "There's a bunch of yours to the right. Your jerseys are still at my dad's, but the T-shirts were too comfortable to leave behind."

Sutton ran her fingers over a row of shirts and stopped on a sky blue one. She picked it up and unfolded it. The shirt was from one of the Hurricanes' first seasons, before their team crest got a face-lift. The back had her name and number. "May I?" Sutton said.

She nodded and looked away as Sutton got dressed. For all their recent intimacy, Kenzie felt differently in this moment. She just wanted to care for Sutton and make her comfortable. She turned around when she felt Sutton's hand on her shoulder. She stopped breathing at the sight of Sutton in her T-shirt. It must've been a size too small, but it looked far from uncomfortable. The worn material hugged Sutton's broad shoulders and biceps beautifully.

"Can we lie down for a bit?"

"Of course," Kenzie said, taking Sutton's hand. She pulled back the covers on her full-size bed and let Sutton get comfortable. She shut off every light but the small lamp on her nightstand. When she got in bed, Sutton curled up against her, resting her head on Kenzie's chest and putting her arm around her waist.

Instinctually, Kenzie brought her hand to Sutton's head and started running her fingers through her hair. Whatever was bothering Sutton must've been big enough for her to need comfort. She kept up the soothing motion until she felt Sutton's breathing even out. And not too much later, she fell asleep, too.

CHAPTER TWENTY

Sutton slowly woke up. She could hear the birds chirping, and the room was bright with sunlight. When she opened her eyes, she was startled to find Kenzie watching her, and Kenzie appeared just as frightened as her.

"I'm sorry," Kenzie said a little too loudly for the morning hour. "Oh God, between this and the shirts, you probably think I'm a mega creep."

"Come here." She pulled Kenzie into her and covered them with the blankets. "I don't think you're a creep. How long have you been awake?"

"Not long. I was staring at you because I was trying to decide if I should wake you up or not, but I got a little lost in the moment." Sutton hummed and closed her eyes when Kenzie started tracing patterns on her stomach. "And you looked so peaceful, not at all how you looked last night."

Sutton opened her eyes. "I'm sorry I just showed up like that. I wasn't going to come here at all. I was going to keep my distance before heading to camp tomorrow." The admission sounded loud and crazy, even more so now. "But I really needed to be with you, and I wasn't ready to talk."

"Are you ready to talk about it now?"

Sutton took a deep breath. As much as she didn't want to, talking about her fight with Taylor would help her work through the problems that arose in its wake. "Taylor and I got into an argument yesterday, and she said some things that got under my skin." She ran her hand down Kenzie's bare arm and let her soft skin soothe her nerves.

"What did you argue about?"

"My relationship with you."

"She knows?"

"We're not exactly subtle." Sutton chuckled. "She's worried the team will suffer when we don't work out."

"When," Kenzie said evenly. "Not if."

She recounted Taylor's concerns, explaining her theory about Sutton's short-lived relationships, and even telling Kenzie that Taylor had called her a fangirl. She felt Kenzie tense in her arms and start to pull away. She wouldn't let her go. "She doesn't really think that," Sutton said with very little confidence.

"I don't care what Taylor thinks." Kenzie struggled to get free from Sutton's embrace. She sat up on one elbow. "I mean, I obviously do because she's my teammate and I want her to like me, but when it comes to something between you and me, I only care what you think."

"I don't think you're a fangirl."

"But I am," Kenzie said, pulling the covers from Sutton's chest and pointing to her shirt. "I just took down your poster before the season started, and I've had a crush on you since your first game with the national team. I used to watch every televised game until the very last second in hopes of the camera showing you wandering the field or stretching."

Sutton knew she shouldn't have been smiling as much as she was, but nothing about Kenzie's confession worried her. "And?"

"And I know that's weird, but if I was only in this for Sutton the superstar, I would've had sex with you by now. I'm with you because I *want* to be with *you*. Because of how funny and caring you are."

"I know this, and I never doubted it. What you said to me in Atlantic City has stuck with me, and you've been respectful since day one. I was upset because Taylor made me doubt myself, not you."

Kenzie fell back on her pillow. "Oh."

She faced Kenzie. "I feel like this is different, like *you're* different, but now all I hear is Taylor's voice in my head." Sutton tucked a thick lock of unruly hair behind Kenzie's ear. "I came here last night because I needed to be surrounded by you to think clearly, if that makes sense. I couldn't figure out how I felt without feeling it." She took a moment to collect herself. "Do you think we're different?"

Kenzie never looked away. "I do."

She took Kenzie's hand and kissed her knuckles and then the inside of her wrist. "Good."

"Can I ask...? Never mind."

"Ask me. You can ask me anything."

"What makes you think we're different? Why am *I* different?"

Sutton grabbed the waistband of Kenzie's yoga pants. She pulled her in until their bodies were flush. "Because I'm not just thinking about how you make me feel today. I'm already thinking about tomorrow and how sad I'll be at camp. I'm thinking about what we'll be to each other months from now. I've never really done that."

Kenzie kissed Sutton and used the sudden force to get her flat on her back. Kenzie straddled her and pulled her to a seated position by the collar of her shirt. She kissed her again, harder this time and with urgency.

Sutton pulled back with a grin. She ran her hands along Kenzie's thighs and up the back of her shirt to touch her bare skin. "We're going to have to tell the team."

Kenzie visibly deflated. "Do we have to?"

"We do, but it can wait until after camp. They're going to figure it out anyway, if they haven't already, and I'm sure a lot of outsiders know, too."

"How?" Kenzie said, placing her hands on Sutton's shoulders. "This is all so new."

"I am really sorry, but I'm in the public eye. My private life isn't very private. I bet we already have a ship name."

"A ship name? Really?"

She got Kenzie's phone from her nightstand. She opened Tumblr and typed her name into the search bar. She scrolled through a lot of older posts, but eventually a new picture caught her eye. "Bingo," she said. She showed Kenzie a post of their Atlantic City pictures side by side. Underneath the post was a caption: *FloShaw Confirmed.*

"FloShaw? I guess I can give them points for creativity," Kenzie said, looking uneasy.

"Is this okay? You're being publicly outed as my girlfriend. Shit, are you okay with being outed at all?"

Kenzie raised Sutton's chin and kissed her sweetly. "I'm okay with telling our team, and I'm okay with other people assuming, but I don't want to make an announcement. I don't want to be looked at as the rookie who's using the star player to get ahead. And as my career grows, I don't know how I'd want to handle a public relationship."

"That's fair," Sutton said. "We can take it one day at a time."

Kenzie bit her lower lip and toyed with the neckline of Sutton's shirt. "What about you? Are you okay with the public assuming I'm your girlfriend?"

"That depends." She let her hands travel higher to the clasp of her bra. She was so happy to discover Kenzie didn't wear a sports bra around the clock like most. "Will you be my girlfriend?"

Kenzie kissed her again through a bright smile. She ran the pads of her thumbs over Sutton's lower lip. "I'd like that very much, and I'd also like to brush my teeth."

"I'm sorry, but that's going to have to wait." She popped open the clasp of Kenzie's bra. "We're in the middle of something here." She tickled Kenzie's stomach before palming Kenzie's small breasts. "This is much more important."

Kenzie's head fell back, and she let out a quiet, sexy whimper as Sutton ran her thumbs around her hard nipples. "I always want your hands on me."

"Kenzie," her mother said from the hallway, but the door swung open before they could move. "You're on your own for—Oh my."

Kenzie screeched and pulled the blanket up. She fell to the side and started to beg her mother to leave. Probably unintentionally, she pulled the blanket away from Sutton, who was left to look Liz in her very amused eyes.

Sutton gave her a sheepish wave and watched as Kenzie's mom left the room. "I think that's my cue to go," she said, looking back to the pile of covers that was Kenzie. "If you'd like, I can take you out to breakfast, and we can go to practice together."

Kenzie pulled the blankets aside just enough to reveal one eye. "I would very much like to get out of here and never come back."

Sutton laughed. "It wasn't that bad."

"My mom walked in on us, and your hands were on my boobs."

Sutton had to admit the situation wasn't ideal. "At least we were dressed."

Kenzie pulled the blanket over her face again and groaned.

After coercing Kenzie to leave the safety of her comforter, they got themselves together quickly and all but ran for the front door.

"Have a good day, sweetheart," Liz said from the kitchen. Kenzie kept pushing Sutton for the door. "And Sutton?"

Sutton froze in the doorway. Kenzie shook her head, but Sutton had to answer her girlfriend's mother. She shrugged and mouthed an apology to Kenzie. "Yes?"

"Is that your black Jeep outside?"

"It is."

"Now I know, and we can avoid another incident like this morning, unless we need to resort to socks on the doorknob."

"Bye, Mom," Kenzie shouted and ran around Sutton to get to her Jeep.

"Bye, Liz." Sutton shut the front door. She could see how rosy Kenzie's cheeks were from twenty feet away. "How are you so beautiful when you're mortified?" She punctuated her rhetorical question with a kiss.

"Just get in the car and drive," Kenzie said, tugging the door open. "And you can't trade this in because now she knows to look for it. We cannot do anything that'll allow *that* to happen again."

"I'll start up the purchase paperwork right away." Sutton laughed hysterically. Every minute she spent with Kenzie had proved to be better than the last. No wonder she couldn't help but imagine their future together.

❖

Sutton's eyes were on Kenzie the entire time the athletic trainers were addressing the team. Staring at her seemed much, much better than focusing on the chill coming from Taylor. They'd eventually talk. They always made it through their fights, but Sutton wouldn't give in easily.

"That being said, Gabby has an announcement for you all," Tyler said, stepping aside to let Gabby command the front of the room.

"First, I'd like to say the level of strength and determination I've seen from you all this season has blown me away. I've worked with this team for five seasons now, and I truly believe this is the our year to win it all." Gabby fidgeted slightly. "Second, this week will be my last." Sutton sat forward along with several other players. The questions grew in volume, and Gabby started laughing. "It's good news, I promise. I'm almost four months pregnant."

The team's complaints quickly shifted to cheers and well-wishing. Sutton stood first and started to applaud. She winked at Kenzie when she followed and even blew out a wolf whistle.

"Thank you. As much as I don't want step away from the team so soon, I have a few health concerns, and my doctor advised me to not travel and take it easy."

"I guess running around and chasing after a bunch of whiney

women doesn't count?" Taylor said, earning a laugh from everyone but Sutton.

"Are you okay?" Sutton said, keeping the focus on Gabby.

Gabby smiled at her. "I am, and so is this nugget." She placed her hand low on her belly. "I hope to be back next season."

Tyler stepped in again. "We'll have a new trainer joining us mid-June. We haven't figured out an exact date, but I'm letting you all know now so you're not surprised when you walk in to a strange face."

"I don't think anyone likes a strange face in the locker room," Brett said as he entered the room. Everyone agreed. "I think that's it for today. Tara and Sutton, good luck at camp with the national team, not that you need it. Everyone else, get ready to face Salt Lake City. The Gulls haven't been doing very well this season, but that's no reason to let our guard down."

"They have one of the best left backs in the game, and their rookie striker is *almost* as good as ours." Chichima walked over to bump fists with Kenzie, who wore a brilliant smile. "We got this."

"Keep that attitude up, and I'll see most of you tomorrow." Brett clapped his hands and dismissed the team.

Tara approached Sutton as she was packing up. "Meet you at the airport tomorrow morning?"

"Of course, I wouldn't want to mess with our routine now." Ever since the first time they were called up together, she and Tara would meet at the airport two hours before their flight and have breakfast in the same chairs at the same Starbucks. Maybe it was superstitious, but Sutton relied on it.

"See you bright and early," Tara said, slapping Sutton's shoulder. She left just as Kenzie walked up with her bag.

Sutton couldn't control her smile. "You had incredible form today, Chicken."

Kenzie shook her head. "Why do I get the feeling you're not talking about my athletic form?" she said quietly.

Sutton bit her bottom lip to control her response. "I was definitely talking about how athletic your form is. I do think you should roll your shorts a little higher next time." Sutton laughed when Kenzie pushed her shoulder, and then she caught Taylor looking at her. Taylor shook her head and left the locker room.

"Do you want to grab dinner?" Kenzie asked.

"I can't. I have to pack, and my flight is super early tomorrow. I can't put it off any more than I already have."

Kenzie lowered her head, clearly disappointed.

"But that doesn't mean you can't come over. We can get something delivered, and you can keep me company."

"Will you actually get your packing done with me there?"

"Maybe, maybe not. Only one way to find out." She walked alongside Kenzie. The desire to hold her hand was overwhelming, but she controlled the urge. Coming out to the team was on her to-do list for after camp. But that didn't mean she didn't want everyone around her to know she'd found a new kind of happiness with Kenzie. For now, she'd bask in the feeling alone.

CHAPTER TWENTY-ONE

Sutton bounced her leg the entire flight home. Two weeks away used to pass in a blur, but things were different now. She missed Kenzie more than she had expected to and couldn't wait to get home to her. Saying good-bye was hard. After a long night of packing and watching movies until they couldn't stay up anymore, Sutton didn't want to let her go.

She had watched the Hurricanes' games online and couldn't be prouder of Kenzie.

Sutton was happy to see Brett recognizing how vital Kenzie could be to their starting lineup. The team had easily won their games against Salt Lake City and Seattle, thanks to goals from Kenzie. Sutton wanted to give her a kiss for each and take her out to celebrate.

She connected to the plane's Wi-Fi and pulled up her most recent message to Kenzie. She had given her the flight information and expected arrival time, which wasn't coming quickly enough. Kenzie hadn't said a word. Sutton pouted at her phone screen. The morning was still early, and Sutton knew the team had an off day.

Maybe Kenzie was sleeping or decided to head to her dad's for the day. If Kenzie had gone to her dad's, then she wouldn't be around to see Sutton. She assumed she'd see Kenzie once she got home, if their recent messages were any indication.

Sutton scrolled up to messages from earlier in the week. She tilted the screen away from the passenger beside her. She really wished Tara had been able to convince the older gentleman to switch with her. She checked to make sure he was engrossed in the in-flight movie before looking back to her screen.

I can't wait to get my hands on you.

Sutton's lower belly erupted in butterflies the same way it did when she first read the message. She scrolled down a few messages and read one of her favorites.

If you knew how much I miss you, you'd probably think I'm crazy. She absolutely didn't think Kenzie was crazy, and she'd told her as much.

She sat and considered the way they felt about each other and how openly they expressed themselves. She had never been in a relationship like this. When she was with Rhea, communicating while out of town was like pulling teeth, even in the beginning. But Sutton wanted to be connected with Kenzie every minute they weren't training or playing. She had skipped several team outings just to talk to Kenzie on the phone. Camp was in California, and the three-hour time difference did very little to keep them from talking. Every night Kenzie fell asleep during their conversation and Sutton would listen to her even breathing for a few minutes before hanging up.

Kenzie showed another side of herself a few messages later. Sutton must've read this particular message a hundred times.

I miss sleeping with you and we haven't even slept together that many times. But I'm in bed right now and it doesn't feel the same. I'm cold.

Sutton had suggested she get another blanket before asking Kenzie what she was wearing. She included a winking emoji just so Kenzie knew she was kidding, but Kenzie's response was anything but funny.

A tank and panties. My pants got in the way when I was touching myself.

Sutton had dropped her phone the first time she read that message, and it made her shift uncomfortably in her seat even now. She put her head back and closed her eyes. She let the memory of their conversation wash over her. Kenzie described, in detail, what she had done to herself and how she still felt unsatisfied. Sutton wanted nothing more than to look at the picture Kenzie included with that message, but that treasure was only for private moments.

Her eyes flew open when her phone buzzed. She looked at it in hopes of seeing Kenzie's name on the screen, but the message was from Taylor. She hesitated before unlocking her phone, in no mood for another lecture. Taylor had been cold to her since their exchange, and Sutton wasn't about to beg her to come around.

Brett wanted me to let you know we're in for a tough game against

New York this weekend. We're down a forward after this afternoon. Training drill gone wrong. So make sure you rest up. Jet lag won't help anyone. Her heart leapt into her throat and she started typing. *Who was hurt? Was it Kenzie?* She stared at her screen, waiting to see Taylor's response. Minutes passed, and she started to sweat.

She looked up when the overhead speakers came on, directing passengers to prepare for landing. Sutton knew she had to turn off her phone, but she waited until a flight attendant stepped up to her and insisted she power down her device.

"My friend was hurt, and I'm waiting for an update," she said, pleading for the woman hovering over her to take pity.

The attendant smiled pleasantly, but Sutton could see annoyance simmering below the surface. "You'll have it back on in no time."

Sutton reluctantly pressed the button and waited for the prompt to power off. She shot the attendant one last glance, but she wasn't buying it. Sutton turned off her phone and fastened her seat belt with a huff.

The plane had a rough landing, but Sutton couldn't care less. She waited for the green light to grab her carry-on and exit the plane. She found Tara and walked to baggage claim, all while waiting for her phone to power on and service to be restored. She could swear the airport had morphed into a black hole over the past two weeks. She wheeled her bag behind her, held her duffel on her left shoulder, and used her right hand to hold her phone up as high as it could go.

"What are you doing?" Tara said.

"I have shit service in here, and I'm waiting to hear back from Taylor about the injury report."

"Oh, yeah. That really sucks."

Sutton stopped walking and stared at Tara. "You know who was injured?"

"No."

"Why can no one tell me if Kenzie's okay or not?" she said loudly.

"I'm okay."

Sutton raised her head so quickly she felt dizzy. Kenzie stood ten feet in front of her, wearing tight jeans and a light sweater, her hair down and wild. She had never looked better. Sutton dropped her bags and rushed to her. Kenzie leapt into her arms and wrapped her legs around her waist as Sutton held her tightly and buried her face into her neck. Her thundering heart slowed, and she felt the warmth of coming home. She lowered Kenzie slowly and took a moment to stare into her bright hazel eyes.

Tara cleared her throat.

Sutton shook her head and laughed. "You knew about this, didn't you?"

"Isabella will miss the next game due to a small tweak to her ankle, but yeah, your girl is fine."

Sutton raised her eyebrows.

"Well, if I didn't know before, I certainly do now."

Sutton turned back to Kenzie. "What about you? Was this your wicked idea?" She pushed a few thick, wavy locks of hair from Kenzie's face.

"No. I was just coming to surprise you, and Taylor knew about it because I was obsessively checking my watch."

"She's very observant."

"But as mean as it was, I'm kinda happy she played you like this. You looked awfully concerned." Kenzie toyed with the zipper of Sutton's training jacket.

"Of course I was concerned. I was freaking out."

"I'm going to get going," Tara said with a raised hand.

"We'll walk out with you." Sutton picked up her bags and followed Tara, happy to have Kenzie at her side.

They talked as they walked, she and Tara recounting their weeks away and the friendly games they'd played against Mexico. Sutton couldn't get over how Kenzie had many of the highlights already committed to memory, like she had watched the games in person instead of on TV with the Hurricanes. Sutton turned the tables and complimented Kenzie's gameplay and her goals. Kenzie turned shy and kissed her on the cheek.

Tara gagged.

"Did you drive here?" Sutton said to Kenzie once they got to the parking deck.

"I asked my mom to drive me so I could keep you company on the way back. I hope that's okay."

Sutton felt the first easy smile in weeks blossom on her face. "That's more than okay." She grabbed her keys from her suitcase and unlocked her Jeep. She handed them to Kenzie and told her to get in while she packed her trunk. She turned back to Tara once Kenzie shut her door. "That was evil."

"It was kind of genius and hilarious," Tara said, shrugging. "Listen, about you and Kenzie—"

Sutton held up her hand. "I already heard it from Taylor. Please, save any lecture you may have for another time."

"*Actually*, I was going to tell you how happy I am for you both. Kenzie is great, and you deserve to be happy. Rhea was fine, but I didn't see you two making it."

Sutton peered through the window and caught a glimpse of Kenzie's profile. "But you see us making it?"

"I don't know how much it's worth, but yeah. I do. I think you're good for each other." Tara squeezed Sutton's shoulder and picked up her bags. "I'll see you tomorrow."

"See you tomorrow." She watched Tara walk across the aisles of cars until she found hers. Once Tara was safely inside, she got in her Jeep and leaned across the center console to kiss Kenzie. Relief and comfort washed over her. Sutton felt whole again. She pulled back just enough to put space between their lips. "This is the best surprise ever."

"I was hoping you'd be happy to see me." Kenzie grabbed Sutton's face and pulled her in for another scorching kiss. "I missed you so much."

"I missed you, too." Sutton closed her eyes when Kenzie ran her hand over her buzzed hair. "Your place or mine?"

"Yours, definitely yours."

Sutton's heart continued to swell as she drove home. She felt Kenzie's hands on her constantly. Whether she touched Sutton's forearm or thigh, Kenzie wouldn't let go. As traffic moved sluggishly down the parkway, they got reacquainted and Sutton soaked up every word. Kenzie started to ramble about her mother and the team, finally touching on the sore subject of Taylor.

"I think she's ready to apologize," Kenzie said.

Sutton kept her eyes on the road as she exited the highway and drove toward her house. "Then she can come apologize."

"You know her better than I do, but I have a feeling she won't go to you."

Sutton rolled her eyes. "She won't, but I don't see why I should go to her."

"Because you're kind, and it's eating you up inside that you're not talking."

"Yeah, and?"

"And meeting her halfway will be easy for you because your big heart already knows it's the right thing to do."

Sutton wanted to argue, but the best retort she could manage was wicked side-eye and a smirk. Whether or not she had a big heart was up for debate, but she knew what her heart was feeling for Kenzie Shaw, and *that* was very big.

CHAPTER TWENTY-TWO

The Hurricanes had no problems when they faced New York, but they wished they could have said the same when they played Chicago ten days later. Every player seemed sluggish on the field, and the Chicago Cyclones were anything but. Their defense was like a brick wall, and their offense moved so seamlessly, Sutton could barely keep up. Each team had one point, and the clock was winding down to the final ten minutes. A player for the Cyclones went down hard, giving them a break to hydrate and regroup. Sutton waited for her whole team to enter the huddle before talking.

"We can do this. I know we can, and you all believe it, too. Shaw, what have you noticed about their defense?"

Kenzie stared at her with a mouth full of water. She shook her head and swallowed. "They're using a two person attack every time we get close. It's hard to get around two players like that."

Sutton nodded as she processed the information. "Taylor, I want you on Kenzie's tail. One, no more than two steps behind her."

"That's not the usual formation."

"I know," Sutton said firmly. "They're expecting the usual formation, and we have to work around that. Stay close behind and hopefully we'll be able to create an opportunity. As far as the rest of the back line, I'll push forward but you all hang back. The last thing we need is to be unguarded."

Lacey perked up and slapped her thick gloves together. "I'm ready if that happens."

The referee blew the whistle, signaling for gameplay to continue.

Sutton tossed her water bottle to Jon, the new assistant trainer, and he fumbled it a bit. "Let's do this."

The Hurricanes charged back out to the field, and Sutton watched as they all fell into place. As soon as the ball started moving toward the opposing goal, Taylor ran up behind Kenzie, and the Cyclones' defensive line stuttered for the first time the entire game. When they'd start to gang up on Kenzie, Kenzie would drop the ball back to Taylor, who'd have enough space to advance.

They worked together three times, each time getting closer and closer to the goal. Sutton ran up the field during their next push, hoping to distract the opposing players just enough to create an open lane for Kenzie to take a shot, and she did. Sutton followed the ball as it soared through the air and bent into the corner of the goal at the last second. The shot was flawless, but Chicago's goalkeeper got her fist on it and sent it flying out of bounds.

Sutton looked at the clock and hoped they could use the extra three minutes of stoppage time to secure a winning goal. Ending the game with a draw wouldn't be terrible, but she wanted the win on the road. She stayed to the far end of the box and took a deep breath.

Chiara set up to take the corner shot. She spun the ball between her hands and set it right on the white line. She stomped her foot once, raised her hand, and started to charge the ball.

Sutton inhaled deeply and held it. She saw the ball launch into the air and soar in her direction. In a split second, she evaluated her options and made the decision to take the shot herself. She used her speed, leg strength, and height to attempt a header shot. She hit the ball with the perfect part of her forehead and pushed the ball toward the goal. The scrambling bodies and confusion inside the box blocked the goalkeeper from reacting quickly enough, and she missed the ball by an inch. Sutton's mouth dropped open as the ball rolled into the back of the net. She dropped to her knees.

Her teammates swarmed her and jumped on her. They piled up and cheered for her, all while she laughed hysterically at the bottom of the bodies. Once everyone cleared off, Kenzie stood above her and offered her a hand. Sutton grabbed it readily and held on with two hands as she was lifted to her feet.

"Great shot, Captain."

"Thanks, Shaw," Sutton said, winking and patting Kenzie's butt.

Taylor rushed up and pushed Sutton's shoulder. "That was insane."

"I honestly can't believe I made it." Sutton gave Taylor's behind a pat for good measure.

The referee blew her whistle again, this time with even more force as the minutes ticked away and the opposing team complained that the Hurricanes were wasting valuable time. Once everyone got back into formation, the ball was on the move for less than twenty seconds when the final whistle was blown. Sutton fell to the ground and lay flat. She looked up at the Chicago sky with a brilliant smile on her face. Scoring goals wasn't part of her usual role within a team, and scoring a winning goal was something she had never done before. All she knew was there'd be one hell of a celebration after the game.

❖

Chicago nightlife was fabulous. Sutton could take her pick of popular bars, but Slippery Slope was her favorite Chicago spot because it had a little bit of everything. She could relax and enjoy a good conversation upstairs or walk downstairs and dance the night away. With adrenaline still running through her after the win, she opted for dancing. She drank her inexpensive craft beer and bopped along to the DJ's nostalgic selections from the 80s and 90s.

A few players chose to relax at the hotel, but most couldn't wait to go out and toast each other for the clutch win. Sutton laughed, watching Kristy, Constance, and Ariana do their best version of the Humpty Dance. Kenzie joined them a second later and tried to mimic their movements. Sutton loved watching her body move, even if those moves were awkward. She gave Kenzie a thumbs-up.

Taylor stepped in front of Sutton and blocked her view. "Hey, Cap, you got a second?"

Sutton could tell by Taylor's tight lips she wasn't about to tell a joke. She checked her beer and nodded toward the stairs. "Let's go upstairs and get refills." Sutton checked over her shoulder when she got to the stairs and noticed Kenzie's eyes on her. She tapped her bottle and shot her a wink, letting her know everything was okay. Sutton flagged down the bartender as soon as they stepped up to the bar and ordered both refills to be put on her tab.

"You're stubborn," Taylor said by way of starting the conversation.

Sutton didn't plan on beating around the bush. "Takes one to know one." She held up her beer and waited for Taylor to clink her highball glass to it. She smiled once they shared cheers.

"Listen, I stand by some of what I said the other day."

"It was almost a month ago, Taylor."

"I know," Taylor said, looking ashamed. "I am worried about the team and what would happen if you two don't work out."

"I'm capable of—"

"Let me finish?"

Sutton took another drink of her beer. She focused on the bubbles dancing on her tongue rather than the reprimand she had cocked and ready.

"That's the only part I stand by. I'm sorry for everything else. You've been a great captain, and you've pushed yourself harder this season than I've ever seen. I think it's a rational worry I have, but I also think after years of playing by your side and being your friend, my trust in you outweighs that concern."

Sutton felt her throat tighten and was shocked at her uncharacteristic swell of emotion. "Thank you. I really appreciate that."

"And I'm sorry for what I said about Kenzie," Taylor said. Her eyes never left the ice in her glass. "I was being a dick. I was hurt you didn't tell me about Kenzie or about your split with Rhea."

Guilt pinged in Sutton's chest. "Everything happened pretty quickly. I knew I liked Kenzie, but I was committed to Rhea. I didn't want her to be another relationship I dumped, you know? I have this reputation, and I hate it. I wanted to do anything I could to make it go away."

"But staying in a relationship when you don't love the other person wasn't the answer."

"No." Sutton thought back to her breakup with Rhea and the inevitable anger that tied into it. She hoped they could find friendly ground again one day. "Kenzie and I had this moment, and I immediately knew something greater was waiting for me. I just had to get my shit together first."

"I'm glad you did."

Sutton chuckled at the memory of Kenzie walking away from her that day on the field. "We were this close," Sutton said, holding her thumb and forefinger an inch apart, "and she just turned away and left me there. She wouldn't give me the time of day again until I talked to Rhea."

"I knew I liked Kenzie for a reason." Taylor took a sip from her drink. "You should've seen your girl while you were away. She's fierce and adapted to new formations without a hiccup. She even rallied and led the front line like she'd been doing it for years."

Sutton straightened her back and puffed out her chest with pride. "She's smart and skilled, talented beyond her years for sure."

Taylor waved her off. "Okay, okay, I don't need to hear about your sex life."

Sutton snorted. "I'm definitely not talking about our sex life."

Taylor regarded her for a minute before speaking again. "Fierce on the field, but a dud in the sheets?"

Sutton gaped. "No, nothing like that." She chewed the inside of her cheek, wondering whether she should share this particular detail with her friend, but Taylor wasn't just any friend. "Kenzie likes to take things slow, so we haven't done *that* yet."

Taylor smirked and slapped Sutton's shoulder. "Buddy, you must've really meant it when you told me she's different, because I've never known you to volunteer for celibacy."

"Ha-ha. I'm not celibate, thank you very much, and it's actually been really nice." A flash of lying beside Kenzie as they watched a movie came to Sutton's mind. "We share this different kind of closeness—it's hard to explain. Don't get me wrong, I will celebrate when the day finally comes, but just knowing she wants me and holding her close satisfies me on a new level."

"Holy shit," Taylor said, clinking her glass to Sutton's bottle again. She laughed into her glass as she drank.

"What?"

"You're in love with Kenzie Shaw."

Sutton stared off into the distance as a flip-book of memories from the minute she first saw Kenzie up until they locked eyes across the club that night played in her mind. "Huh."

"Are you planning on going public with your relationship?"

"It's not a secret."

"I know, but the speculation and confirmation are two different beasts. You never went public with Rhea."

Sutton thought about that for a second. She never realized. "Kenzie is worth going public for, but that's not really what she wants."

"I'm sure you'll figure it out together when the time comes. Speaking of, let's head back downstairs before your girl starts to miss you too much."

The downstairs was more crowded than it had been when they left, and Sutton worried she'd have a hard time finding Kenzie, but that wasn't the case. Something about the energy in the room led her directly to her girlfriend, and she felt Kenzie's eyes on her before she even spotted her. She walked toward the far back corner and the bodies on the dance floor parted to reveal Kenzie dancing with Chiara. Their bodies were fused together, and Chiara was rolling her hips slowly. Kenzie tossed her long hair over one shoulder, and she slapped the side of Chiara's thigh as she welcomed her backside into her crotch.

Sutton watched, irrational jealousy bubbling deep inside and warring with arousal for her attention. Two could play at that game. She stepped up behind Kenzie without being noticed. She grabbed Kenzie's hips and pulled her into her body.

"Replaced already?" Sutton said, pressing her lips to Kenzie's warm ear.

Kenzie reached behind her to grab the back of Sutton's head and held her in place. The rhythm of her dancing faltered slightly, and Chiara turned around.

"You stole my dance partner, Flores."

Sutton shot her a wicked smile. "I never said you had to stop dancing with her." She felt Kenzie shake with laughter.

"As hot as that threesome idea is, I'm going to pass since I'm really just a third wheel. Chichima is a better dancer anyway. No offense, Shaw."

"None taken," Kenzie said, waving her hand dismissively. She faced Sutton. "Hi."

"Hey, you." Sutton knew Kenzie was talking, but she couldn't hear her over the music. She leaned forward. "What?"

"Is everything okay with Taylor?" Kenzie shouted.

"We're good." Sutton leaned back and gave Kenzie two thumbs up to ensure she got the message. Kenzie's smile was radiant when she mirrored Sutton's pose and continued bouncing to the music.

Damn, she really was in love with Kenzie Shaw.

CHAPTER TWENTY-THREE

K enzie couldn't move. She just stared at the front door.
"Are we going in?" Sutton said. "These are starting to get heavy." She held up the two cases of beer they brought for Kenzie's father's Fourth of July celebration. Since they'd had a game, though, it was on the fifth. Kenzie knew most of the cars lining the street were here for the party. She swallowed hard and looked up at Sutton with the best smile she could. She wanted to ask Sutton to promise she wouldn't break up with her after being subjected to what she was about to deal with.

As if reading her worries, Sutton leaned in and kissed Kenzie's cheek. "Don't be nervous. I'm not."

"You're not?" Kenzie said with a hint of awe.

"No, and I wasn't nervous when I met your mom, either."

Kenzie chortled. If only it were that simple. "We weren't together when you met my mother, and she's just my mother. You're going to meet my *dad*." The words visibly sank in and Sutton's entire demeanor changed.

Sutton put the beer down and smoothed her collar. "Do I look okay? What's he like when you bring people home? Does he know we're together? I should've grabbed something just for him at the liquor store." She even bent to make sure the cuffs on her pants were even and boat shoes tied properly.

Kenzie couldn't get over how cute Sutton could be when she was nervous. "You look incredible. I love this preppy look on you." She ran her fingertip down Sutton's buttons. "You're not losing a point for not bringing him a drink because he doesn't drink often." Sutton's shoulders relaxed. "He doesn't know we're together, and I've never brought anyone home, so I'm not sure how this is going to go," she said in one rushed breath.

"I should've asked these questions beforehand."

Kenzie pouted. "Would you have not come then?"

One side of Sutton's mouth turned up. "Of course I would've, but I could've prepared myself by popping open one or ten of these bad boys on the way over," she said, holding up one of the cases.

Kenzie grabbed the knob and opened the door. Loud chatter could be heard from the back of the house. "Are you ready?"

"Only if you are."

Kenzie took every ounce of reassurance Sutton sent with just a glance and stepped into the house. She followed the sounds and recognized most of the voices. Her father called out the moment she rounded the corner into the kitchen.

Her dad wrapped his arms around her and held her tight. They hadn't seen each other in months since she'd come home during her break, and his happiness was palpable and matched hers. As much as she wanted him to make it to her games, he had crowned himself a bad luck charm years ago. She stepped back and into Sutton by accident. She looked at Sutton with an apologetic broad smile.

"Dad, I hope you don't mind I brought someone. This is—"

"Sutton Flores," he said, extending his hand. "Like I wouldn't recognize you."

Her parents were very different people, but this was where they differed the most. Kenzie never worried her father would embarrass her. She was overwhelmed with happiness and love as she watched them meet. Even just the small gesture of shaking hands meant the world to her.

"It's very nice to meet you, sir. Kenzie speaks very highly of you. I'm happy to meet the man who made her the special person she is today."

Her dad waved off the praise like he normally did. "She is her own person and always was. I'm the lucky one here. And please, keep the formalities for someone else because I definitely do not feel like a *sir*. Louis is fine."

Kenzie took a deep breath to bolster her bravery. She noticed her aunt and a few other family friends who had made it to every party they had thrown through the years. She opened her mouth to finish proper introductions, but her dad wasn't finished.

"I can't believe you're standing in my kitchen right now. I knew you were Kenzie's teammate, but this is unexpected. We watched a lot of your games together."

Kenzie looked at Sutton just in time to catch her wink. Her stomach fluttered. "I actually brought her home as more than my teammate." She expected her father to catch on, but his face remained in a simple smile. "She's my girlfriend." All chatter in the kitchen stopped. The small smile fell from her dad's face.

He looked between her and Sutton, completely expressionless. "I'm about to put some burgers and dogs on the grill. I hope you're both hungry." He left through the back door without another word.

Kenzie could read the silent question on Sutton's face. "I have no idea what that was about."

"Maybe I shouldn't have come."

"No," Kenzie said, grabbing Sutton's hand. "I want you here, with me."

Sutton softened. "Anything you want."

"I'm going to go find out what his problem is."

Sutton tightened her grip on Kenzie's hand. "Kenzie, don't. This is his party. Let everyone enjoy the food and have fun. You can talk to him about this later."

"But I want you to enjoy the food and have fun," she said, pouting. Kenzie knew she was being a bit of a baby, but this wasn't what she expected when she imagined bringing Sutton home.

"And I will because I'm here with you."

"It's sweet how you're pretending this isn't driving you crazy."

"I'm dying, and you know it, but I want you to have fun with your family."

One of Kenzie's more boisterous teenage cousins interrupted them. "Hey, Kenzie, did I hear you say Sutton Flores is your girlfriend?" He looked up at Sutton.

"Yes, she is my girlfriend."

"So, like, you're together?"

She narrowed her eyes at him. "Yes."

"She's an Olympic gold medalist."

"I know."

"And a World Cup champion."

"Definitely know that, too."

"So what's she doing with you?" he said with a snort.

She wanted to palm his pimply face and push him away. "Jimmy, I swear to God…"

"I'll answer your question, Jimmy." Sutton wore the fakest smile Kenzie had ever seen. "I'm with Kenzie because she's really, really hot."

"Gross," he said, cringing. He ran off to join a few other cousins.

"Took care of that."

Kenzie couldn't decide if she was more amused by Jimmy's reaction or how proud Sutton looked. "Now my family is going to think you're only with me because I'm pretty."

"You are awfully pretty."

Kenzie wanted to get lost in the softness of Sutton's eyes and her open expression, but they had a house and yard full of guests to mingle with. "Win over the rest of these people and leave my dad to me."

"You don't think it's because I'm…because of the gay thing, do you? I'm not exactly subtle."

Kenzie held Sutton's face in her hands. "No, it's not that. When I came out to my dad last year, he was nothing but supportive."

"But if I'm the first person you brought home, maybe it's too much."

"Trust me when I say that's not it."

Sutton held Kenzie's wrists and nodded. "Okay. Let's do this, then."

Kenzie kissed Sutton softly and didn't pay any mind to Jimmy's sounds of disgust. Before they made it out the door, her aunt commented on how cute they were, and one of her neighbors stopped Sutton for a picture. Kenzie had to politely ask them not to post to social media, and it dawned on her she'd be doing that a lot. She still wasn't entirely comfortable sharing their relationship with the public, and she knew Sutton understood.

The barbecue was nothing but eating and laughing. Kenzie couldn't believe how easily Sutton fit in with her family and neighbors. She held everyone's attention with stories of games gone awry and recounting the final minutes of championships long in the past. The only person not giving in to Sutton's pull was her dad.

Kenzie waited for him to walk alone to the cooler to talk, and she wasn't going to soften her words for his benefit. "What's your problem with Sutton?"

He cracked open a can of Sprite and shrugged. "I don't have a problem with Sutton."

"Yes, you do, and you're not hiding it very well. You were so pleasant when we first walked in, and then I tell you she's my girlfriend and you turn to stone."

"Honestly, kiddo, I wasn't ready for this. A heads-up would've been nice."

"You're taking my spontaneity out on Sutton?"

"I didn't know you were seeing someone, let alone Sutton Flores. You walk into the house with a superstar, and then drop it on me that she's your girlfriend." He fiddled with the tab on the can and pulled his lip between his teeth. "It feels like just yesterday you were idolizing her and begging me to buy you her poster."

Her father's attitude had nothing to do with Sutton and everything to do with Kenzie growing up. "I'm still your little girl."

"Yeah, okay. Tell that to your empty room upstairs." His eyes grew misty. "One minute you're here every day, and then you're gone, and before I know it, you're standing in my kitchen with someone special. I didn't expect watching you grow up would be this hard."

Kenzie leaned into his side. "It's okay, Dad. I miss you, too. But I'm having a great time, and I'm doing really well with my team. You're always welcome to come to a game." She'd never stop trying to get him to drop his silly superstition.

"No can do. If you're doing well, it's because your old man watches from the couch," he said with a steady shake of his head. "I never doubted you would be great." He put his arm around Kenzie and pulled her into a side hug. "Tell me this—you always thought Sutton was so amazing as a player, how is she as a person?"

"She's wonderful. Lucky for you, you can find out for yourself because she's right over there." Kenzie pointed to where Sutton sat on the steps of their wooden deck. "Get to know her. I really like her."

"Anyone with eyes can see that."

"Come on. You're going to make this right." Kenzie left her father and approached Sutton slowly. Just the way Sutton watched her made Kenzie's insides quiver. She placed her hand on Sutton's shoulder as she passed. "I'm sorry."

"For what?" Sutton stood. Her father approached them a second later.

He fidgeted with his hands in his pockets. He looked every bit as uncomfortable as Sutton did. "Are you enjoying yourself?"

"I am. Thank you for having me."

He bobbed his head a few times before scratching the back of his neck. "Look, I'm sorry for how I treated you earlier," he said, rubbing his shaved head. "I was a bit shocked."

"It's okay. I completely understand." She looked him in the eye.

"Good. Maybe you'll also understand how I don't think there's one person on this planet good enough for Kenzie."

"Dad."

Sutton laughed nervously. "You and I can agree on that."

"Are you saying you're not good enough?"

"That's exactly what I'm saying," Sutton said, turning to look at Kenzie, "but I think I can be. Every day I feel like a better version of myself because of her."

Kenzie's breath caught. In that very second, a piece of her heart fell into place and she felt awash with love. Sutton was so much more than someone she was dating—she was the person she wanted to share *everything* with.

"As long as you treat her right and respect her, you'll have no grief from me." Her dad smiled at her. "And I don't care how many medals or trophies you have—I'll come after you if you hurt her." His threat settled heavily in the happy atmosphere. His smile never faltered, like he had been waiting years to deliver that particular threat.

Sutton mock-saluted. "Message received, loud and clear."

"We should probably hit the road," Kenzie said, feeling overwhelmed and in need of having Sutton all to herself.

"You're not staying?" He looked genuinely disappointed.

"I have to hit the gym early tomorrow."

"Okay, well, make the rounds so no one thinks you disappeared." Her dad hugged her.

Kenzie rushed Sutton around to get all of their good-byes in and practically pushed her out the door and to the Jeep. Once they were finally buckled up, she looked at Sutton in relief. "I'm sorry about that, but I just wanted to get out of there."

"I thought you wanted to stay. Your dad was under the same impression."

"I did, but I changed my mind. I just want to be with you tonight." Kenzie felt her nerves come to life. Sutton put the car in drive and started on their way home without asking questions. She had no idea how to explain what she was feeling anyway. All she knew was Sutton made her feel everything she had been waiting for. Their connection went far beyond attraction. Sutton made her feel valued, respected, and wanted. Her eyes were trained on the way Sutton's long fingers hooked around the steering wheel. Her desire flared.

She was done waiting.

CHAPTER TWENTY-FOUR

Kenzie didn't expect to be so nervous, but she felt like she was losing her virginity all over again. She followed Sutton into her house and all the way to the bedroom. Instead of focusing on her nerves, she pretended they lived together already, and she was just entering her own bedroom at the end of a long day. She removed her Keds and put them against the wall. Sutton entered the bedroom a minute later and started her own nightly routine. Kenzie could guess her every action before she did it.

Sutton took off her watch first and then her bracelet. Next came her shoes and then her shirt. She always brushed her teeth without a shirt, and every time Kenzie teased her about it, Sutton would say she'd lost too many shirts to a glob of toothpaste. She smiled as Sutton walked into the bathroom attached to the master and started the sink. From afar, she followed each flex of Sutton's back and felt her own pulse quicken. Kenzie started to undress slowly, but it took little effort to be left in nothing more than her bra and panties. Her skin was sensitive to the chilly air in the room. She quickly crawled between the covers.

"Your family is very nice. Are they all from your dad's side?" Sutton changed into a fresh pair of boxers and threw on a soft T-shirt. She turned off every light except the small lamp on her bedside table.

"Most of them. My uncle Craig is actually my mom's brother, but he and my dad were close before anyone got married."

"That's cool that they stayed friends even after the divorce." Sutton got in bed and scooted closer to her.

She took a deep breath and let it out slowly. "Thank you for coming with me today. It really meant a lot to me."

Sutton turned on her side and gave her a lazy smile. "I'd go anywhere with you."

She kissed Sutton, hoping to pour out every ounce of her pent-up passion and want or she'd be consumed by it. The kiss was a slow exploration meant to drive them wild with shared desire.

She got on top of Sutton, one of her favorite positions because she was able to feel Sutton everywhere. Sutton gripped Kenzie's ass with her strong hands, and Kenzie lifted her hips, pushing herself into Sutton's palms. She grabbed Sutton's hand and directed it between her legs.

"Touch me," Kenzie said. Her eyes were closed, and she felt Sutton freeze with her hand on her inner thigh.

"Look at me, Kenzie. Are you sure?"

"I want you so bad, and I can't remember any of the reasons why I wanted to wait. I trust you, and I feel safe with you." Kenzie dipped her head to kiss the side of Sutton's neck, feeling Sutton's pulse quicken. "I've never felt this way about anyone." She moaned at the first contact of Sutton's fingertips. The sensation was intense, even through her panties. "I want to be yours, completely."

"If you change your mind, just tell me. All I care about is you."

Kenzie bucked against Sutton's hand. "What about you?"

"What about me?"

"Are you ready?"

Sutton pushed her finger beneath the band of Kenzie's panties and ran it the length of her soaked entrance. "About as ready as you are."

Kenzie started to pant and moved her hips. She rid herself of her bra, and in the next second found herself on her back beneath Sutton.

Sutton trailed kisses over Kenzie's neck and down her sternum, followed by a bite to the underside of her right breast. Kenzie couldn't control her whimpers and yelps.

"You are so incredibly sexy," Sutton said when her mouth wasn't busy. She nipped at Kenzie's hipbone. "I really am the luckiest person on earth." She swirled her tongue around Kenzie's navel and bit at the flawless skin an inch lower. Sutton hooked her thumbs into the sides of Kenzie's panties and lowered them slowly, her eyes never leaving the juncture of Kenzie's thighs.

Kenzie never expected being undressed by someone could feel so sexy, so empowering, and the effects were stronger than a lethal drug.

Sutton tossed Kenzie's panties aside and kissed the inside of both her knees. "I love your legs and your stomach, but I really love your freckles. You have so many," Sutton said, running her hands up Kenzie's freckled thighs and stopping at her hips. "And then they seem to disappear, and only a few lone survivors get to be here." She connected the few freckles on Kenzie's stomach. "You even have a few here." She ran her index finger into the small patch of red curls between Kenzie's legs.

Kenzie threw her head back. Her body wanted to focus on the physical feelings engulfing her, but her heart wanted to revel in the emotional. She decided her body had waited long enough, and she deserved release.

She pulled Sutton's shirt off and threw it aside. She palmed Sutton's breasts and pinched her nipples roughly. The pleasurable pain must've kicked Sutton into gear, because she finally took pity on Kenzie's writhing body and rubbed her clit.

She called out loudly, shouting Sutton's name into the dark room. "You feel so good. Faster, please."

Sutton kissed along Kenzie's collarbone and up to her ear. "You're very polite. Too bad I plan on taking my time with you." She flicked Kenzie's earlobe with her tongue. Sutton spread small kisses across her sweaty torso and spent extra time sucking on her nipples. She tugged at them with her teeth and switched to lavishing them with her tongue when Kenzie started to beg.

"Please, I need more." Kenzie moved her hips frantically in search of more pressure.

Sutton stopped her motions. She crawled back up Kenzie's body and kissed her sweetly, slowly, and smiled down at her. "Don't close your eyes."

Kenzie gasped as Sutton circled her entrance with two fingertips. She kept her eyes on Sutton's as she took Sutton in inch by inch, relishing the pleasurable sting of being stretched. Once they were fully connected, she took Sutton's lips in a sloppy kiss.

Sutton started pumping slowly and lowered herself to her waiting pussy. Sutton hummed at the first contact of her tongue to Kenzie's clit. "You taste wonderful," she said, running the flat of her tongue over it in no certain pattern, but with just the right amount of pressure that drove Kenzie crazy.

"Please," Kenzie whined. "I need to come. Holy shit, I need to come so fucking bad." She weaved her fingers into Sutton's hair and pulled her face more fully into her wetness.

Sutton increased her speed and force, while setting a steady pace with her tongue. She'd stop only to suck Kenzie's clit between her lips, bobbing her head to alternate sensations. Sutton caressed Kenzie deep inside with her long fingers in such perfect rhythm that Kenzie quickly approached orgasm.

"I'm coming, I'm—" Kenzie's mouth fell open in a silent scream as she clamped her thighs around Sutton's head. She rode out her orgasm, writhing against Sutton and whimpering unintelligible sentences. Every inch of her body buzzed and shook with pleasure, and her heart pounded. If she'd had any doubts the wait was worth it, they were banished the second her body melded with Sutton's.

Sutton kissed her way back up her body, stopping at different spots here and there before meeting her mouth. Sutton's first kiss was chaste, the second tender, and the third a burst of Kenzie's flavor between them. She wore a cocky smile when she pulled back. "You doing okay, Chicken?"

Kenzie let out a throaty chuckle, and her limbs fell to the bed lifelessly. "This is no place for the use of *Chicken*, got it?"

"Yes, ma'am." Sutton pressed her hips forward into Kenzie's pulsing center.

Kenzie twitched and burrowed her head more deeply into the pillow. "Mmm…How are you so good at everything you do?"

"Am I?" Sutton said with a goofy smile. "Maybe I'm just good at things I love to do."

"You must really love doing this."

Sutton kissed Kenzie's chin. "I do, especially with you."

The sincerity in Sutton's eyes fueled Kenzie's soul and body. She sat up slowly and pushed at Sutton's shoulder, encouraging her to lie on her back. Kenzie pressed her body along Sutton's side and draped one leg over hers. She rested her head in her hand and took in Sutton's full breasts and dark nipples, the impressive hardness of her muscle, and the slight gap between her feminine hipbones and the waistband of her simple white boxers. She walked her fingertips down to them.

"You make these look very sexy. You're so tan and the way they hug your thighs…" Kenzie scratched her short nails along the inside of Sutton's thigh, watching as Sutton's nipples hardened in response. "But I can't help but be more invested in what's under them." She lifted Sutton's waistband and peered underneath before reaching in to cup Sutton's mound. It was warm and wet. She glided her fingers over Sutton's folds effortlessly, and she basked in her satisfied sigh. She licked Sutton's parted lips. "What do you like?"

Sutton pulled Kenzie's hair to one side. "Anything you're willing to give—just don't stop touching me."

Kenzie tasted the pulse at Sutton's throat and down to her breast. She smiled before scraping her teeth against the soft skin. Sutton's whimper electrified her. If most of the team already knew they were together, why bother holding back now? Kenzie sank her teeth in harder, claiming Sutton. Her hand never moved, and her fingers never stilled. Circling Sutton's clit felt like the most important and special task she had ever been given.

She watched in awe as Sutton bucked beneath her, her taut body glistening with sweat and marked with small red indentations. Sutton's eyes were clamped shut, and she moved her full lips in soundless words. Kenzie could just make out her own name from time to time, and each whisper felt more significant than the last.

Sutton suddenly reached up to hold Kenzie's chin in one hand while she held Kenzie's hand in place with the other. She pressed her open mouth to Kenzie's as she cried out and shook.

Kenzie held on to Sutton as her thundering heart calmed. She used her fingers to soothe and draw out their connection. She reached a little lower to Sutton's contracting and soaked entrance. She slid her middle finger in with ease, and Sutton pumped her hips.

Sutton's second orgasm was quick and silent, but no less intense for either of them. Sutton finished and flipped her on her back. Kenzie erupted into a fit of giggles.

"What's so funny?" Sutton said as she laughed along.

"I can't believe I'm having sex with Sutton Flores."

"You are."

"Millions of women wish they were me."

"I've got news for you—there's a lot of people who wish they were in my position, too."

"Stop."

"It's true."

Kenzie brought her finger to her mouth and licked it clean. "I guess we really are the lucky ones."

"The absolute luckiest." Sutton pulled the covers up to completely cover them and proved, well into the night, that Kenzie was very, very lucky.

CHAPTER TWENTY-FIVE

The Hurricanes suffered a loss to the Boston Blazers on the road, and although their record remained good enough for a chance at the playoffs, the players were glum for the entire flight home.

After deplaning and claiming her baggage, Sutton climbed the bus stairs and searched for Kenzie. She was in her usual back row seat, headphones already on. Sutton took a deep breath and approached slowly. She felt like she'd let Kenzie down more than any other player on the team. She held on to the back of the seat and waited for Kenzie to notice her.

Kenzie smiled up at Sutton, but it never reached her eyes. Kenzie's natural glee was absent. She moved her book from the seat next to her and waited for Sutton to sit. "How are you holding up?"

She shrugged. "Not good. What about you?"

"This was my first loss playing a full ninety, so…I'm doing about as well as you are."

"Hey," Sutton said, shifting in her seat to angle her body toward Kenzie. "You played great, like you always do."

Kenzie shook her head so strongly her headphones shifted. She removed them and said, "I had multiple opportunities to score and missed every single shot. I shouldn't have. Maybe I'm not ready to be a starter."

"This loss is on me. I didn't stop their offense, and I could've communicated more with everyone." She looked around the bus before taking Kenzie's hand and lowering her voice. "You're a starter and the best forward on this team. I won't let you doubt that."

Kenzie leaned in close. "You're very sweet." She pulled her hand away from Sutton. When they were with the team, they were professionals and made sure to act that way. "I think we both need to wallow and lick our wounds for a bit."

"Okay, yeah. You're right." She assumed Kenzie meant go their separate ways once they got home. She couldn't blame her. Every player handled a loss differently, and as much as she wanted Kenzie next to her at all times, she had to respect Kenzie's process as an athlete.

"Season two of *Wynonna Earp* isn't going to watch itself."

She looked back at Kenzie in surprise. She couldn't fight the grin that took over her face. Kenzie knew exactly what she needed. Kenzie *was* exactly what she needed. Always.

"I lo—" She paused. This wasn't the appropriate place for what she felt compelled to say. After clearing her throat and collecting her thoughts, Sutton spoke carefully. "I really want to kiss you right now and hate that I can't."

Kenzie's eyes twinkled. "There's a lot of things I want to do to you. Thankfully, I don't have to wait much longer."

Sutton felt that promise between her legs. She realized they had already discovered the best method of post-loss therapy. "Soon."

"Gross." Taylor's head popped up over the seat in front of them. "Can you keep all that information to yourselves? I'd prefer to not puke on this bus. Thanks."

Sutton laughed loudly. "Sorry, Taylor."

"Yeah, sorry." Kenzie shot her a sugary smile. She shared a knowing smile and giggle with Sutton. They weren't sorry. Taylor fell back into her seat with a grunt.

Sutton passed the time with her phone. She had a few messages and emails to catch up on. A flagged contact caught her eye. "Got my schedule for the next national team camp. I leave right after our game against Chicago next week for the Tournament of Nations."

"That's it?" Kenzie said, peeking at Sutton's phone screen. "You get notified, and you know when to leave?"

"Pretty much. Sometimes it's a call, sometimes an email. Then there's usually follow-up information sent shortly after. Flights and stuff like that."

"Do you get excited anymore?"

"I am excited."

"You don't seem excited."

She considered her feelings for a minute. "I'm honored every single time I get called up, and once I get there, I can't believe I get another chance to play for my country. But you know how much I miss this team and my home." She never looked away from Kenzie, trying her best to silently tell her how she was part of that home now. How did one loss make her so emotional?

"I can understand that. I get homesick very easily. I was lucky to be drafted to the Hurricanes because I'm just a drive away from my home and my dad."

Sutton felt a pang in her chest. "Is Jersey starting to feel like home at all?"

Kenzie nodded. "Definitely, but I don't know how so many players go overseas and things like that. I could never. I'd be so depressed all the time."

Sutton had never considered what Kenzie would do once the season was over. She just assumed she'd stick around with her. "What are your plans for the off-season?"

"My dad's company is holding a temp job for me. I just file and make phone calls, but it's a paycheck and will supplement what I'm not making until the preseason starts up."

The prospect of Kenzie going back to Pennsylvania for months felt like an even darker cloud over her now. "That's good, that's really good."

"I see that frown, Sutton. Tell me what you're thinking."

"I just thought you'd stay with me."

"It's not news that our pay sucks, especially in comparison to the men's teams, and some of us don't have endorsements and national team duties to help pay the bills." Kenzie smirked, taking away some of the sting of her words. "Plus, Pennsylvania is my home."

Sutton looked at her sadly. "Forever?"

"For now." Kenzie opened the music app on her phone and started to pull her headphones back on. "We'll talk more about this later when we're alone. I promise."

"Okay. I just—"

Kenzie's phone vibrated. "Huh. Who's calling me?"

"What?" Sutton looked between Kenzie and her phone in concern.

Kenzie pulled her headphones off and pressed the phone to her ear. "Hello?" She moved to the other side of the bus.

Sutton watched Kenzie talk on the phone, hating the way Kenzie angled her body away from her. She couldn't make out a word Kenzie was saying, but her tone was unlike anything Sutton had heard before. When Kenzie returned to her seat, Sutton stared at her expectantly.

"Is everything okay?"

"I'll be with you," Kenzie said.

Sutton racked her brain to try to complete that riddle. "With me where? Pennsylvania?"

"San Jose, apparently. That was Coach Weller. I'm being called up. Sutton, I got my first call-up to the national team." Kenzie held up her phone.

"Holy shit, that's great!" She wrapped her arms around Kenzie. Memories of her first call-up came flooding back and she wanted nothing more than to celebrate Kenzie's achievement. "You deserve this. You're incredible. Can I announce it?" She felt Kenzie nod against her.

Sutton stood and took a breath deep enough that'd allow her to speak over the bus's engine. "Can I have everyone's attention?" Everyone on the bus turned toward her. "We may be a little down after our loss, but there's some good news. Our own number twelve, Kenzie Shaw, just got her first call-up to the national team." Hoots, exclamations, and applause rang out in the bus. She looked at Kenzie proudly.

"Way to go, Shaw," Taylor said, raising her hand for a high five over the back of her seat.

Happiness radiated off Kenzie, but they couldn't bask in it for too long. The national team frowned upon members being in a public relationship. The decision to come out as a couple was no longer theirs to make, and she was going to have to break that to Kenzie.

❖

Sutton rushed around her Jeep to open the door for Kenzie. She adored the small smile Kenzie shot her every time she did something simple and chivalrous. "Did you enjoy yourself?"

"We went to a hibachi restaurant, what wasn't to enjoy?" Kenzie said, patting her stomach. "It was very nice of Taylor to pick up the tab."

"Taylor knows how big a deal it is to get your first call-up." Sutton walked beside Kenzie slowly. She wanted to get inside and start to enjoy their alone time, but she knew she'd have to address the elephant in the room. An elephant only she could see, but one that weighed on her heavily nonetheless.

"I'm surprised she's never been called up. She's so good."

"She was," Sutton said as she pushed open her front door. "Once about six years ago."

"But not again after that?" Kenzie took off her heels and placed them by the front door. She flexed her painted toes against the hardwood floors, stretching languidly and letting out a large yawn.

Sutton always laughed at the stereotype of lesbians bringing a U-Haul to a second date, but Kenzie made her understand why so many people believed it. Every time Kenzie was in her house, she wanted to ask her to stay for good, to move in and be there for every sunrise and sunset.

"Sutton?"

Sutton snapped her attention back to Kenzie. "Sorry. Looking at you distracted me."

"Is everything okay? You were really quiet during dinner but—don't take this the wrong way—you're rarely quiet."

Sutton tossed her keys on the kitchen table and walked up to Kenzie. She held her face in her hands and kissed her sweetly. "I'm beat." She started to turn away, but Kenzie never budged.

"That's not an answer, and you've been acting a little weird since I found out about my call-up, come to think of it."

Sutton read between those lines pretty clearly. "It's not about that."

"But something *is* bothering you."

Sutton took a deep breath and let it out slowly. "Taylor was only called up to the national team once because there's a level of politics involved, just like with any other federation or organization. There're rules, regulations, and a lot of fine print in our contracts. A lot of that didn't agree with Taylor, or rather she didn't agree with a lot of it."

Kenzie rolled her eyes and walked out of the room. Sutton looked after her, confused by her sudden departure and behavior. She had answered Kenzie's question about Taylor and thought she had explained herself rather well. She followed Kenzie into her bedroom and was shocked to see her packing up her overnight bag.

"What are you doing?"

"I'm going home."

"Why?"

Kenzie zippered her bag. "Because you're being weird and not talking to me about whatever is actually bothering you. Today was a great day. I got the biggest news of my career, and all I wanted to do was celebrate with some of my teammates and my girlfriend, but now whatever this is," Kenzie said, waving between them, "is kind of ruining it for me."

Sutton's heart sank. "I'm sorry, and please step away from the bag." She placed her hands on Kenzie's shoulders and moved her away from the duffel bag. "I am so happy and proud that you got your call-up today, and I truly believe you're going to make an even bigger impact on the national team than you did with the Hurricanes." Sutton looked into Kenzie's hazel eyes and waited to see some of the softness return before speaking again. "You are right, my mood tonight is purely selfish."

"What is it?"

"I can't be with you and be on the national team."

"That's a weird code to live by. Does it happen often for you?"

She chose to ignore Kenzie's zinger. "It's not my code—it's the federation's code." She saw the confusion on Kenzie's face. "If we're both on the national team, we can't be in a relationship, at least not publicly. It's not a rule, but it's pretty well-known that the higher-ups don't like it. Taylor didn't like how they tried to dictate the players' lives, so she passed. I think they're small cons that are outweighed by the pros."

Kenzie appeared to relax. "Well, shit, I guess it's a good thing we didn't make a big public display."

Sutton frowned at how easily Kenzie accepted this setback in their relationship. "Yeah, I guess it is."

"We'll be teammates in public and girlfriends behind closed doors and with close friends."

"I know a few players who have made it work."

"I doubt it's easy."

Sutton couldn't stop herself from pouting. "It's not."

Kenzie ran her hands over Sutton's shoulders, tracing the seams of her T-shirt with her short fingernails. "You know what, though?"

"What?"

"The national team isn't forever, and I'd like to think that, maybe, what you and I have will last longer than this opportunity," Kenzie said, never looking up from Sutton's neck. "I know that probably sounds crazy—"

"It doesn't," Sutton said quickly. She pulled Kenzie against her and held her tight. "It sounds perfect."

"Can I ask you something?"

"Anything."

"As a national team member, is the sex better?"

Sutton let out a deep laugh. "I haven't really noticed, but with two national team members working at it, I'm sure we can come up with a definitive answer."

Kenzie started tugging on the button of Sutton's jeans frantically. "We should get to it, then. For scientific purposes."

"I always did love science."

CHAPTER TWENTY-SIX

W here did that back line come from?" Kenzie pulled off her jersey and tossed it into her locker. "This is not the same team we played a few weeks ago."

Chiara dropped into the seat beside Kenzie's locker and didn't move. She was just as out of steam as the rest of them. "They must've practiced a lot, or we caught them on an off day last time."

"But we still won," Sutton said over the chatter in the locker room. She was already in her sports bra and compression shorts.

Kenzie allowed herself a moment before turning back into a professional. "We did, but I have to admit, I thought we were going to lose."

"Me, too," Sherri said. She hadn't spoken to Kenzie much since the incident with Rhea, but the chill between them had started to thaw. "We barely had the ball in the first half, and things weren't looking much better at the start of the second."

Jon, the newest addition to the athletic staff, interrupted their conversation. "I'm sorry to barge in like this, but I want to check on Shaw."

Kenzie looked at him in confusion. No one had ever sought her out like that. "What's up?"

"You took quite a spill in the ninetieth minute and came down pretty hard on that right shoulder. I want to make sure you're okay."

"I'm fine."

"I was sent. I should assess your movement and stretch you. At the very least."

She looked at Sutton, who offered a noncommittal shrug. She supposed it was better to have a training staff who hovered and worried than one who'd neglect a hurt player. She followed Jon into the area of the locker room where they had ice baths and tables to lie on. Kenzie took a seat and rolled her shoulders.

"I really am fine. The fall looked a lot worse than it was."

"I knew a player once who was so focused on how her legs and feet felt that she never noticed she'd sprained her elbow and torn her rotator cuff."

"Ouch. Really?"

"Yeah," Jon said, running his hand over Kenzie's bare shoulder. "You female soccer players are a rare breed. Everything you care about is from the waist down." He started to knead her shoulder joint. "Raise your arm up."

Kenzie reached her hand up as high as she could, her entire arm straight and rigid. "No pain."

"Very good. Bring it down and bend your elbow to ninety degrees. Make a fist and move your arm back and forth, like it's a swinging door."

Kenzie followed Jon's instructions. She was always patient with medical protocol, but right now she just wanted to change and start on her way home. She had national team camp to prep for. "I feel good."

"Let me just move you a little and we'll be done." Jon placed his hand over the front of her shoulder, fingers under the strap of her sports bra. Kenzie shifted uncomfortably but let him work. He grabbed the inside of her elbow and moved her arm back and forth, stretching and rotating the joint each time. "I bet you're excited to play with the national team."

"I am."

"Once you hit that level, there's no turning back. Guys will be lining up to try to date you. Better watch out." He laughed goofily, and Kenzie joined in to be polite.

She pulled away from him and stood up. "Thank you. I actually do feel a little better now, but I have to get changed. I hate waiting too long after a game."

"Let me know if you wake up with any stiffness or if anything doesn't feel right."

"I will." Kenzie walked back to the crowded locker room, slightly unsettled but just ready to get out of there. Sutton had already showered and was getting dressed. She waved off Sutton's curious look. She quickly changed into a training outfit and packed up her gear. She'd shower at Sutton's.

Sutton waited for her at the door, and they walked to her Jeep together. "Everything check out with your wing, Chicken?"

"I'm good. I didn't even need to be evaluated."

"Tyler can be a little overprotective of us, especially once we get into the second half of the season. Every game is do or die in his mind, and he wants us at one hundred percent at all times."

"I get that." She tossed her bag into Sutton's back seat and climbed into the Jeep. "That just seemed weird, not to mention Jon commented on how guys will be *lining up* for me once I'm on the national team," she said, using air quotes.

"Little does Jonny-boy know people are already lining up for you." Sutton smiled at her and started to drive.

She still felt unsettled. "I just thought it was odd."

"He probably has a crush on you. Can you blame him? I know I'm crazy about you."

Kenzie's unease started to melt away. "You are?"

Sutton cast her a quick glance. "You know I am."

"If you're crazy about me, then you'll draw me a bubble bath when we get home." Kenzie realized what she'd said and tried to backpedal. "Home to your place."

Sutton patted Kenzie's thigh. "How about an ice bath? I bet your muscles need it."

"No. Hot, with bubbles and a sexy defender washing my back for me."

"I don't have any bubble bath."

"Lucky for you there's a Walgreens on the way to your place."

"Lucky for me."

❖

Kenzie woke slowly the next morning, allowing herself to indulge in the softness of Sutton and her expensive sheets. She buried her face in the crook of Sutton's neck and wrapped her arm around her waist. She loved this, but she wasn't sure she truly understood the feeling.

She loved her family and her friends, but that was the only love she'd ever truly known. The kind of love that was rooted in friendship and fed passion and adoration until it grew into something uncontrollable and powerful? Kenzie was just starting to figure out what that love felt like, and she was more than a little terrified because she didn't know if Sutton felt the same. So she refused to say a word, let alone *those* three.

Instead, she relished their time together and waited for Sutton to say them first.

"Are you nervous?" Sutton's voice was sleep-ridden and sexy.

"Yes, I'm nervous. I'm actually pretty scared."

Sutton shifted just enough to draw Kenzie's body farther into her own. She entwined their legs and started running her fingers through Kenzie's hair, a movement equal to a double dose of sedatives. "What are you scared of?"

"I'm scared of everything. I'm scared of meeting new people, of playing poorly…" She paused to breathe deeply. She placed her palm over Sutton's heart and allowed its steady beat to soothe her. "But most of all I'm scared of disappointing you."

"That's impossible."

"What is?"

"You disappointing me."

"What if Coach Weller puts me in, and you lose because of something stupid I do?"

"Won't happen."

"What if I score an own goal?"

"Happens to the best of us."

"What if I don't tie my boot tight enough, and it flies off just as I'm about to score the winning goal?"

"That's a bit much."

"What if I get a bad concussion in the first minute of my first cap and miss the rest of camp and never get called up again?"

Sutton started to laugh. "Kenzie, as remarkable as your imagination is, I think your concerns are getting out of hand. Anything can happen when you're out on the field. I've seen crazy injuries and embarrassing mistakes, and I've made more than a few myself."

"Not helping."

"What I'm trying to say is I know how good you are and how deserving you are of this opportunity. You couldn't do one thing to disappoint me."

Kenzie thought hard to come up with the craziest idea yet. "What if it's too much pressure, and I decide to quit."

Sutton stayed silent for a minute before kissing her forehead. "I would be sad, but only because I know you'd be disappointing yourself." Sutton rolled over and covered Kenzie with her body. "I think it's a little too early for this kind of stress, and it's my duty to turn off your mind."

Kenzie hummed with satisfaction. Lying naked with Sutton was quickly becoming her favorite thing in life. She dragged her hands up Sutton's sides, caressing her firm muscles and palming her breasts. Kenzie loved teasing Sutton's nipples. She had discovered they were incredibly sensitive, and the soft skin surrounding them blushed every time Kenzie touched her.

"We have a few hours before we have to leave for the airport, and I think it'd be best for us to stay right here." Sutton kissed the side of Kenzie's neck.

"I wouldn't mind staying right here forever," Kenzie said, the confession coming out in a whisper.

Sutton leaned up to kiss her softly. She reacted immediately and deepened the kiss. When they separated, Sutton wore a satisfied grin. "Looks like you're getting over your aversion to morning breath."

Kenzie was done being playful. "I need you." She stared up at Sutton's puffy eyes and mussed hair. She really did need her in so many ways. "I need…"

"What?" Sutton kissed her cheeks and her brows. "What do you need?"

Kenzie pinched Sutton's nipple before trailing her right hand down her abdomen, scratching her bronze skin along the way. She ran her fingertips into Sutton's growing wetness and rubbed her hardening clit. "I need to come with you. Together." Sutton kept her eyes locked on hers as Kenzie entered her slowly.

"You're going to be amazing," Sutton whispered against Kenzie's lips. She started to work her hips in time to her thrusts. "You're going to leave the team wondering how they functioned before you, and the fans will fall in love with you, too."

Kenzie's heart started to hammer against her rib cage. Sutton's encouragement did more to her body than dirty talk ever could. They touched and kissed and loved each other until the last possible minute. Kenzie couldn't imagine a better start to a day, let alone the beginning of one of the most important days of her life. She counted her blessings as she readied herself for their flight. Sutton sat at the top of that list. Having a partner at your side during the best and worst times was what love was all about. Kenzie was finally starting to understand that.

Chapter Twenty-Seven

Training with the United States Women's National Team was unlike anything Kenzie imagined. Not because the drills were special or the routines out of the norm, but because she was surrounded by talented players who had more accolades and awards than she ever hoped to. More than half the players were from the World Cup champion team, and several more were Olympic medalists. Kenzie understood she was a nobody on this roster, the lowest player on the totem pole, but she still felt a pang of disappointment when she wasn't named to the starting eleven in their game against Japan.

Sutton pressed her shoulder into Kenzie's. "You'll get your chance, and when you do, you'll crush it."

She shot Sutton her most convincing smile and finished getting ready. Regardless of the slight disappointment she felt, her giddiness shone through when she pulled on her jersey. She felt a little silly for thinking it, but she actually felt different wearing the uniform.

Tara Best walked up to her and raised both of her hands, giving Kenzie a double high five. "Welcome to the national team, Shaw."

"You do look good in red, white, and blue." Sutton's smirk told Kenzie a million things she couldn't say aloud. "Are you ready?"

"To warm the bench? Absolutely," Kenzie said lightly. She didn't want anyone thinking she wasn't grateful to be there.

Coach Tammy Weller called out for the team to gather at the center of the locker room. "This is our last tournament before we enter a World Cup year next year. Consider these games your auditions. I've kept my eye on all of you for years—that includes the rookies," she said, looking directly at Kenzie. "Don't showboat or strain yourself in order to prove something. Show me you can play smart and as a team. Do *not* compete with each other, because nothing is more powerful than a group of women who work together. We represent the best parts of the United States of America, so let's get out there and prove it to the crowd who came here to cheer you on."

Kenzie stood taller as she fell in line and got ready to walk out. She took her spot on the bench after warm-ups. The national anthems played, and the wait for the first whistle to blow seemed endless. Her eyes were on Sutton the whole time. Watching her command the national team was an unexpected aphrodisiac she'd gladly revisit when she wasn't at work.

The United States dominated Japan in the first half of the game. Even when Japan had possession of the ball, they were unable to convert any of their plays to a shot on goal. Japan had a very talented roster, but they looked like they were sleeping on the field. At the start of the second half, the US was up by four points.

The trainer for the national team started clapping. Roger looked at everyone on the bench. "Get up and start jogging. Come on, down to the corner and back."

Kenzie jumped up, grateful to move. She jogged up the sideline and kept her eyes on the gameplay. Sutton had just stripped the ball from the opposing team seamlessly and passed it off to their midfielder. The best part of watching Sutton play was how deeply into the game she got. Kenzie could've been naked, and Sutton wouldn't have noticed. When she was in the zone, her attention and focus were rock solid.

Kenzie went back to the bench with the rest of the substitutes, but the coach called out to both her and another rookie, Mary. Weller instructed them to start stretching, which usually meant they'd be seeing minutes soon.

Roger and the assistant coach directed them through a few stretches they were both very familiar with, but they followed along anyway. She ran through a few drills, her heart pounding more from nerves than exertion.

"Shaw, you're going in for Narvaez up top. Let Amelia know we're dropping back to a four-two-three-one. You're the one."

Kenzie squared her shoulders and looked the assistant coach in the eye as she nodded. If only she felt as confident as she led him to believe. She had practiced in this position before, but she hadn't expected it to really happen this soon. "Let's do it."

He handed Kenzie her substitution slip, and she walked up to the official at the sideline. She handed him the paper but hesitated before letting go. He eyed her curiously before jotting down the info.

Kenzie looked around the stadium. She shook out her limbs and jumped up and down a few times, trying to ready her body for the game. The whistle blew and she knew she'd be stepping onto the field as a national team player in a matter of seconds. She was about to earn her first cap for her country.

The referee held up the digital sign that told everyone who was out and who was going in. Kenzie stared up at her number two, lit in green. Narvaez jogged to the sideline, taking her time to run down the clock. She pulled Kenzie in for a quick hug. "Good luck," she whispered in Kenzie's ear before releasing her and patting her butt.

Kenzie dashed out on the field, engulfed by the sound of the crowd cheering around her. She knew in that moment her life was exactly what she had always hoped it'd be. This was the start of *everything* for Kenzie Shaw.

"We're dropping back to a four-two-three-one. I'm up top," she said to Amelia, who nodded and fell back a few yards. When the whistle blew again, Kenzie wasted no time attacking the ball.

Japan did their best to keep possession, employing every bit of fancy footwork they were capable of, but they were no match for Kenzie's trained eye. Everything Sutton taught her on the field the day their relationship changed course came flooding back. She surged forward and stripped the ball from a player's foot just as she was about to pass it, causing her to stumble. By the time she regained her balance, Kenzie was already on her way toward Japan's goal.

Japan's defensive line formed a wall, so she slotted the ball back, knowing one of her midfielders would be there to receive and advance with it. As they distracted the defenders, she moved to the post. When she turned back, she saw Sutton wide open and waving to Tara, who passed the ball.

Kenzie ran to the top of the box and waited. Sutton looked up from the ball for a split second before launching it in Kenzie's direction. Kenzie followed it as it drifted slightly to the left. She received the pass with the perfect first touch and turned her whole body as she took the shot. The ball torpedoed directly into the back of the net.

She couldn't believe it. She had just scored in the first minutes of her first cap with the national team. She looked back at Sutton, who was running toward her to celebrate. Kenzie did the first thing that came to mind: the chicken dance. Sutton was in hysterics by the time she reached her. Kenzie launched herself into Sutton's arms and wrapped her legs around her waist. The rest of the team followed and surrounded them. Kenzie could hear everyone cheering for her as they patted her back or head, or playfully tugged her bun. Sutton left the huddle first, and just as quickly as it all started, Kenzie stood on her own again.

She didn't score another goal, but by the time the whistle blew in the ninety-fourth minute, the US was up six to two. The team's cooldown was jovial and fun, everyone laughing and recounting the most exciting moments of the game. A few players surrounded their keeper and tried to make her feel better about giving up two goals. Kenzie felt beyond grateful.

Once they started for the locker room, a few players went to sign autographs at the sidelines. Kenzie was far from surprised to see Sutton surrounded by excited fans. Sutton waved her over, and Kenzie smiled at the group of young girls asking for pictures with Sutton. One turned to Kenzie with a smile so broad it looked painful.

"Would you please sign my ball?" She held up an official ball with more than a few signatures on it already.

"I'd be honored," Kenzie said, taking the ball and finding the perfect place to sign. She handed it back, and the girl's mother stepped in.

"You're one of her favorite players."

Kenzie didn't hide her surprise. "Wow, thank you. She's officially one of my favorite fans." The little girl's face lit up even more.

"Would you mind taking a picture with her? It would mean a lot."

"Of course." Kenzie bent slightly and leaned over the wall to put her arm around the girl's shoulder. She smiled for the picture and waited while the mother took a few. When she stepped back, she noticed the little girl was wearing her Hurricanes jersey.

"This is what it's all about, Chicken," Sutton said into her ear. "Also, look at the sign all the way to the right. Girl with the Uncle Sam hat."

Kenzie scanned the crowd of spectators waiting or lingering. She noticed the sign immediately. *World Cup bound #FloShaw.* She felt panicked when she turned back to Sutton.

Sutton wore an easy smile and kept signing and posing. Kenzie took a deep breath and decided to follow her lead. If Sutton wasn't worried, then she shouldn't be, either.

Kenzie stayed with the fans until security came over and insisted they get back to the locker room. With a final autograph and a sad smile, Kenzie stepped away.

"I feel amazing," she said to Sutton.

"You should. You may have broken a record today with how quickly you scored."

"Not that. Well, okay, maybe a little about that, but really meeting those kids."

"It's my favorite part, win or lose. I wish I'd had more female role models growing up. I'm not saying I'm a great role model for those kids, but I try to be, for that reason. Young girls deserve the chance to see themselves in someone they look up to. Every time I sign a jersey or pose for a picture, I want them to know nothing is stopping them from being in my position one day."

"You're remarkable."

"So are you," Sutton said with her hand on the locker room door handle. "And you're just getting started."

In the locker room, the team presented Kenzie with a game ball signed by everyone, a custom started years ago for any player who got their first cap with the national team. Kenzie soaked up the praise of her teammates and the positive words Coach Weller shared before they split up to shower and head back to the hotel. Kenzie looked forward to recovery. The excitement of the day, the physical drain of playing, and the emotional toll of meeting fans had worn her out. She just hoped her roommate wouldn't mind keeping it quiet for the rest of the night.

CHAPTER TWENTY-EIGHT

The team spent the next day traveling to another stadium, and they usually spent the first night in a new hotel resting up for the following day of training. But not everyone followed that plan.

Sutton knocked on the door to Kenzie's room three times. She leaned against the doorframe casually, but inside she was itching just to touch her. Playing beside Kenzie while being in a secret relationship with her was both torturous and invigorating. All day she watched Kenzie's unbelievable body display its strength and agility, while knowing what it felt like to have Kenzie stripped down and writhing beneath her. She jumped when the door swung open.

Kenzie looked beautiful with her hair down and framing her face. The hotel lighting cast breathtaking shadows along her cheekbones. She hated that she had to keep her hands to herself.

"Hey," Kenzie said softly.

Sutton noticed movement behind Kenzie. Her roommate was shuffling around. Sutton liked Jenny just fine, but right now she stood between her and getting to touch Kenzie. Sutton let out a small grunt of displeasure.

"Some of the girls are getting together in Tara's room to watch a movie. Would you like to join me?"

Kenzie appeared as though she really had to think about it. "I suppose I could be persuaded."

"It's a horror film," Sutton said as she started to lean in a bit. "You can hold on to me if you get scared."

Kenzie took her lower lip between her teeth, her eyes set on Sutton's mouth. She backed into the room and grabbed her phone off the desk by the door. She told Jenny where they were heading and politely extended an invitation to join. Jenny declined.

"Let's go." Kenzie started down the hall.

Sutton caught up to her and grabbed her elbow gently, guiding her into a nearby cubby with soda and ice machines. She kissed Kenzie sweetly, just long enough to sate her hunger.

"I miss you."

Kenzie giggled. "You're with me."

"You know exactly what I mean because I know you feel it, too."

Kenzie wrapped her arms around Sutton's waist and held her close. Kenzie's face was cool against Sutton's neck, and she could feel how cold the tip of her nose was. Kenzie stepped away without a word and walked back into the hallway.

Sutton caught up with her and gave her shoulder a nudge. The small touch was her way of wordlessly asking if she was okay. Kenzie shot her a reassuring smile and a wink just as they arrived at Tara's room. The door was already ajar, and they were greeted the moment they pushed it all the way open.

"You made it just in time—I'm about to hit play," Tara said from her place on the floor in front of the TV.

"Where should we sit?" Sutton looked around the crowed space. Nine other players were crammed into the double room. An empty space called to her from the far bed. They'd be able to sit against the wall together. Sutton stepped around the sprawled bodies and pulled back the covers. She signaled for Kenzie to get in first. "Right side is for you," she whispered as Kenzie climbed in.

They settled in under the covers, pressed against one another's side. Thankfully, most teammates were close enough for behavior like this to go unquestioned. Someone turned out the lights, and Kenzie grabbed Sutton's thigh under the covers as the screen lit up with blood-red lettering.

Sutton turned slightly and leaned into Kenzie's side. "Do you not like scary movies?" she said.

"Not particularly. But I like holding on to you."

The opening scene of the film started with a loud noise, causing everyone in the room to jump. Sutton laughed. Everyone was so engrossed in the story line of demonic possession they didn't move for a while.

"Oh, hell no," Amelia shouted when the possessed character's neck bent at a ninety-degree angle. "Why do the heads have to do that?"

"It's Possession 101," Sutton said. "You're not possessed unless your head does some crazy shit." The possessed woman opened her mouth and screamed suddenly. Kenzie hid her face in Sutton's shoulder. "It's okay." She rubbed Kenzie's arm, jumping herself as Kenzie felt her way up Sutton's inner thigh.

"Big bad Sutton finally got scared like the rest of us." Tara's eyes shone with challenge, but Sutton could only manage a dumb nod.

Kenzie tugged loose the tie on the inside of Sutton's waistband. Sutton swallowed hard. "Wh-what are you doing?"

Kenzie's breathed heavily into the crook of Sutton's neck. "I need a distraction."

Sutton looked around, relieved to see everyone's eyes on the screen. "Are you not scared of getting caught?"

"Sure. I'm also scared that the possessed lady will be waiting in my room for me later. Life is all about what we do with our fears." Kenzie stared at the TV, seemingly still watching the movie, but under the covers, she traced featherlight circles on Sutton's mound through her boy shorts.

"That's pretty deep, Chick—" Sutton bumped her head against the headboard, thankful for its padding. Kenzie ran her finger along Sutton's covered entrance. She was growing wetter by the second and her muscles pulsed to take Kenzie in. Sutton hated the barrier between herself and the touch she needed so much. When Kenzie applied a little pressure, Sutton's whole body jerked. She looked at Kenzie and stared at her profile. Her face was so innocent as she watched the movie, but her hand was doing devilish things beneath the covers. Sutton spread her legs a little more when she felt Kenzie move her hand to slip into her underwear. Kenzie's fingertips were cold as they traced her intimate flesh, the contrast in temperature bringing with it great pleasure.

Sutton fought to keep her hips still and her breathing even as Kenzie worked her clit at a painfully slow pace. The circles she drew were driving Sutton mad with want. Subtly, Sutton reached under the blanket and grabbed Kenzie's wrist. She pushed her hand down farther, guiding Kenzie's fingers back to her hungry entrance. She bit back a moan as Kenzie entered her quickly.

A loud scream sounded from the movie and everyone jumped. Kenzie pulled her hand back and put distance between them. Sutton took the opportunity to catch her breath under the guise of being scared. Sutton swallowed hard when she saw Kenzie licking the tips of her fingers.

"I'm getting kind of tired, guys," Sutton said a little too loudly for the quiet room. "I'm going to head back to my room." She got out of bed.

"I'll come, too." Kenzie followed her lead less gracefully as she fought to free herself from the sheets.

"You two aren't fooling anyone," Tara said.

They both froze. "What are you talking about?" Sutton said. She hoped Tara wouldn't spill their secret to the national team, even if it wasn't the best-kept secret to begin with.

"You can admit it, Sutton."

"Admit what?"

"You're scared."

Sutton smiled. "Yeah, you're right. I admit it. We're scared, so instead of crawling under the covers, we're going to head out and go watch something with happy times and rainbows. Good night, everyone." She backed out of the room and nudged Kenzie along, too.

Kenzie didn't speak until they were in the hallways and the door shut. "Holy shit."

"I know." Sutton stuffed her hands into the pocket of her sweatshirt, resisting the temptation to touch Kenzie. "We need to get back to my room. Now."

"Do you think that's smart after what just happened in there?"

She got close enough to be in Kenzie's personal space but far enough away so they didn't look suspicious. "The only thing that happened in that room was a lot of teasing, and you're going to pay for it, Chicken."

Kenzie flinched, her eyes growing momentarily heavy. "Yes, Captain."

They walked down the hallway as quickly as they could without drawing attention. Sutton's hand shook as she unlocked the door to her room and swung it open. She locked the door as soon as it shut. "We have about an hour." Sutton took Kenzie's face in her hands and kissed her fiercely, with no preamble, before sliding her tongue into her mouth.

Kenzie went to work on Sutton's shorts. She pushed her fingers into the waistband, pausing with her palms on the naked skin of Sutton's ass, before shoving Sutton's shorts and boy shorts down.

Sutton welcomed the cool air on her skin. She made short work of their sweatshirts and the training T-shirt Kenzie had on underneath.

They undressed each other fully before falling on Sutton's bed. Kenzie straddled Sutton's hips. She felt powerless as she stared up at Kenzie. She reached up and palmed her small bare breasts.

Kenzie ground her wetness into Sutton, placing her hands below Sutton's breasts and leaning forward. "Where do you want me?" Kenzie said.

"Right where you were before." Sutton sucked in a breath as Kenzie entered her with two fingers. She tilted her head back and sighed when Kenzie kissed her throat.

"Why am I so tempted to bite you?"

"Because you know you can't." Sutton canted her hips, inviting Kenzie to press into her more deeply. "Not while we're here."

"I can't get enough of you like this," Kenzie said in a whisper, her breath tickling Sutton's ear. "Wide open and at my mercy. I used to fantasize about this, about having you. I'd watch your games and then lie in bed at night with my hand between my legs. I'd call your name every time."

Sutton opened her eyes and stared at the ceiling. She keened low when Kenzie turned her attention to her clit. Kenzie knew exactly how to touch her to make her come quickly. Kenzie nipped at her earlobe and returned to Sutton's mouth. She matched Kenzie's passion head-on. She flipped Kenzie on her back, careful to not lose their connection. She entered Kenzie swiftly and swallowed her sudden cry. Sutton pumped her hips against Kenzie's hand. The pulsing warmth brought her incredibly close to orgasm. She could feel the wildfire in her belly and the pull at her clit.

"I want you to come with me," she said, licking Kenzie's full lower lip.

Kenzie whined. "I'm so close."

Sutton pulled out and collected Kenzie's juices on her fingertips. She rubbed Kenzie's clit at a steady pace, exactly how Kenzie liked it. Kenzie brought her free hand up to hold the back of Sutton's neck and their foreheads together. They stared into each other's eyes as their passion mounted. Sutton's body started to shake as Kenzie's breathing grew ragged.

Kenzie tightened her grip on Sutton's neck. "I love you," she said just before she closed her eyes and threw her head back. Kenzie was exquisite when she came. Sutton watched as red patches erupted on her glistening chest.

Sutton had no choice but to let her orgasm take over then. She grunted as quietly as she could. Her body moved erratically, and every muscle joined the intense release. Kenzie went slack beneath her. She rested her head against Kenzie's chest and listened to her heartbeat return to normal.

The first time Kenzie moved was to cover her face. "I can't believe I just did that."

Sutton looked up. "What? Fingered me in our teammate's bed?"

"Yes. Let's go with that. That was definitely the most mortifying thing I did tonight. I'm sure of it."

Sutton eyed her curiously. Her hair was a mess of runaway red waves, and her nipples were still hard. Sutton lowered her head and took one rosy peak between her lips. Kenzie bowed her back off the mattress. She traced her tongue around Kenzie's breast, enjoying the salty taste of her sweat.

Kenzie ran her fingers through Sutton's hair with one hand and scratched Sutton's shoulder blade with the other.

"Kenzie?" Sutton felt the rumble in Kenzie's chest when she hummed. "What did you do that you can't believe?"

Kenzie's eye flew open wide. She wouldn't look at Sutton. "I can't believe I said *that* for the first time during sex. It's so cliché."

Sutton grinned. She moved up from Kenzie's chest to place a sweet kiss on her lips. "I think you should tell someone you love them the moment you feel it." Sutton felt that indescribable but immediately recognizable warmth blossom in her chest.

Kenzie looked at Sutton with soft eyes and a barely there smile. "You do?"

"I do."

Kenzie nodded and started to turn her head away, but Sutton didn't want to lose this moment.

"And you know what, Chicken?"

Kenzie rolled her eyes and laughed. "What?"

"I love you, too. I should've told you a while ago." She kissed Kenzie's forehead and her eyelids, tasting salty wetness against her lips. She pulled back to see tears in Kenzie's eyes. "Are you okay?"

Kenzie kissed Sutton with so much passion and emotion, it took her breath away. "I'm so much better than okay."

Sutton pushed a few strands of hair from Kenzie's face. "I think we have enough time for a quick shower." She wiggled her eyebrows.

"Say no more." Kenzie squirmed out from underneath Sutton and practically skipped to the bathroom.

Sutton watched after her and laughed. She was so in love with Kenzie. She couldn't believe it had taken her until this moment to say it, but Sutton knew she'd be saying it every day for a very long time.

CHAPTER TWENTY-NINE

The United States swept the Tournament of Nations, leaving Japan, Brazil, and Australia in their dust for the third year in a row. The last game against Australia was the toughest. Sutton had her work cut out for her, going against one of the deadliest forwards in the sport. But Kenzie took the brunt of Australia's brute force. In the last ten minutes of the game, an Australian defender took Kenzie down hard. Kenzie went down on her knee with such force, she slid a few feet. She stayed on the ground to regain her composure. Once the referee and a few teammates checked on her, Kenzie stood and received a round of applause.

After the end of the game and trophy presentation, Sutton rushed to Kenzie to check on her. She knew Kenzie was trying hard to conceal a limp. "Hey, Chicken, how's the leg?"

"I'm fine."

"Kenzie," Sutton said, grabbing her hand and stopping her from getting on the bus. "As somebody who knows your body and how you move, I know you're lying."

Kenzie rolled her eyes. "It's a small tweak. My knee will be good to go by the time we get home. Trust me."

"I do trust you, and I also believe you'll put playing before what your body needs."

"Can we get on the bus?" Kenzie said, tilting her head subtly toward the crowd taking their picture.

Sutton followed her on the bus and picked up their conversation as soon as they sat. "Promise me you'll tell Brett or Tyler if you're not okay."

"I promise. Now, please, can we just enjoy the night? I played my first games and first tournament with the national team. Can you just… can you be my teammate for the night?"

Sutton sat back, slightly hurt. "Yeah. If that's what you want." She turned to look out the window. She didn't know why she was being punished for showing concern. If Kenzie expected her to just shut off her feelings, she was in for an unpleasant surprise.

Kenzie must've noticed Sutton's mood change because she leaned in to her a minute later as the bus pulled out onto the highway. "I'm not asking you to stop being my girlfriend."

"That's exactly what you just asked me to do, Kenzie, and you got it. You played a great game today." She patted Kenzie's shoulder stiffly and looked back out the window.

"Please don't be like this."

"I'm going to talk to Tara about our next game."

Sutton changed seats and plopped down beside Tara, who looked at her like she had fifteen heads.

"What?" Sutton said.

"You've never sat next to me on the bus, not even before Kenzie came along."

"I needed a change of scenery, and I figured we could talk strategy against Boston."

"We play three up top because their defense is their weakness. That's been our strategy since day one, and this is our third game against them. There's no surprises." Tara closed the magazine she was reading. "What's really going on?"

Sutton looked at her thumbs and noticed one nail was trimmed shorter than the other. That was going to bother her until she fixed it. She dropped her hands in her lap. "I'm worried about Kenzie because I know her leg is hurting, but she won't talk to me about it."

"Why not?"

"Because we just won a tournament, and she wants to focus on that. She wants me to be happy for her as her teammate," Sutton said in her best mocking tone.

"Can you blame her?"

She shot a deathly glare at Tara.

"Listen, this was her first camp. She's probably the closest to high as she's ever been, and she's walking away a champion. She doesn't give a shit about her knee, and she probably just expects you to feel the same way."

"And I don't because I care about her, and as a teammate I'm affected by her well-being."

"Are you this hard to talk to when you go to Taylor with your problems?"

"Taylor usually doesn't listen for this long."

"What would Taylor say?"

Sutton let her annoyance show on her face. "She would've cut me off two words in and told me Kenzie's an adult, and I should do whatever would make her happy."

"Taylor can be so smart, and more people would probably know it if she wasn't so dang annoying."

Sutton smiled, but she pushed the small cheerful moment away and forced a frown back on her face. "Whatever. I'm still hurt and pissed, and I'm allowed to be."

"I never said you weren't," Tara said, opening her magazine again. "I just think this is a really silly thing to let hurt both of you." She licked the tip of her forefinger and turned the page loudly. "I wouldn't want to be Kenzie right now. I'm having a great day and then my girlfriend ruins it with a temper tantrum."

"Hey!"

"I was channeling Taylor."

Sutton sulked in her seat and remained silent for the rest of the drive. She hated Tara right then, but she didn't want to change seats again. Thankfully, the hotel wasn't too far from the stadium, and she wouldn't be stuck on the bus forever. She waited for Kenzie to get off first and felt a chill in her chest when Kenzie looked back at her sadly.

In her room, Sutton tried her best not to picture Kenzie's sad eyes or the defeated sag of her shoulders. But the fact was unavoidable. She was wrong. She should've believed Kenzie instead of pushing her. If the roles had been reversed, she would've acted the same way, except she would've never asked Kenzie to be *just* a teammate. That's what hurt. She dropped her bag on her bed and left the room. She cared about Kenzie, loved her more deeply than anyone she had ever been with, and she wasn't going to let this small argument ruin what should be a great night.

She marched down the elegantly decorated hallway of the hotel and turned the corner to Kenzie's room. She bumped into Kenzie, who stumbled back and grabbed the wall to steady herself.

"Oh my God," Sutton said, reaching out to hold Kenzie. "I am so sorry. I was on my way to see you and wasn't watching where I was going."

Kenzie started to giggle. "I was doing the same thing."

"I'm sorry."

"I'm sorry."

Sutton desperately needed to set things right and started talking before Kenzie could get another word out. "I should've believed you and let it drop. Tonight is supposed to be a great night, and I'm ruining that for you. I acted out and switched seats because I was hurt."

"And I shouldn't have asked you to be anyone other than who you are." Kenzie reached out to touch her but pulled back and balled her fists at her sides. "This is harder than I thought it'd be."

"It won't get any easier, but you're worth it."

"I'll get checked out by Tyler first thing when we get to practice. I feel fine, but I will make sure I'm in good shape before I play any more minutes."

"I trust you to do whatever you think is best with your body. I've never played on a team with someone I'm involved with before, so this is new and a little hard for me to juggle. It's going to take me a while to figure out when to be your teammate, your captain, or your girlfriend. But no matter which role I'm playing, I love you so much."

Kenzie grinned. "I'll never get tired of hearing that."

"Do you still love me after I acted like an idiot and ruined your first tournament with the national team?"

"I still love you, and you didn't ruin anything. Now we'll always remember when we had our first real fight."

Sutton grimaced. "That's not good."

"It's a milestone for a couple."

"Great," Sutton said with a grumble, but her smile belied her tone.

"Can we go someplace private now? I really want to kiss you. It's been forever," Kenzie said in exasperation.

"The team is going out tonight to celebrate, so we should probably get ready. But if I were to follow you back to your room for a few minutes…"

"Jenny's there."

"Amelia is probably in my room already," Sutton said. "She was only a few steps behind me coming up." Sutton looked up and down the hallway before directing Kenzie into a small alcove with an emergency exit. She kissed her quickly. "Looks like we'll have to wait." Sutton knew the rest of the night would be a true test of her restraint.

❖

The next morning, Sutton was grumpy and tired as she wheeled her suitcase through the airport. Even Kenzie's sunshiny demeanor couldn't break through her funk. "I need coffee and a scone," Sutton said.

"Somehow, someway, I still think you're adorable even when you're being a grump." Kenzie stepped up to the Starbucks counter and placed the order for herself, Sutton, and Tara. She even went as far as ordering one of each scone they had available. Tara enjoyed that.

Sutton yawned. "How are you two in such a good mood? We didn't go to sleep until after four in the morning." Sutton checked the time on her phone. She'd only gotten two hours of sleep.

"Our Chicken is a spring chicken." Tara laughed at her own joke. "She's nice and young, made for sleepless nights and partying. I, on the other hand, snuck out at midnight. I can't hang like that." Tara took her coffee from the barista and thanked her.

"I thought you went missing." Sutton took her coffee from Kenzie and refrained from kissing her.

"Nice to know I'm missed when I'm not around," Tara said with an eye roll. "Sutton, can I ask you a personal question?"

Sutton looked at Tara over the white lid of her cup and then to Kenzie.

Kenzie looked between the both of them. "Do you need me to step away?"

"No, you can be here. I'm sure Sutton would tell you anyway."

"Okay," Sutton said. "Go ahead."

"Is Taylor seeing anyone or interested in anyone?"

Sutton felt a fraction more awake. "Are you asking for a friend or for yourself?"

"Would that change the answer?"

"Maybe."

Tara sighed. "For myself."

Kenzie hummed as she sipped at her drink. "You two would be really cute together."

Sutton nodded. "You would. Taylor is single, and she's not interested in anyone as far as I know. I thought you said Taylor was annoying. Is that something you like in a woman?" Tara laughed and started to blush. Sutton had never seen her teammate act like this before. She had to admit, Tara was charming when she had a crush.

"Not necessarily, but after talking to you last night, I realized Taylor is blunt and honest, and those *are* qualities I appreciate in a woman. And she's cute—like, really cute."

"She is," Kenzie said enthusiastically.

Sutton looked at Kenzie in surprise. "Are you trying to tell me something, Chicken?"

Kenzie shook her head. "I've only had eyes for you since day one, but Taylor is cute, and she has a nice butt."

Tara slapped Kenzie's shoulder. "Doesn't she?"

"Okay," Sutton said while holding up her free hand. "Let's stop talking about my best friend's butt for a minute. How do you think Brett will handle four of his players being in a relationship?"

"First, Taylor and I would be in our own relationship, but thank you for the invitation."

Kenzie snorted, and Sutton couldn't help but laugh, too.

"Second, he doesn't get a say. We'd be just as professional as the two of you. Plus, she won't play for the national team again, so we won't have to do this awkward dance." Tara motioned to Sutton and Kenzie.

"What awkward dance?" Sutton took a scone from Kenzie's bag and had to hold back from kissing her.

"That, right there," Tara said, pointing to Sutton. "You so obviously want to touch each other but can't. It's kind of sad, but also funny. To anyone who doesn't know better, you look like you can't stand being near each other."

Sutton smirked at Kenzie, knowing the complete opposite was true. "I'd envy you and Taylor for not having to hide, but watching Kenzie's national team dreams come true from the same field feels even better."

Kenzie paused with her cup in front of her lips. "I love you," she said from behind her coffee.

"Best part is Taylor and I can take turns rubbing each other's backs when we vomit because of you two."

"Shut up." Sutton felt much more awake now and couldn't wait to get home behind closed doors where she could show Kenzie just how much she loved her back.

Chapter Thirty

Kenzie knocked on the doorframe to the training staff's small office. "Hey, Tyler, do you have a minute?"

"Of course. What's up, Shaw?" He put the papers he was holding on his desk.

"I was wondering if you'd be able to take a quick look at my knee. I took a hard spill against Australia." Kenzie could tell by his sympathetic wince he knew the fall she was talking about.

"Did they check you out after the game?"

"No. They looked at me on the field, and I said I was good to keep playing. Afterward, I just wanted to celebrate."

He shook his head. "Athletes and their trophy high. You should've been evaluated by the trainer immediately after the game if you were feeling any pain."

Kenzie felt appropriately scolded. "I feel fine."

"Your movements were smooth during practice. I didn't notice you favoring one foot or one leg more than the other." Tyler crossed his arms over his chest and stared at Kenzie's legs for a moment. "But we're in the second half of the season and can't take any chances."

Kenzie almost laughed at his predictability. Sutton had known exactly what he was going to say. "That's why I came to you."

"Go see Jon. He should be in the back, prepping ice baths."

Kenzie immediately tensed. "Wouldn't it be better for you to take a look since we have more history? You know exactly what to look for and know what's normal for my body."

"I'm sure you're fine," he said. "Plus, I'm swamped with this fitness data. Jon will take a quick look and sign off on you playing against Boston tomorrow."

Kenzie wanted to argue but didn't know what to say. She didn't feel comfortable because the guy *might* have a crush on her? She told herself to grow up. A rookie shouldn't seek special treatment or attention, not if they wanted to have a good reputation. She thanked Tyler and went in search of Jon, who was exactly where Tyler said he'd be. She considered skipping the evaluation altogether, but with Tyler and Sutton both knowing about her knee, she'd look unprofessional and reckless. The last thing she wanted was to lose minutes because of something she could've been making up.

Jon looked up and saw her standing there. He almost dropped the bucket of ice he was holding. "Kenzie. Hi."

"Tyler sent me back to get my knee checked after last game."

"That was a pretty bad fall you had. Simon shouldn't have been that rough with you. I hope the Aussies' coach talked to her afterward."

Kenzie saw a few players and staff members milling around, so she felt safe enough to sit on a nearby bench. "I haven't had any pain since that night, and all of my movements feel good. It's just a little scratched up." She looked up at Jon as he loomed over her.

His clean-shaven face was deeply set with concern. "Better safe than sorry. Let's have a look," he said, moving toward a private exam room.

"We can do it right here." Kenzie lay back and started flexing her leg.

Jon laughed. "Come on, Shaw." He waved for her to follow and kept walking to the back.

She followed him, already weighed down by foreboding. She sat on the exam table and refrained from asking him to not close the door. *Standard procedure. He's just doing his job.*

"Lie back and put your feet on the table, knees bent." Jon put his hand on her knee as soon as she followed his instructions. "Very good." He poked at a few points around her kneecap and gave her knee a squeeze, concentrating his pressure on the sides of the joint. "Flatten your legs." He repeated the touches with her flat knee, never saying a word. The quiet was disconcerting. "No pain?"

"None."

Next, he held her knee in both hands and manipulated the tendons and muscle behind her knee. "You don't have any swelling, so that's good."

"Great." Kenzie started to sit up, but Jon pushed her back down.

"Not so fast, champ." He grabbed her ankle and raised it, so

Kenzie's foot was level with his shoulder. He touched the inside of Kenzie's knee with his other hand. "Any tenderness in your thigh or shooting pains?"

Kenzie blinked at the blank white ceiling. "No. I hurt my knee."

"Hamstrings can be tricky like that." Jon walked the tips of his index and middle fingers up the back of Kenzie's thigh, applying pressure as he went in search of swelling or a sore spot.

Kenzie had been playing soccer for most of her life, and she was no stranger to hamstring injuries. She also knew where the hamstring tendon ended, and Jon was getting very close to that point. "I think I'm good."

He ran his palm the rest of the way over her thigh and around to the front, his fingertips slipping below the hem of Kenzie's training shorts and ghosting over the edge of her panties. Kenzie's stomach twisted, and she sat up quickly.

"You check out fine, but that doesn't mean you shouldn't be careful. I know a few exercises you can do to help avoid an injury. I could explain them over dinner later."

She tried to control her breathing. Jon's face was innocent, and he stood with his chest puffed out, like he was proud. She dropped her gaze to the noticeable bulge in his uniform shorts. She looked away quickly and stood.

"No," she said, reaching for the doorknob.

"I'd hate for you to miss the game against Boston."

Kenzie froze. "What?"

"Let me take you to dinner. We'll talk about ways we can work your legs out." He ran his hand over the front of his pants.

"I'm not interested."

"I'm going to suggest to Tyler you sit the next game out. Or maybe even the next few."

Kenzie pushed past her discomfort and anxiety to find the anger building in her chest. She allowed it to fuel her rigid stance and response. "My knee is fine, and my ability to play is not in question here. What I am ready to question is what makes you think threatening and harassing players is okay?"

"I didn't hear a threat," he said, looking over her shoulder at the covered window of the exam room, "and neither did anyone else."

Kenzie opened the door and all but fell out of the exam room. She rushed through the locker room and gathered her bags. She had told Sutton to head out without her, knowing it would take some time to get her knee evaluated. Now, she was regretting that decision. Maybe if Sutton had been around, Jon wouldn't have threatened her.

Kenzie burst through the stadium doors and into the humid summer air. She gulped the thickness into her lungs, desperately trying to catch her breath, but the tightness in her chest didn't subside. She gathered herself enough to make it to her car. The moment she closed the door, her resolve broke on a wave of sobs.

❖

Sutton stared at her phone screen. She read Kenzie's message over and over, but no matter how many times she read the words, they gave her no more information than the first time.

Everything checked out fine with my knee, but I can't make it tonight. Sorry. See you tomorrow before the game.

Sutton frowned. "Sorry, guys, Kenzie's not coming." She turned to Taylor and Tara, who stood against her kitchen counter. They had opened a bottle of sparkling water and were nibbling on fruits and cheeses. The whole plan for the evening was to get Tara and Taylor in the same room to gauge their compatibility, and Kenzie had orchestrated it—another reason her absence was so strange.

"Is everything okay?" Tara grabbed a bunch of grapes and started to eat them.

"She didn't say, but I'm sure she's fine. Her mom has a tendency to get her involved in projects and stuff." Sutton's words sounded rational, but they did very little to quell her worry. She decided to respond to the text.

Tara and Taylor say hi and are sorry to miss you. But I miss you more.

"I'm surprised she doesn't live with you yet. How many nights a week does she stay here?" Taylor popped a cube of cheddar into her mouth.

"Most of them, but she goes home after away games to get clothes, do laundry, or to just check on her mom, a woman who does not need to be checked on," Sutton said with a laugh. "But truthfully, I've been thinking about asking her. I'm just afraid she'll freak out because it's so soon."

Tara pulled her long chestnut hair over one shoulder before reaching for some brie and apples. "I don't think time should have any factor in decisions like that."

Taylor turned to Tara slowly and hitched an eyebrow. "You don't?"

"Do I think a couple should move in together after the first date? No, but if you're together for a few months, I think it's perfectly acceptable to consider it. We know what's best for us, no one else. Don't you agree, Taylor?"

"I don't know, honestly. I've never really been with anyone I've wanted to live with."

"My last girlfriend and I talked at length about moving in together, but she cheated on me while I was on the road with the national team." Tara ate a strawberry like being cheated on was no big deal. "It's fine, but the point is just do it if you want to. We kept talking about it because neither of us wanted to actually do it. Clearly."

"Idiot," Taylor said. She sipped her water. "I'm sure you're with someone way better now."

"She's not," Sutton said too loudly and too quickly.

Tara glared at her.

"The flatbread should be warmed through," Sutton said. She stalked off to the oven but listened in on Tara and Taylor's conversation, storing details in her memory to share with Kenzie later.

"I swore off relationships for a bit after that."

"Understandable. I'd swear off women altogether if someone cheated on me," Taylor said.

Sutton pulled the flatbread out of the oven but hovered for a few seconds, wanting to give them a little more time alone.

"You've never been cheated on?" Tara sounded genuinely surprised.

"Not that I know of."

"You're lucky."

"You *are* lucky," Sutton said, joining the conversation again. She put the flatbread in the center of her large kitchen island. "I've been cheated on four times." Both Taylor and Tara looked at her in disbelief. "I swear."

"And I was always jealous of the way women flocked to you," Taylor said. "I guess I'll count my blessings that the few that do come my way are good people." She tapped her glass to Tara's.

Sutton had to force herself not to smile. She really wished Kenzie could see the success of their matchmaking. "Sometimes I think I deserved it because I'm always on the road."

"Or you make yourself unavailable," Taylor said.

Sutton glared at Taylor. "Or that."

Tara shook her head. "No one deserves to be cheated on, and I hope you never feel that pain, Taylor. It sucks."

"Are you seeing anyone?" Sutton said over the rim of her water glass. She knew Taylor would see right through her facade, but things were going so well, she decided to go in for the kill. "You haven't mentioned anyone recently."

Taylor had a glint in her eye when she looked at Sutton. "No, I'm single, but there may be somebody." She turned back to Tara, who was eating grapes directly from the cluster. "We'll see where it goes."

Sutton mentally high-fived herself. She couldn't wait to give Kenzie the play-by-play. She checked her phone again and was discontented to see she had no new notifications. She hoped Kenzie was okay.

Chapter Thirty-One

Kenzie arrived at the stadium late for the game, wanting to avoid as much time in the locker room and with the staff as possible. She couldn't even bear to look at Sutton. She knew she'd crumble the instant she looked into her dark eyes. She kept to herself as she got changed and readied herself for the game, only shooting Sutton a fake smile and small wave. She knew Sutton had a million questions, but she'd have to wait to ask them.

Brett stepped into the locker room and announced the starting eleven. Kenzie held her breath as he listed player after player, and she felt bile rise in her throat when her name was never called.

"Shaw, you're out for the next two as per trainer orders. We need your knee to be fresh against Kansas City."

Kenzie saw Jon standing at the edge of the locker room and fought against the retching her body demanded. "Of course. Would it be okay if I went home? I'm actually not feeling very well."

Brett looked at her skeptically. Even if they were injured, players usually sat in during the game. "Sure. I'll see you at practice."

"Thanks." Kenzie picked up her bag and rushed out the door with her boots and shin guards still on. She turned the corner of the building and bent at the waist. She wanted to vomit, but nothing came up. She heaved and heaved, coughing until her throat was dry and hurting. A touch at her shoulder made her jump. She turned to see Sutton, her eyes full of worry.

"Hey," Sutton said gently. She pressed her hand to Kenzie's forehead.

Kenzie pressed back, hungry for the warm and comforting touch. "Hey."

"Were you sick last night?"

Kenzie stared up into Sutton's big eyes and nodded, at a loss for what to say. She had been sick, but she couldn't tell Sutton what had happened. She wasn't even sure she could say the words aloud, but more importantly, she couldn't distract Sutton from the game she was about to play.

"Go home and get some rest. I'll come see you after the game."

"You don't have to do that," Kenzie said. "In case I'm contagious."

"I'm not scared of your germs." Sutton started back toward the door but turned when Kenzie called her name.

"Go kick some ass."

"Always." Sutton winked and ran back into the stadium.

Kenzie's eyes filled with tears. She stared up at the cloudy sky and begged any force that might be listening to give her a sign and tell her what to do.

She took a long shower when she got home, the fifth in the last twenty-four hours, and was finally starting to feel clean again. She turned on *Bend It Like Beckham* and crawled under the covers. Between the sound of rain hitting her window and the comfort of her favorite childhood movie, Kenzie started to relax. She pulled up the hood of her sweatshirt to cover her wet bun and drew her thick comforter up to her chin. One of her favorite feelings in the summer was the chill of the air-conditioning in a house. She watched the opening scene of the movie and felt exactly the same rush she always did.

Kenzie knew she should be watching her team play, but she wanted to avoid any reminder of what had happened, and a broadcast of the game would likely show the faces on the sidelines. She already saw Jon's face when she closed her eyes, so she didn't need any help picturing him. She heard the doorbell ring and didn't budge. Her mom was home and could get the door. Her mother was squawking, which meant she was excited to see whoever was at the door.

Sutton pushed open her bedroom door a minute later, all smiles and wet hair. "How's my sick Chicken?" She had a bag in her hand, and Kenzie melted a little.

Kenzie paused the movie. "You shouldn't have come."

Sutton waved her off. She placed the bag on the bed and started going through its contents. "I brought you some essentials. Gatorade—blue, red, and yellow because I didn't know which your favorite was when you're sick. Mine is yellow, by the way." Sutton placed the bottles on the bed and pulled out a bag and a box next. "Classic Saltine squares and oyster crackers. I also brought bananas and applesauce."

Kenzie couldn't move. She couldn't speak. She stared at Sutton, the soft smile she wore and the pride in her eyes over the small buffet she'd just bestowed. "I love you," Kenzie said, unable to keep her eyes from tearing up. "I love you so much."

"Hey, hey." Sutton got under the covers next to Kenzie and pulled her into her body. "Everybody should be taken care of when they're sick."

Kenzie took consecutive deep breaths and focused on Sutton surrounding her. The strength and safety she felt in her arms was the first hint of normalcy she'd felt since the incident. "My mom was home," she said into Sutton's chest.

"It's not the same and you know it." Sutton pulled back Kenzie's hood and kissed the top of her head. "You smell nice."

"I've showered a hundred times."

"Showering when you're sick is invigorating. Oh, man, you're watching *Bend It Like Beckham*. I love this movie."

Kenzie felt Sutton reach for the remote but stopped her. "It's my favorite. I watch it when I'm sick or sad, and I definitely watch it if I'm having a really bad day."

"Showers and the best movie ever." Sutton pulled the bag she brought closer. "Now all you need is to pop some oyster crackers like they're popcorn, and you'll be on the mend in no time."

Kenzie couldn't look at Sutton for another second without telling her the truth. "I'm not sick," she said weakly.

Sutton rubbed circles on her back. "Maybe not anymore, but you have to take the time to heal."

"I wasn't ever sick, not like sickness sick." Kenzie felt Sutton pull away and she tightened her grip. She needed Sutton's physical presence to draw strength from. "Please don't go."

"I won't," Sutton said, renewing her tight hold on Kenzie. She rested her chin atop Kenzie's head. "What's going on?"

Kenzie took another deep breath and for the first time felt strong enough to tell someone what had happened. "I went to Tyler about my knee yesterday."

"Yeah, I was shocked they put you on the injured list. I thought you said everything checked out fine."

"I *am* fine. There's nothing wrong with my knee. Tyler sent me to Jon for my evaluation because he was busy." She took a steadying breath to settle the rolling of her stomach. "He checked my knee, but when his evaluation should've stopped, he proceeded to touch my thigh...and higher."

"Was your thigh bothering you?"

Kenzie let her silence answer for her.

Sutton's next words were quiet. "How much higher?"

"High enough to touch my underwear." Kenzie heard Sutton grind her teeth. "And then he..." Kenzie paused to breathe. "He touched himself and offered to take me to dinner to talk about *ways to exercise my legs*. When I said no, he threatened to give me a bad evaluation and cause me to miss games."

Sutton got out of bed and started to pace. "What exactly are you saying?"

Kenzie wouldn't look at her. She lay against her pillows and studied the paisley print of her comforter.

"Did you tell Tyler?"

Kenzie shook her head emphatically. "I came straight home."

Sutton sat on the edge of the bed and took Kenzie's hands in hers. "I'm so sorry, Kenzie. I feel like this is my fault. You told me he made you uncomfortable, and I didn't even consider something like this could happen. Your team should be a safe place, and I should protect you."

"You don't have to protect me—"

"And I didn't," Sutton said with a resigned sigh. "You have to go to Brett and demand to speak with Bob. This is something the general manager needs to take care of. Jon needs to be reported, fired, and arrested."

Kenzie's head started to spin. "I have no proof."

"You don't need proof. Brett and Bob will listen to you. They put the well-being of the team and its players ahead of anything else. Promise me you'll make a report."

Kenzie nodded. She was so tired. What she really wanted was to sleep for days, and after telling Sutton, she felt like maybe she'd be able to sleep. Kenzie panicked when Sutton stood again. "Where are you going?"

"To kill Jon."

"Sutton."

Sutton turned back to Kenzie, her face red with anger and sadness.

"Please come watch the movie with me. I need you to hold me. That's all I've needed since yesterday."

Sutton got back in bed and took care to pull up the covers around Kenzie. She tucked her in and held her close. Sutton held the small remote to Kenzie's Apple TV in her hand but didn't hit play. "I want to ask you something, but I don't want you to think I'm trying to make you feel guilty or anything."

Kenzie pressed her palm softly on Sutton's stomach, up high and just below her sternum. She could feel her heartbeat. This had become the most addictive feeling. Nothing compared to the steady calm of Sutton's heart. "Ask me."

"Why didn't you tell me last night?"

"I couldn't. I was processing it, and I knew Tara and Taylor were heading to your place. I didn't want to ruin the night."

"I love you, Kenzie, and that means more than a cheese platter and setting up our friends."

"I know that, and please believe me when I say nothing made sense to me after it happened. I couldn't rationalize my feelings or what to do. I was just sick and weak and sad. I was questioning everything, including what I did to deserve it."

"You did nothing."

"I must've led him on in some way," Kenzie said, her throat tightening with each word. "For some reason, he thought his actions were okay."

"Because he's a terrible person. You did absolutely nothing to deserve or welcome this. You are a victim, and I am so sorry this happened to you." Kenzie saw a teardrop fall on Sutton's shirt. She looked up to see Sutton's wet cheeks. "We'll make it right. I will do anything and give anything to ensure it."

"Out of the millions of thoughts that consumed me, one stood out amongst the rest as a solid truth."

"What's that?"

"I know I will overcome this."

"You will."

"Because I have you."

Sutton leaned in slowly, as if waiting for cues from Kenzie. The respect Sutton showed her made her fall even more deeply in love. They shared a soft kiss before finally turning on the movie.

She added Sutton to the list of her comforts. Her favorite movie was even more healing now, and the sound of rain against the glass windows even more soothing. The chill of the air conditioner was an even greater contrast to the warmth of Sutton's arms. Kenzie felt herself start to heal. She knew it would be a very long road, but those first few pieces falling back into place held a promise she'd thought impossible just one day earlier.

Chapter Thirty-Two

Sutton paced in front of the general manager's office. Kenzie had been in with Bob, Brett, and Tyler for almost an hour, and she was starting to grow anxious. She'd tried to go in with Kenzie, but Brett kindly told her she wasn't welcome. She even tried to play the team captain card, but Brett reminded her that role was mainly for the field, not for business matters. She would've had a few choice words for him, but she could see he felt bad for blocking her.

She pulled her phone out of her pocket and checked it for what felt like the hundredth time that hour. Her need for a distraction was so intense, she decided to read through the comments on her picture from that morning.

On the way to the Hurricanes' main office, she and Kenzie had stopped for breakfast at a quaint café which offered healthy food options. She snapped a picture of her espresso and avocado toast. For such an innocuous picture, the comments were ridiculous. Someone always had to announce when they were the first *Like* and comment. Some bordered on vulgar, many declared love, and a few hinted at her relationship with Kenzie. One begged for an update on *#FloShaw*, saying they were worried about the rumors.

Intrigued, Sutton pulled up Tumblr. Sure enough, many users were concerned. Rumors had been flying for over two weeks, pointing out the lack of content and pictures together. Sutton read an entire thread between multiple users arguing about national team members being in a relationship. Sutton was amazed. These people were more thorough and intense than the FBI when it came to digging for evidence. As soon as someone started to point out Sutton's average relationship lifespan, she exited the app and locked her phone screen.

The door to the main office swung open a minute later. Tyler walked out first and offered Sutton a friendly good-bye. Brett was next, his face impassive, but he wasn't her concern. Two minutes later Kenzie walked out and headed right to Sutton. They had discussed this moment earlier and decided to put professionalism before feelings. She knew Kenzie wanted to be held as much as she wanted to hold her. Sutton didn't ask a question until they were sitting in her Jeep.

"How did it go?"

Kenzie picked at the frayed knee of her tight jeans. "I don't know, actually. They told me they'd do an investigation."

"That's it?"

Kenzie shrugged and looked at Sutton with tired eyes. "They made me go over it again and again. Brett and Bob were both taking notes, and Bob did call his legal team while I was sitting there."

"Okay, that's a step in the right direction, but why do you look like you lost?"

"I'm not sure. Out of all three of them, Tyler was the only one who seemed bothered or surprised. He wanted to take full responsibility because he hired Jon. But then Bob said something that really bothered me."

"Bob isn't the most articulate guy."

"He told Tyler to wait and see if there's something to take responsibility for, like he didn't believe me."

Sutton bristled. It took all of her control to not get out of the car and march back into the building. "Let's see what they say after the investigation. The guy is guilty, we know it and Tyler believes it. They can't run a team where their players are at risk like this, and they can't expect you to keep showing up where your harasser is. I hope they at least suspend him for the duration of the investigation." Sutton started the ignition. She needed to get away from the stadium and bring Kenzie home where she could relax and feel safe again.

"I asked about that. He will be suspended without pay until the investigation is over, but I feel like they're just doing that to keep me from being distracted, and my performance from dropping."

"I'm just happy he's out for now. I would've attacked him on the spot."

"You sound very macho right now."

"It's not about being macho or butch or whatever you want to call it. It's about this anger I feel," Sutton said, bringing her fist to her diaphragm. "I can't take back what he did, but I could definitely make him regret it."

"Hopefully he'll pay for what he did *legally*, and I don't have to worry about you going to jail."

Sutton took a deep breath to calm herself down. She had been running through the incident over and over and all the ways she could've done something to prevent it, but that wasn't helping anyone. Especially not Kenzie.

"I'm sorry, baby, I'm making this about me again."

"Baby? That's new."

She took Kenzie's hand and kissed her knuckles. "It just sort of slipped out. I hope you don't mind."

"I do not mind at all. I am very much in favor of Sutton Flores calling me sweet, lovey pet names."

"Shnookums?"

"Love it."

"Sweetie?"

"So cute."

"Love?"

"Every minute of the day, please."

Sutton pursed her lips in thought. "Darling?"

"Old-time charming and gets my heart racing."

"Chicken?"

Kenzie laughed loudly. "Even that has grown on me, as much as I hate to admit it."

Sutton held on to the moment and cherished the look of genuine happiness on Kenzie's face. She knew the dark cloud wouldn't leave her for a while, but these minutes where her sunshine broke through were little gifts. She leaned across the console to kiss Kenzie, only to have her flinch and pull away when Sutton dropped her hand to her thigh.

"I'm sorry," Sutton said, pulling her hand away as quickly as if she had touched a glowing ember.

Kenzie's eyes were closed, and her breathing was rapid. "I should be the one apologizing."

"Absolutely not," Sutton said firmly. She continued driving and chose her next words carefully. "You went through something I can't even begin to understand. Whatever you need from me, I will give it to you." She took Kenzie's hand again and entwined their fingers.

Kenzie put her other hand over Sutton's and traced the tendons of her wrist. "Don't stop touching me, okay?"

Concern outweighed Sutton's willingness to accept Kenzie's request. "But what if I make you uncomfortable?"

"Then I'll say something. Sutton, one of my worries is that you'll look at me or treat me differently. I don't want anything to change between us. What Jon did has already changed so much of my life, my work, and the way I feel inside, but I need to know that you, that *we*, are the same."

Sutton heard and felt Kenzie's words. Instead of sounding like she was compromised because of what had happened, Kenzie sounded strong. "You got it, love bug."

Kenzie's smile was more blinding than the early afternoon sun.

❖

A full two weeks passed before any news came from management about the investigation into Jon's behavior. Kenzie got called to the main offices the day after the team returned from their away game against Kansas City, a game they lost.

"Kenzie," Bob said, greeting her loudly. He stood behind his small wooden desk and motioned for her to take a seat in front of him. Brett and Tyler were noticeably absent. "I hope you are well, even with yesterday's loss."

That depends on this meeting. Kenzie smiled stiffly. "I'm fine." She waved off his offer of water.

"I'm sure you have better things to do than sit here on your off day, so I'll cut right to the chase." He straightened his orange polo after sitting. The color was ugly with his pale complexion and salt-and-pepper hair. "After speaking with our legal team and with Jon, I'm sorry to say we don't have a case."

Kenzie could only blink as she tried to understand what he had just said. "Wha-what exactly do you mean?"

"There's no case against Jon."

"My case," Kenzie said, pointing to herself. "*My* case is against Jon."

"With no witnesses, it's his word against yours."

"And what exactly is Jon's word?"

"I shouldn't share with you as his accuser."

"Since when does the accused get more respect than the accuser?"

Kenzie slapped her palm on Bob's desk. "If you told him my side of the story, you at least owe me his."

Bob seemed thoughtful and steepled his fingers. After tapping them to his lips several times, he sighed. "He said that he examined your hamstring after feeling a hint of swelling at the back of your knee. When he said he was going to recommend you sit out for a couple of games to recover, you threatened him."

"*I* threatened *him*?"

"That's what he told us."

"I can't believe this." Kenzie stood. "Do *you* believe this?"

"It's not about what I believe, it's about what can be proven. Considering the circumstances and your status with the team, we can't write off the possibility you'd make poor decisions to protect your reputation."

Kenzie couldn't believe he kept a straight face as he fed her that line of bullshit. "Wow. And here I thought I was lucky to be drafted to this team." She marched out of his office, never turning back when he called her name or continued to talk. No words would make up for his lack of empathy and respect.

"Kenzie?" Sutton jumped up from where she was sitting and waiting. "Kenzie, what happened?"

Kenzie kept walking, exhausting her energy and trying to focus on not crying. She had done more than enough of that lately. "Jon is still employed because there's no evidence to support my story."

"What?"

Kenzie stopped suddenly and spun around. "And—get this—he had his own story to tell. Now Bob thinks I'm a manipulative rookie who'd threaten a staff member if they tried to make me sit out a game."

"Hold the fuck up."

"Don't make me repeat myself because I can't say it again."

"Bob is believing Jon's word over yours? A douche who's been with the team for a hot minute? Nope." Sutton turned around and started to march back to Bob's office.

Kenzie caught up with her and grabbed her arm. "Sutton, don't. It is what it is."

"No, it's not. I'm going in there for two reasons. Because this is my team, and I believe the Hurricanes, even as an organization, are better than this. I'm not going to sit back and let a skeeze stay employed and be handed the opportunity to molest players."

Kenzie flinched at her choice of words, and Sutton took a few breaths to calm down.

"The second reason is because I love you. You do not deserve the punishment of seeing his face every day you come to work, and I know how to make sure that doesn't happen." Sutton walked into Bob's office before Kenzie could stop her. "We need to talk," Sutton announced loudly. Bob looked up from his paperwork.

She stood beside Sutton, not wanting to look like she sent her girlfriend in to fight her battles for her.

"If you're here for the reason I think, I cannot openly discuss the case with you, Flores."

"I'm not looking to discuss anything. I'm here to tell you, you have a choice to make. You either start caring about your players and remove Jon from your staff, or make some phone calls to start up a trade."

"I hardly think sending Kenzie to another team is an appropriate solution," Bob said, scoffing at her.

"The trade will be for both of us."

Kenzie looked at Sutton in shock.

Bob tried his best to backpedal. "Let's talk about this."

"There's nothing to talk about. It's one or the other, and you have until we get back from national team camp to decide." Sutton nodded for Kenzie to follow her, and they left the office.

"Are you crazy?" Kenzie whispered harshly, gawking at Sutton the moment they were far enough from the office to not be heard.

"No, I'm very sane. He made choices that changed the fundamentals of the team I call home. If he's not willing to make the right decisions, the ones with his team's best interests at heart, then it's time for me to find another home team."

Kenzie was astounded. "You're not crazy, you're brave."

"No braver than you are. Now, let's get out of here. We have a trip to get ready for."

"I didn't get my call-up yet. How are you so sure I'm going to camp with you?"

"Weller would be insane not to call you up again."

"I'll probably have to stay here and be tortured by the wait."

"Check your phone."

Kenzie took her phone from Sutton, who'd kept it during her meeting with Bob, and right on the home screen was an alert. Coach Weller had called her and left a voicemail. "You saw this, didn't you?"

Sutton nodded.

Kenzie checked the message and inhaled deeply.

"You're going to be okay," Sutton said reassuringly. "*We're* going to be okay."

Despite the unexpected turn her afternoon took, Kenzie didn't let the negatives overshadow the potential of the future. She saw a light at the end of this very dark tunnel.

CHAPTER THIRTY-THREE

Sutton felt like she'd be smiling for the rest of her life. She had never felt so good after returning from training with the national team. As much as she loved representing her country, she normally returned home fatigued. But this time, she felt rejuvenated and hopeful because her life was going to change, and she embraced change. Regardless of the shitty circumstances leading her and Kenzie to this moment, she knew big things were coming.

"How was camp, bud?" Taylor dropped her gear next to Sutton's and slapped her on the back. "We missed you around here."

Sutton winced, not expecting the force behind Taylor's enthusiastic welcome. "Camp was good. What did I miss around here? Anything that would qualify as the *best*?" Sutton said, hinting at the few messages she had exchanged with Taylor about her blossoming relationship with Tara. She winked rapidly just to be obnoxious.

"Calm yourself. I swear, you turn back into a gossipy teenager the moment you find out someone is in a new relationship."

"So you're saying it *is* a relationship?"

Taylor glanced around the locker room before leaning closer to Sutton. "I'm saying Tara and I are exploring the option."

"So you're saying you're exploring each other?"

"I hate you so much sometimes." Taylor smiled at her. "But it's good. It's really good."

Sutton's desire to be immature melted away at the softness she saw written so plainly on Taylor's face. "I'm really happy for you, Taylor. You deserve to be happy, and I know for a fact Tara is a good person."

"She is. Speaking of reasons for our happiness, where's Kenzie?"

Sutton twisted her face up. "Kenzie didn't handle the travels as well as she usually does. She overslept this morning."

"Keeping her up too late, Flores?"

"No. I think she's nervous about coming back here." Sutton sat on a bench. The Hurricanes were doing fitness training, saving Sutton the time of changing her socks and shoes. She had some time to unload a few worries. "I hated not being able to room with her during camp. Every morning she'd be exhausted during breakfast. I can't wait for this to be over."

"You still won't tell me what happened?"

"It's Kenzie's story to tell, and now's just not a good time. I don't want to give anyone ammo against me or Kenzie."

"You know I won't say anything."

"I know. I trust you more than anyone, but we have to be careful. I'm already afraid Kenzie will be mistreated just for being in a relationship with me."

"You're actually scaring me, but I'll let it go for now. Just know you can talk to me. Kenzie, too, since she's basically an extension of you at this point."

Sutton laughed, and God, it felt good. "Everything will work out for the best. I know it."

"Flores." Brett's voice carried across the room. "My office. Now."

Sutton's positivity drained away instantly. The moment she stepped into his office, he motioned her to have a seat.

"I just got off the phone with Bob, and if I'm understanding things correctly, you gave him an ultimatum?"

Sutton gripped the plastic armrests of the cheap office chair. She'd expected the news to make its way to Brett well before this. "I did."

"You're one of the best players in the world," he said evenly, despite his scowl. "Named to FIFA's best eleven twice, and a nominee for player of the year."

Sutton had a hard time reading Brett's long pause that followed. "That's correct."

"And I have enough experience coaching you and knowing you as a person to feel confident in assuming you are not stupid."

"I am not, no."

"Then why the hell would you give an ultimatum to your boss?" Brett's voice was at a new volume, the tone unlike anything Sutton had heard on or off the field. "Do you think your accolades make you untouchable or above the chain of command here?"

"No."

"Could've fooled me."

"My *accolades* have nothing to do with my decision to do what's right. This entire situation is being mishandled, and one of our best players is being mistreated in the process."

"You can't put your personal feelings here."

"My personal feelings have very little to do with what I said and what I did. I'm the team captain, I'm a senior member of this team, and I am a woman who has the right to feel safe and protected when I show up to work. You know what Kenzie *doesn't* feel when she's here? Safe or protected, and now she doesn't feel respected."

"Kenzie should speak for herself."

"She tried, Brett." She stood up and paced. "My voice is louder, and I decided to use it as a way to protect everyone in that locker room," she said, pointing out the door. "Because clearly no one in management cares about them."

Brett sat back and rubbed at his temples. "There's procedures to follow."

"Procedures that protect the reputations of men and organizations."

"It's not about that."

"The hell it's not." Sutton wanted to pick up the chair and throw it. Her frustrations were mounting, and she needed to escape before she said things she'd regret. "I appreciate your concern. I'm heading back to the gym."

"I didn't call you in here to share my concern. I just got off the phone with Bob."

"Is he on his way?"

"No. He's currently giving Kenzie the information for her new team."

Sutton choked out a hollow laugh "Unbelievable. He'd rather trade us than believe Kenzie and follow through accordingly." Bob was not the man she thought she was playing for all along. "Where are we heading?"

"I don't have details of what team Kenzie is being traded to yet, but you're not going anywhere."

"Excuse me?"

"You're under contract, Sutton. You're legally bound to the Hurricanes for the remainder of the season. If you try to back out, you'll be penalized, and Bob will have no problem dragging it out and making it impossible for you to play for at least that long."

Sutton flexed her jaw and let out a slow breath. "I want to talk to Kenzie before anything is finalized."

"It's done. And I was told to tell you that if you make another ultimatum or cause any more problems, Bob will pull the trade, and Kenzie will have to choose between playing here or not playing in the league at all. And if he lets other managers know about her storytelling, no one will want her on their team anyway."

"So if I try to go, I'm damned, but if I stay, I can't open my mouth or else Kenzie will be punished? What about Jon working with these women every day? I can't say anything to them?" Flames of anger hurt Sutton's chest. The only relief she had was seeing the sadness on Brett's face as he delivered Bob's message. "You're not happy about this, are you?"

Brett shook his head. "I didn't want to lose Kenzie, and I don't think Bob is handling this the proper way, but my hands are tied."

Sutton felt nauseous with uncontrollable fury and anxiety. "I'm taking the rest of the day off, and you will not penalize me for it."

Brett hung his head. "Go. I'll see you tomorrow."

Sutton marched out of the office, slamming the door behind her as she went. She had no idea where to go next. She knew she had to talk to Kenzie, but what could she say? On the one hand was her loyalty to the woman she loved, and on the other was Kenzie's future in the sport she loved. Sutton was about to make a choice she never saw coming.

❖

Sutton was staring out into her backyard when Kenzie arrived. She listened to the listless cadence of Kenzie's footsteps as she walked through the house to the large sliders overlooking the patio. She had barely spoken to Kenzie since running from Brett's office earlier, and now the sun was setting on what was sure to be one of Sutton's worst days in recent years.

"Hey," Kenzie said sadly.

Sutton willed herself not to smile when she turned around. "How did your mom take the news?"

Kenzie folded her legs beneath her as she sat on a lounge chair. "She's sad. We were in a good place, but she understands why everything went this way. That was how we ended things, after a thirty-minute rant where the words *castration* and *murder* were overused."

"Can't really blame her." Sutton wanted to join Kenzie on the chair, but she had to keep her distance. She stayed put, leaning against the doorframe with her arms crossed. "What about your dad?"

"I didn't go into details with him. I told him management and I didn't agree on a few things, and I was being traded." Kenzie took off her sneakers and socks and flexed her toes. Sutton stared, soaking up the fleeting moment. "One thing they both agreed on was how happy they were to hear you'd be going to Kansas City with me, and my dad was especially happy it didn't push me to quit and give up my dreams."

This moment arrived sooner than Sutton had hoped, but she promised herself she'd tackle it right away. "About that…"

"I know going to play for our rivals isn't ideal, but as long as management is better to us there, that's all that matters to me. But I may throw the championship game if we play against the Hurricanes," Kenzie said with a smirk.

"I'm not going to Kansas City with you."

Kenzie looked at Sutton, studying her face with a concentrated frown. "Bob traded you to a different team?"

"No. I'm staying with the Hurricanes."

"I don't understand. Would he not trade you?"

"It was my choice." She looked just beyond Kenzie, to a row of small shrubs, and concentrated on not showing her true feelings on her face. "I'm not ready to leave my team, my home."

"What about everything you said?" Kenzie stood up and walked over to her. "What happened to wanting to do what's right?"

Sutton looked into Kenzie's eyes, the hazel brightening as they grew wet. She pressed her tongue to the roof of her mouth to control her rising emotion. When she knew she could, Sutton finally spoke. "I have to do what's right for me."

"And this is it?" Kenzie said.

Sutton nodded.

"I don't believe you."

"Come on, Kenzie, we both knew this wasn't going to last," Sutton said with as much strength as she could feign. "I couldn't pack up my life for something like this." A tear traveled down Kenzie's cheek. Sutton memorized the way it connected her freckles.

"You're lying. You have to be, because this isn't the person I fell in love with. *You* are not the person I fell in love with."

"I doubt I was ever that person. I would've liked things to last a little longer, but now we're at this fork in the road. I think it's time."

"How could you…? Everything you've said to me…"

"You're going to move on," Sutton said, ignoring the sting of the truth in her throat. "You'll be great in Kansas City. You'll flourish, and you'll thank me eventually."

Kenzie snorted. "Don't hold your breath." She sat heavily and pulled on her shoes. "You know, I really doubted Taylor, but I should've known your best friend would be right about you."

Sutton prepared herself for what Kenzie was about to say, for the pain she so rightly deserved. "Taylor knows me better than anyone."

"You're selfish, and you treat people like they're disposable." Kenzie started to leave but stopped just inside the doorway. She turned back to Sutton slowly. "Even before I met you, I thought you were incredible. I thought you were the kind of player, the kind of *person*, more women should look up to. I get why they say you should never meet your heroes."

"You were wrong to ever see me as a hero in the first place."

"And that's probably the only true thing you've ever said to me. Good-bye, Sutton."

Sutton fell into the lounge chair heavily and covered her face with her hands. She started to sob, shedding tears of mourning, love, and guilt. She cried until her throat hurt and her eyes burned. She cried until she felt like she said a proper good-bye to the love she had. She'd expected to feel better, maybe even a little proud of herself for making such a big sacrifice for someone she loved, but instead, she felt she had betrayed Kenzie and herself. The tears finally stopped once she accepted the end was inevitable, because Kenzie had always deserved better.

CHAPTER THIRTY-FOUR

Sutton loved autumn in the Northwest. The chill in the air was unique to the area, teasing of the winter to come but smelling of colorful leaves. Seattle's dampness and gloom matched her disposition well. In the two months since Kenzie's trade, Sutton had kept to herself. She even shut Taylor out, not wanting her melancholy to taint what was growing between her and Tara. She showed up and did her job, focusing solely on her teammates and pushing the Hurricanes to be more successful than ever. Only one game stood between them and the finals.

She sat in a quiet café off Main Street and people-watched. Much like every other day, her mind wandered to what Kenzie would've ordered or what she would have thought of the place. She knew Kenzie would have made fun of her for ordering two avocado toasts and an oatmeal. Sutton smiled sadly at her breakfast as the pang of heartbreak ebbed in her chest.

She'd expected to feel better as time passed, or at least come to terms with what she had done, maybe even start to believe it was the right thing. But she didn't. For the first time in her career, Sutton couldn't wait for the season to be over, to be a free agent and escape the villains behind the scenes. Maybe she'd even talk to Seattle's coach after the game and let her know she was interested in playing for the Mist next year. She sipped her latte. Sutton could make Seattle her new home. It didn't matter where she went because she'd always be missing Kenzie.

She checked her phone. Soon she'd have to head back to the hotel and get ready for the game. She'd lost the spark she used to feel before big games. Now it was about routine and performance, not drive and passion. She was going through the motions—something she'd never expected to happen with soccer.

She walked the streets of Seattle slowly, trying on the city like a new pair of shoes. Could she take this walk every day and never grow tired of it? Was Seattle the kind of city she'd beg her family to come visit? Would her dad approve of the team? She pulled her wool peacoat around her. October in Seattle felt more like a Jersey November.

Sutton wasn't at all surprised to find Taylor waiting for her in her hotel room. "What's up?" Even her tone was flat.

"Chiara let me in."

"How nice of her," she said. She paid more attention to the buttons on her jacket than she did Taylor.

Taylor looked up at Sutton from where she was seated on the end of her bed. "I just wanted to check on you. Today is a big game—"

"I am well aware."

Taylor let out a heavy breath. "What is up with you? You tell me you broke up with Kenzie *after* Brett makes an announcement that she was traded to Kansas City, and that's it. Now, you mope around, avoid me at all costs, and are so furious on the field I'm convinced you'll get a red card every game. Or kill someone."

"I'm going through some stuff, but I'm still here. I still show up and give one hundred percent."

"And that's it—you're just there. It's been two months, Sutton. We barely speak, and I only see you when we're working."

"That's all I'm capable of right now."

"I tried to be respectful and give you your space, but I'm over the bullshit. Tell me what happened. I need to figure out a way to help you."

Sutton scrubbed her face with her hands. "I can't. You can't."

"I told you—I'm over the bullshit."

Sutton looked Taylor in the eye. She had one game left, two if she was lucky, with New Jersey. Bob's threats could only last until the end of the season. He couldn't touch Sutton's career after that, and Kenzie should be in the clear, too. Maybe she could finally share a bit of her burden with Taylor. "Kansas City acquired Kenzie through a trade."

"And the sky is blue."

"Do you want me to tell you or no? Because I don't have to."

Taylor put up her palms. "I'm sorry. Sometimes I forget when to check my sarcasm. I want you to tell me. Please?"

"Smoke acquired Kenzie through a trade we started, and I was supposed to be part of it."

Taylor stared blankly before her face twisted in confusion. "Wait. You were going to be traded and you never told me?"

"Taylor—"

"What the fuck, Sutton? We've been friends for years and some girl comes along that suddenly you're ready to leave your team for?" Taylor stood and leveled Sutton with her stare. "I knew you were serious about her, but *Jesus*."

"We asked for the trade."

"Is that supposed to make me feel better?" Taylor started for the door. "Forget I asked. I don't need this before a big game."

"Jon touched her."

Taylor froze. "What do you mean?"

"He *touched* her, Taylor. An athletic trainer who was hired by our manager, someone we're supposed to trust, assaulted and threatened Kenzie." Sutton stared out the big windows in her room, the sun breaking through the fog.

"What did he do to her?"

"I can't even say it without wanting to throw up."

"Why didn't you tell us? He checks Tara after every game." She ran her hands through her short hair. "What the fuck is he still doing on our staff?"

Sutton looked at Taylor again, this time with wet eyes. "It's a he said–she said situation. They wouldn't fire him, and the best offer we could agree on was a trade. I had to go with her because I believe her. Without a doubt."

"And Bob doesn't." Taylor slammed her fist on the desk by the door. "We should all threaten to walk out."

Sutton shook her head.

"No? Why the fuck not?"

"Kenzie thinks I stayed with the Hurricanes because I didn't want to leave my team. She can't know the truth until after the season's over."

"What is the truth?"

"Bob threatened to sue me for breach of contract if I left the team."

"You may be breaking your contract, but he's also responsible for the safety of his team. Like not hiring dirtbags."

"He made it clear how deep his connections went. I couldn't cause any problems or push the trade issue without major consequences to my career, which is why I didn't tell you, either. But I promise you, Tara was safe the whole time. I've been watching Jon," Sutton said, wiping away a tear that managed to escape her lashes.

"You could've told me…"

"He threatened to destroy Kenzie's career, too, if I said anything. They'd blacklist her, Taylor. I couldn't let him do that." She sat on the bed and broke down. Every emotion she had muted over the past months finally got the best of her, coming to the surface as hot tears.

Taylor approached Sutton slowly and started to pat her back. Emotional displays didn't often happen between them. "Why didn't you tell Kenzie?"

"I couldn't handle the thought of her not playing because of me or sticking around here and having to see him. I needed to know she was as far away from him as possible. I pushed her to come forward about Jon, and I told her everything would be all right."

"What about playing overseas?"

"She wouldn't leave her dad." Sutton inhaled deeply and stood. Her sadness was turning back to anger. "She hates me now."

"For what it's worth, I don't think she hates you. She may hate what you've done, but not you."

"I hate me."

"You'll make it right."

"I don't know if I can, but what I do know is I have to make it right for the team, too."

"I'll help you with that."

"I can't drag you into this."

Taylor placed her hands on Sutton's shoulders. "You're my best friend. I'm in this with you. We should talk to Tyler. He works with Jon directly and probably knows better than anyone what can be done."

Sutton thought back to everything Kenzie had told her about the first meeting with Bob, Brett, and Tyler. "Kenzie said Tyler was the only one who seemed genuinely shaken and upset by her story. Tyler really cared about what she had gone through."

Taylor's lips tightened into a small smile. "I always liked Tyler. From the first day he was hired. He really cares about the players."

"You're right." Sutton pulled out her phone and sent Tyler a message. "I'll meet with him before the game."

"Before? Do you think that's smart? It's sort of a semifinal."

Sutton let out a quiet, genuine laugh. "I've played well this far—I doubt this meeting will change that. If anything, he'll piss me off enough to make me play harder or give me some relief so I'll be cooler on the field." She patted Taylor's shoulder before grabbing her bag and heading out of the room.

She rushed through the hotel, double-checking room numbers along the way. She pounded on Tyler's door and pushed her way in the moment he opened the door.

"Jesus, Sutton, I know you said it was urgent but calm down."

She was out of breath. "I'm sorry," she said, dropping her bag and rubbing her face. "Can we talk about Jon?"

His face fell. "We really shouldn't."

"What would it matter if we did? The season is almost over, and I can't handle the thought of this guy sticking with the team. What if he does this to another player? What if he already did? Can you live with that?" Sutton watched Tyler closely, but his expression never changed. "Wait. Do you not believe Kenzie?"

"I do, it's just…" Tyler looked like he felt completely helpless, a feeling Sutton knew very well.

"Bob threatened you, didn't he." Sutton read it all in his eyes. "I won't say anything, I promise. He threatened me, too."

"I heard about that. I'm so sorry, Sutton. I tried to talk to him after the meeting, but he wouldn't listen to me. He cares about the team's reputation more than anything. He doesn't want to be known as the team with the molester on it."

"Which wouldn't be a thing if he had fired Jon. Now we're *literally* the team with the molester."

"I know." Tyler shifted uncomfortably and scratched at his shaved head. "I've been subtly limiting Jon's duties ever since. I don't want him to do the same thing to another player."

"Kenzie knew something was off with him from the first time you sent him to check on her."

Tyler looked at her curiously. "What time?"

"Her shoulder. She fell pretty hard during our game against Orlando, and you sent Jon to make sure she was okay."

He shook his head. "I never sent Jon to check on any player one-on-one."

"Huh." Sutton placed her hands on her hips and looked up to the ceiling. So much could have been avoided if she had taken Kenzie's discomfort seriously right away and encouraged her to talk to Tyler then. "Are you sure you didn't?"

"I'm positive. I don't send anyone to check on players. You know the drill, Sutton. If I think anyone is injured and keeping it to themselves, I seek them out personally after practice or after a game. The other trainers aren't my messengers. I even keep notes of any injury that catches my eye."

Sutton felt like she was going to explode. "I thought it was weird, but who am I to question these things?" Now she regretted that she hadn't. "But at least now we have some kind of evidence."

"It's too late. The season's almost over, and Kenzie's already on another team. Bob got what he wanted."

"But Jon's still employed. We need to do the right thing—I promised Kenzie I would." Sutton thought of the other promises she'd broken and knew this was one she had to keep no matter what. "Let's just get through this game, and then we expose Jon, Bob, and every other scumbag who allowed this to happen. We owe this to the nineteen other players on this team. Are you with me?" Sutton extended her hand and smiled when Tyler took it immediately.

"What kind of person would I be if I wasn't?"

Sutton shook his hand and felt hopeful for the first time in months. She knew the process of uncovering the truth and exposing the team wouldn't be easy, but knowing she could help Kenzie heal made the challenge worth it. Even if she didn't get to experience doing the right thing with Kenzie at her side.

Chapter Thirty-Five

Kenzie thought about Sutton constantly, even when she demanded of herself to stop. She tried dating to rid herself of her desire and need for Sutton, but nothing worked. Kissing someone else reminded her of the way Sutton made her feel. She even sought out intimacy to wash her skin clean of Sutton's touch, but the moment someone else tried to touch her, she'd start to cry.

Everything was impossible to enjoy. She watched her teammates at the bar, celebrating their semifinal win. She had been with Kansas City for two months, but no one felt like a real friend. She missed Chiara and even Sherri. Marybeth was the only Kansas City player who even seemed interested in welcoming and getting to know her. But still, Kenzie couldn't bring herself to walk over and infiltrate the small group Marybeth was with. She remembered how long it took her to warm up to the Hurricanes. She had very little desire to warm up to the Smoke players, which meant it would take her forever to feel at home.

"Hey, Shaw," Lucy Aaron, the Smoke's captain, said as she stepped up to Kenzie. "What're you doing over here all by your lonesome? The party's over there." She pointed to the group currently entertained by Marybeth.

"I'm not much of a party person."

"I know we're not your team, but you should be celebrating anyway. The Hurricanes won their semifinal, and we won ours. That means you'd be heading to the finals no matter what. Cheers to that." Lucy held up her beer.

Kenzie touched her empty glass to Lucy's drink. "Cheers." She drank, hoping for a few drops of alcohol to drip from the melting ice. "This *is* my team—I'm just having a hard time adjusting."

Lucy leaned forward on the bar to get the bartender's attention.

Kenzie admired her lean back and the sliver of skin on display between her jeans and crop top. She turned back and handed Kenzie a shot. "Here's some really good whiskey to make up for what you missed in your glass."

Kenzie took the shot and threw it back, grimacing. She sucked in a breath to quell the fire in her throat.

Lucy looked only mildly uncomfortable after her shot. She ordered two more while Kenzie tried to shake off her reaction. "One more."

"I can't."

"You absolutely can." Lucy took Kenzie's hand and gripped the shot with it. "You don't have to, but I have a feeling you want to."

Kenzie liked how playful Lucy's eyes were. They sparkled and hinted at a happiness that ran deep. "You're right." She waited for Lucy, and they drank at the same time. This shot went down much smoother than the first. Kenzie only shuddered a little.

"We're all really happy to have you on our team, Kenzie. It was hard at first because of how sudden we traded Richards for you and the secrecy of it all, but we knew how good you were. You know what they say about a gift horse." Lucy laughed when Kenzie covered her mouth. "I should've said this two months sooner," Lucy said, looking a little ashamed. "Whatever you need to feel more at home with this team, tell me or tell the coach. We want you to be happy here."

"I really appreciate that. When I moved in with Katie and Jane, they said something pretty similar, even though I was the stranger coming out of nowhere."

"I'm happy to hear my players were nice to you." Lucy tapped her glass on the bar top and looked thoughtful. "So, what did happen with the Hurricanes?"

Kenzie opened her mouth, her tongue loose from the liquor and ready to spill secrets, but she caught herself at the last second. "It was a management issue. I'm just glad it was resolved as quickly as it was and in a way that was beneficial to me."

"And us. Want another?" Lucy said, pointing to the empty shot glass Kenzie rolled between her palms.

She studied Lucy's chiseled face and long black hair. Maybe she just had a thing for team captains. She wanted to laugh and yell at herself. She'd learned her lesson with Sutton. "Sure." The season was almost over, so her ban on drinking should be as well.

"One more and then you're coming over there with me."

Kenzie actually enjoyed the third shot and had no fear when she followed Lucy over to the rest of the team. She danced and drank some more, letting the alcohol break down the walls she'd so careful constructed around herself. She was grateful, because she really liked her new teammates. Marybeth kept everyone laughing well into the night, and Kenzie knew she wouldn't need to work out her abs anytime soon. She felt much more positive by the time she was ready to head home. She checked in with Jane and Katie before calling an Uber. They wanted to stay for a little longer, but Kenzie needed a tall glass of water and her bed before she started to get sloppy.

She had a text waiting for her when she looked at her phone. Clara had messaged her twenty minutes ago asking if she'd like to come over. Clara was tall and blond, with strong broad shoulders and a smile that could melt someone on the spot. But Kenzie couldn't force a spark for her.

She felt a flush of embarrassment when she recalled the last time she was with Clara, sitting on her couch watching an apocalyptic action movie. Clara was sweet and respectful, moving slowly and letting Kenzie approve or disapprove of her next move. Everything was going so well that Kenzie could even feel herself getting lost in the softness of Clara's lips, but then Sutton's face came to mind. And only then did Kenzie feel any real physical response to her date. She ran from Clara that night and never called her again.

When Kenzie first sought out physical connection after leaving New Jersey, she'd struggled with thoughts of Jon, picturing him when she closed her eyes, but eventually she had pushed his ghost out of her mind with the help of her therapist. Now she struggled to forget Sutton, and so much of her didn't want to let go.

The longer she stared at Clara's message and wondered how to respond, the angrier she got. Sutton shouldn't have this kind of power over her. Not anymore.

❖

A strange noise woke Sutton from her fitful sleep. She opened one eye first before blinking hard and opening both eyes wide. The moonlight streamed through the windows and painted bright shapes on her wall. She finally recognized the sound as her phone buzzing. Her heart sank when she saw Kenzie's name on her screen. She checked the time before answering. It would be close to two in the morning in

Missouri. She slid her thumb across the screen and put the phone to her ear.

"Hello?" she said, her voice raspy with sleep. No distinguishable sounds could be heard from the other side. "Kenzie?"

"I miss you." Kenzie's voice was low and broken.

The weight of Kenzie's words felt heavy in Sutton's chest. She couldn't breathe. She sat up. "Are you okay?"

"No." Kenzie exhaled. "Yes. I'm fine."

Sutton listened closely and could make out music and voices in the background. It sounded like Kenzie was at a party. Probably celebrating her team securing their spot in the finals. "Congratulations on the win."

"Looks like we'll be playing each other after all."

"Yeah. Looks like it." Sutton pressed the phone harder to her ear, desperate to hear anything that could clue her in to what Kenzie was doing or thinking.

"Imagine if I had been drafted to Kansas City first. Life would be so much easier. We'd just be two players on rival teams, and that'd be that. No history or mistakes made."

Sutton clamped her eyes shut. Hearing Kenzie refer to their relationship as a mistake reopened every wound that had barely scabbed over. "I'm glad that's not how it all went down."

Kenzie choked out a laugh. "Of course you're not, but that's not why I'm calling."

"Why *are* you calling me?" Sutton pulled the covers away from her bare legs. The anxiety of her late-night phone call made her hot.

"I don't really know."

Sutton picked up a detail in Kenzie's tone, something different but familiar. This tone was one she had only heard a few times before. "Have you been drinking?"

"It's a party, Sutton, what do you think?" Kenzie said harshly. "I'm sorry. I don't know why I'm calling you, I just…"

Sutton's mind raced. She shouldn't allow the call to go on. If Kenzie had been drinking, talking would lead to nothing more than rehashing the past when neither of them was at her best. She should tell Kenzie to head home, to be safe, and to rest. But her heart couldn't understand reason. Her heart demanded she hold tight to any connection she had.

"You just what?" Sutton held her breath.

"I miss you so fucking much."

Her heart broke a little more. "I miss you, too."

"No. You don't get to say that. You don't get to miss me because you did this."

"I know, and I'm sorry."

"Do you tell Richards how sorry you are? How much you miss me?"

Sutton shook her head, trying to clear the fog still lingering. "Richards?"

Kenzie made a disgusted sound into the phone. "I see the pictures. She's pretty and new. The perfect type for you to move on to."

Sutton had no clue how to tell Kenzie she couldn't possibly replace her. "I'm not moving on."

"You have no idea what it's like for me. You know I still feel you sometimes? God, I swear I can still taste you. I get so lonely, but it's like you're still there, haunting me from the inside out."

"Kenzie—"

"I just wanted you to know that. You broke me and ruined me for anyone else, but I'm going to get over it. I will."

Sutton's stomach twisted at the thought of Kenzie with someone else, no longer caring about emotional attachment and just searching for something physical. "I never meant for any of this to happen."

"I fell for your game, just like every other rookie before me." Kenzie's voice was instantly rid of any latent sadness. She was full of mirth. "I thought I was smarter than that. Anyway, I'm sorry for waking you. I should've never called." Kenzie disconnected the call.

Sutton stared at the picture of her and Kenzie on her phone screen for a moment before falling back on her pillow. She needed Kenzie to know the truth, but how was she ever going to explain this situation? How would she ever get Kenzie to believe and forgive her? She reminded herself she only had to make it to the end of the season. Then she could come clean to Kenzie and allow her to decide their future. Sutton's eyes flew open. The scariest thought was whether Kenzie could ever see a future for them again.

CHAPTER THIRTY-SIX

Kenzie braided her hair for the fourth time. The first three times became a mess halfway down when she got distracted. The Smoke's flight from Missouri to Texas was bumpy, and the drive from the airport to their hotel in Dallas was stifling thanks to a broken air-conditioning unit in the bus. Why did the final game have to be in Texas? The state was sweltering even in November.

Kenzie felt nervous, uncomfortable, and completely out of sorts. She even took an unusual number of spills during training because her own feet got in the way. She picked up her headphones from the hotel bed and checked her appearance one last time in the mirror. The Smoke's gray and violet colors complemented her pale complexion, a small sliver of positivity. She wasn't ready to play in her first final with Kansas City, but at least her braid finally looked good. This day was about fighting her way through the biggest game of the season. She had to forget about everything else. She had to leave her embarrassing phone call to Sutton behind, and she had to focus beyond the thought of seeing Sutton for the first time in months. But if she really thought that was true, she would've left her room ten minutes ago.

Her phone buzzed, and she frowned. She expected it to be a teammate telling her the bus was going to leave without her or a coach yelling at her for being a space cadet, but the name on the display shocked her. Tyler wanted to meet up with her in the lobby. She was curious what he wanted, but she didn't have time to find out. She messaged him back and explained she was short for time, but he insisted. They agreed to meet at the elevators and walk out together.

The elevator ride to the lobby was unbelievably long, but Kenzie chalked that up to her tardiness and nerves. The doors opened on Tyler pacing the sparkling floor of the hotel's lobby. He looked at her with a smile that faded quickly into sadness.

"Tyler, it's so good to see you." Kenzie walked up to him and gave him quick hug. Kansas City had a great training staff, but she would be lying if she said she didn't miss the supporting members of her former team.

"You, too, I just wish the circumstances were different. Let's walk. You can't miss your bus." He extended his arm toward the door.

Kenzie fell in stride as she walked and waited for him to talk. The walk wasn't long by any means, so she spurred him on. "What did you want to talk about?"

"I wanted to formally apologize to you."

"You don't owe me an apology."

"I do," he said, reaching for Kenzie's arm and stopping her before they stepped outside. "I believe you, and I did from day one. I should've stood up then and forced Bob to take the situation more seriously. I let you down."

"It's okay. I think everything worked out the way it was supposed to."

"Sutton told me about the first incident with Jon, and that's why we're pursuing a case against the team."

Kenzie stepped back in surprise. "You're what?"

Tyler looked at her oddly for a second. "Sutton didn't tell you?" He scratched his forehead when she shook her head. "I never sent Jon to check on you for your shoulder. I have proof of that in my injury journals. That was enough to file a new report against him and have him removed from the team. We're moving forward. I can't believe Sutton didn't tell you any of this."

Kenzie looked over Tyler's shoulder and lost herself to the revolving door's soothing whoosh. "Because it wouldn't change anything."

"What?"

"Nothing. Thank you for telling me. The safety of the team should be first."

"And we're hoping it'll go to the top. Bob has threatened his last player, and he's in for a rude awakening once Sutton's out of her contract and free to walk away, along with the three other players who'll be free agents. He single-handedly destroyed the Hurricanes."

Kenzie was overwhelmed with new information. She had a million questions for Tyler, but she had to get moving. "I appreciate and accept your apology, Tyler. I wish both you and Sutton the best of luck turning the Hurricanes back into the team she so obviously believes in."

"Like I said, she's gone after this game. She's been miserable since Bob forced her to stick around, but she'll be happy to be on the field with you again. Even if it is as rivals."

Kenzie struggled to keep her face neutral while her mind reeled with possibilities. "Thanks again."

"Good luck today." Tyler patted Kenzie's shoulder and walked out the door.

She stared at the bus idling outside the large glass doors. If Sutton had been threatened and forced to stay with the Hurricanes, then everything she told Kenzie when they broke up was a lie. Kenzie needed to know why. But first, she had to make it through ninety minutes of soccer against Sutton.

"Easy-peasy," she mumbled to herself as she put on her headphones. She stepped on the bus with only the game on her mind.

The ride to the stadium took fifteen minutes, so Kenzie listened to four and half of the most upbeat songs she had downloaded to her phone. She had to get in the zone. She had to pump herself up for the most intense game of her life. If she stepped out on the field with any other expectation, she could cause her team to lose. She was lucky enough to be a starter for the game, and she couldn't blow it.

When the bus came to a stop, everyone stood. The bus was oddly quiet, and the mood ebbed and buzzed with nervousness and excitement. Kenzie looked straight ahead to the front of the bus, and when the heads parted enough, she saw the Hurricanes' bus parked right by them. She said a silent prayer that the players had already stepped off and were long since changing in their locker room. She rolled her shoulders and waited her turn to walk off the bus.

She did a little hop when she came off the bottom step, proceeding toward the stadium. She heard the sound of another set of bus doors opening. She told herself to ignore it and kept putting one foot in front of the other. But something stronger than her own will screamed for her to turn around. She turned and felt her world tilt just enough to rebalance on its axis.

Sutton stood next to the bus, just looking in Kenzie's direction. Sutton's face held no hint of emotion, but she was watching Kenzie and never looked away.

Kenzie understood in that moment that the last two months they were apart meant nothing. It didn't break down what made them so special in the first place, and her love for Sutton had never faded.

The Smoke's coach, Diana, placed her hand on Kenzie's back and encouraged her to keep walking. "I'm sure this isn't easy for you, Shaw, but I need you to focus."

"You have my full attention, Coach, I promise. I want this win just as much as every other player on this team."

"I have no doubt you want to win. I also have no doubt you're going to be a key player in our win. When I got the call about the trade, I was surprised but very excited. Your talent didn't go unnoticed this season."

"Diana," Kenzie said, wanting to start the conversation but understanding she had to be cautious. "I want to ask you something about the trade, but I understand it's not really my place."

Diana tilted her head. "I can tell you anything I know. I'm actually surprised it took you this long to even mention it." She walked into the locker room and motioned for Kenzie to follow her into the small coach's office.

Kenzie had to laugh at that truth. She was sure her teammates asked way more questions during her first weeks with the Smoke than she'd said words. "Was Sutton Flores ever mentioned as part of the trade?"

"She was," Diana said, shaking her fist in frustration. "Bob called me and very vaguely explained the situation. I'm sorry, by the way." The sympathy in her eyes struck Kenzie as genuine. "I thought I struck gold. He knew we had a couple players who weren't locked in and wanted to know if we'd be willing to trade. What coach gets the most talented senior and rookie players dropped in their lap midway through the season? But it was too good to be true. He called me back the very next day and explained Sutton's contract was binding, and he refused to let her go."

"Did he say anything else about it?"

"No, and I didn't ask. I was still in a very good position acquiring you."

"This is so crazy."

Diana looked completely confused. "Kenzie, forgive me if I sound a bit harsh, but this happened months ago."

"I know, but I didn't question anything then. I was in a weird place after everything that happened, and I just wanted to get into the swing of things."

"And now?"

Kenzie looked into Diana's eyes and couldn't help but answer honestly. "Now I'm questioning everything."

"Except your place on this team."

Kenzie smiled. "Correct."

"And how we're going to win."

"No question there."

"Great. Now go suit up. This one won't be easy, but it'll definitely be fun."

Kenzie left the office with a new lightness accompanying her steps. For the first time in months, she felt like herself again, the Kenzie Shaw who played sharply and confidently. She was going to go out on the field and fight to win a title.

Chapter Thirty-Seven

Sutton twisted her foot into the turf and focused on the resistance of the ground beneath her cleat. The national anthem played, each note echoing loudly through the stadium. She had her eyes closed as she took in the moment, the start of the final game of the season, her final game with the Hurricanes. She had no idea what exactly was going to happen for her next, but as the last note of the song faded, she understood only this game mattered for now. Everything else in her life would wait for the next ninety minutes.

Following the song, she took off her training jacket on the sideline and waited for her teammates to surround her. She might not believe in the team's management anymore, but the heart and soul of the team was the group of women she played with, fought with, and bled with. She owed it to herself and to them to share one last speech.

"This season was full of surprises, and not all of them good," she said with her eyes on Brett. "We had ups and downs, and we lost someone I believe helped us become the team we are today." She shook off her emotion when Taylor placed her hand on her shoulder. "But regardless of circumstance, we are here—*I* am here—today, and I am so proud of all of you. We have ninety minutes standing between us and the trophy we should've won last year. How about we go out there and prove that we really are a force of nature?"

"Hell yes!" the team shouted in time.

"Who are we?"

The team answered immediately, "Hurricanes."

"Who are we?" Sutton said again, louder than the last time.

"Hurricanes!"

"Now let's go blow the Smoke away." Sutton put her hand out and everyone followed suit. "We're coming for the trophy, so let me hear *Take it back* on three. One…two…three."

"Take it back!"

Sutton jogged out to the middle of the field. She could swear her hand shook as she greeted the head referee and the opposing team's captain. Sutton had met Lucy on several occasions, always on the field and never truly friendly. She nodded to Lucy and waited for the coin toss. The Smoke would have possession of the ball first, but Sutton didn't mind. She'd rather her team start the second half with the ball, just in case the score wasn't in their favor by then. And if she remembered anything from last year's upset, losing to Kansas City could happen quickly.

She hustled toward the back line and called in her fellow defenders for a quick huddle. She checked over her shoulder to evaluate the Smoke's front line. Her stomach quivered at the sight of Kenzie stretching, but she wasn't sure if it was from nerves or sadness. She looked back to Tara and Erin.

"I'm sure this will come as no surprise, but we need to keep an eye on Shaw. We know how she plays, but we don't know how she plays with them. We've played the rest before, which means some of their moves should be old news. Let's be smart and play with our heads."

"Do you want any one of us specifically on Kenzie if she gets near our box?" Erin said.

Sutton nodded but didn't really have an answer. All she knew was she couldn't be the one to cover Kenzie directly. "Tara, keep your eye on Kenzie. Erin, if Tara is busy, then you're up. It looks like Aimee Brock is up top with her. She's good but not a threat." Sutton knew her time was running out, and she bumped her fist to her teammates'. "Department of defense has been called in."

They spread out into formation and stood tall. Sutton's back was rigid, and she held her hands in fists at her sides. She had to win this game, if not for proof that she hadn't wasted her time on a team that no longer cared, then to prove to Bob he had no idea what he was losing.

Adrenaline coursed through her as soon as the first whistle blew. She followed a well-known pattern as she ran, careful to stay with the ball but giving her midfielders enough space to do their job. Excitement buzzed all around when Taylor stripped the ball from a Smoke player and carried it well into Kansas City's territory. No one, not even Sutton, would have predicted the Hurricanes going in for the first scoring attempt of the game.

She stood on the midfield line and calculated each pass as Taylor, Chiara, and Sherri played a game of keep-away. But then Kenzie had the ball no less than ten feet in front of her. Sutton willed herself to only see the ball. She dropped back, moving backward and faster with each step while Kenzie dribbled at her.

Sutton stopped suddenly, and Kenzie stepped into her reach. Sutton took the ball with minimal contact. She pushed her shoulder into Kenzie's to gain leverage and she ran away with the ball, a hint of Kenzie's scent in her nose. Sutton fumbled a little, but she regained her composure and rocketed the ball to Chiara, who stood wide open on the opposite side of the field. The whistle blew, and an offside flag went up.

"Fuck," Sutton said under her breath. Nothing killed a team's momentum quite like an offside call. Sweat was already collecting on her brow, and she struggled to calm her breathing. Kansas City wasted no time putting the ball back into play, clearly not wanting to lose the buildup, either.

The next fifteen minutes passed in a blur. Sutton had to work double time in the Hurricanes' box when Tara focused on Kenzie. There seemed to be more Smoke players than Hurricanes surrounding her and that made Sutton nervous. The next play caught Sutton off guard, and she slid to block a low shot from ten yards outside the box. She cleared it, but the ball went out of bounds, giving Kansas City the first corner kick of the game.

Many players loved corner kicks because the chances of scoring ran high, but as a defender, Sutton hated them. She had seen one too many injuries happen as a result of a corner kick.

The player taking the kick placed the ball in the designated corner spot and took a few steps back. Her nerves were palpable, and Sutton shared the feeling. She took a deep breath, spared a glance to the jumble of players in the box, and raised her hand in the air.

The ball was soaring in the next second, nowhere near Sutton, who breathed a sigh of relief when Tara cleared it easily. She could hear Smoke fans in the crowd groan in disappointment. Sutton shouted for her team to spread out and press forward. She always felt silly yelling at them to do what they already knew to do, but it always just came out.

The game was scoreless by the end of the first half, and Sutton hated how uneventful the game had been. She felt like she was playing a regular season game against Kansas City. No spark or fireworks had ignited yet. She rushed into the locker room to hydrate and adjust her shin guards. She straightened out her uniform and sports bra, which had gotten bunched up after a particularly hard tackle.

Brett started to pump the team up, but Sutton couldn't care less what he had to say. As far as she was concerned, he was no longer her coach. How was he able to act like he cared about these athletes when he didn't try to protect them?

Tara knelt beside Sutton, tightening the laces of her boots. "How are you holding up?" Tara said, her voice husky from exertion.

"This has been a very strange game."

"Playing against Kenzie?"

"Well, yeah." Sutton ran her fingers through her hair, pushing it off her face and back in place. "But even the rhythm of the game is weird. Normally, Kansas City is more aggressive and offensive."

"Maybe they're having an off day."

"Maybe. Let's try to capitalize on it if they are."

"Aye-aye, Captain." Tara saluted her with a corny smile. "I'm going to miss you."

"We'll be on the national team together, and my home is still in New Jersey. Hell, you're dating my best friend. I'm not really going anywhere."

"But you won't be here doing what you do best, which is whipping us into shape when we need it."

Sutton helped Tara to her feet even though she didn't need it and placed her hand on her shoulder. "Either you or Taylor will be captain next season, and you're both very good at whipping."

Tara's eyes went wide. "Taylor told you about that?"

"Ew. Gross. No."

Tara's expression changed into a sly smile. "Just kidding."

Sutton threw back her head and laughed. "I'll miss you, too."

Taylor walked up to them, clapping her hands wildly. "Let's go win this."

The energy in the stadium was vastly different when the Hurricanes took the field. Sutton knew everyone felt it, from staff and players to fans. A light mist had started to fall, giving the stadium an eerie feel but cooling the players off. The next forty-five minutes were going to be a fight. A fight Sutton was ready for.

Brett made one substitution at halftime, bringing in the striker who'd replaced Kenzie. Maybelle Richards was fast and very talented with her feet, but she wasn't known for making good split-second decisions. Hopefully, the newbie was up for the challenge.

Sutton started moving the moment the whistle blew. She could feel the fatigue starting to set in. Her calves burned slightly, and her legs felt sluggish to start. But her body always knew when to tap into reserves and rebuild her speed. Both teams wasted some opportunities back to back, and the frustration grew on the field. The fog had turned into a steady drizzle, turning the turf slick and unreliable. Trying to read a ball as it bounced on a wet surface was impossible.

Sutton ran full speed to catch an opposing midfielder who had spent most of the game trying to set Kenzie up for a goal. Sutton couldn't allow that. She squared up and dug her foot forward for the ball. Her toe made some contact with the wet ball, but not much. She tried to go for it again, but the midfielder worked around her attempts and broke free. Sutton turned quickly, hoping for a second chance, but she ran into Lucy, the Smoke's captain, instead.

Lucy shoved Sutton with a shoulder to the chest, and Sutton fell to the ground in a breathless lump. She lay on her back on the wet turf, gasping for breath and in a slight daze, although she heard the whistle and the referee admonishing Lucy. She saw Lucy smiling smugly. Kenzie stood not too far from her captain, her eyes locked on Sutton's.

"Are you okay?" Maybelle said.

Sutton coughed and sat up. "Yeah, I'm fine." She gave the trainers on the sidelines a thumbs-up, letting them know she didn't need to be evaluated. Next thing she knew, Maybelle was kneeling next to her and placing her hand on her shoulder. "I'm really okay."

"Do you need help standing?"

"No," Sutton said. She rushed to her feet and brushed the dirt from her shorts, a useless endeavor thanks to the rain. "Thanks." She jogged away from Maybelle, feeling only slightly guilty for brushing her off. But they had a game to play and Kenzie was watching.

Sutton tried to find Kenzie again, but she had run off to fall back into another formation. Sutton took the ball from the ref with a grimace and placed it on the ground for her free kick. She kicked the ball amazingly well given the wet turf, and she watched it land right on target. She had two strikers open to receive, but much to her dismay, Kenzie was faster.

The play turned around so quickly, the Hurricanes couldn't react quickly enough. They were still on the wrong half of the field and couldn't gain enough speed to catch up. Kenzie faced Sheridan head-on and took her shot, the ball hitting the back of the net.

Sutton watched as Kansas City celebrated their goal. Kenzie grinned and laughed as Lucy lifted her into the air. Everyone cheered and the announcer's voice bellowed through the stadium. The moment was perfect and everything Kenzie deserved. Sutton knew she was smiling while the rest of her team was frowning.

No one scored another goal that night.

Chapter Thirty-Eight

Sutton paced outside the Kansas City locker room, grateful the rain had stopped. She could feel the sweat drying on her skin and her damp uniform clinging to her, making her itch. Every Smoke cheer from within hurt Sutton's ego, but her ego wasn't the priority anymore. Kenzie was.

All Sutton could think about was seeing Kenzie, congratulating her on her win and pouring her heart out to her. She was surprised she even made it through the game. Her heart leapt when she heard the door open, but it was just someone carrying equipment.

Sutton nodded and offered a small wave. "Are they coming out soon?"

"Should be," she said while dragging the equipment to the team bus.

Sutton rocked back on her heels and readjusted her own equipment bag. She'd spent less than ten minutes in her own locker room. She didn't need to grumble with her teammates about their loss. Sutton knew exactly why they didn't win. Aside from her own distraction, the team was missing one critical piece.

The locker room door opened again, and players started to file out. Sutton greeted everyone, knowing most of them on a fairly personal basis. One of the first things you learned as a professional was to leave the game on the field. Even if you just lost the championship. Again.

Sutton's courage for this confrontation faded the moment she saw Kenzie come through the door. Her cheeks were rosy, and her hair was wet and piled on her head. Sutton knew she'd smell of lavender shampoo and Irish Spring. But Kenzie stopped smiling the moment she saw Sutton waiting for her.

"I'll see you on the bus," Kenzie said to Lucy, who looked at Sutton pointedly.

Sutton offered Lucy a pleasant nod out of courtesy. The sun might have gone down, but the parking lot lighting was bright enough to highlight Kenzie's unimpressed look.

"What are you doing here?"

Sutton pulled at the strap of her bag nervously. "I just wanted a minute with you, face-to-face." When Kenzie said nothing, Sutton played it safe. "Congratulations."

"You played a very good game."

"We did, and we would've won if we still had you." Sutton couldn't help but flash Kenzie a charming smile. She was telling the truth and wanted Kenzie to know it.

Kenzie started to smile back before she forced it away. "I could've stayed," she said in a small voice.

Sutton shook her head. "No, you couldn't."

"Yes, I could have, and if you'd told me the truth, I would have."

Sutton flinched. "What do you mean?"

"Why didn't you tell me Bob wouldn't let you out of your contract and threatened you?"

"I...how did you know?"

"Tyler came to see me before the game. He apologized for not supporting me when I came forward, and he told me about the way Bob treated him. And you. Sutton, I would've stayed and faced Jon every day if it meant figuring this out with you."

"I am so sorry."

"Why didn't you tell me?"

She had no choice now but to tell Kenzie the whole story. "Because he threatened your career."

"I can handle myself, Sutton."

"I never doubted that. But he could've ended your career with the league, and I would've never forgiven myself if that had happened."

"I could've stayed with the Hurricanes and been with you when you took action against Jon and the team," Kenzie said, stepping up to her. She stopped a foot away. "Why did you lie and let me believe you didn't love me?"

Sutton closed her eyes. The pain she'd felt that day still lingered. "Because it came down to one choice. I could either live with a broken heart and make sure you got all the success you deserve, or put my feelings and my needs first."

"My heart was broken, too."

Sutton laughed as tears ran down her cheeks. "I had no doubt you'd find someone else and be happy. Maybe somebody more mature who'd act more like a partner, not a protector. Someone better for you than me, more deserving."

Kenzie reached out to grab the strap of Sutton's bag. She shook her until Sutton looked up. Somehow, Kenzie's smile was still bright. "There's no replacing you, not in this world or in my heart."

"I love you, Kenzie, and I have never stopped. Letting you go was the worst thing I could've ever done. Every day without you was miserable, like I was missing a piece of myself." She flinched when Kenzie ran the back of her fingers along her cheek. She didn't feel worthy of the gentle touch.

"You are the strongest, most loyal person I know. You love so strongly and fiercely, it's a little scary sometimes," Kenzie said with a giggle. "I guess that's why I believed you when you said you chose the team over me. I didn't think you could fit all of us in your heart."

Sutton shook her head frantically. "You are in my heart. You'll be there forever."

"Forever is a long time."

"Not long enough." Sutton took Kenzie's hand and held it to her chest. Just feeling her warm skin rejuvenated her spirit. "Can we do this? Can you forgive me, and can we please try again?"

"That depends."

Sutton's soaring heart sank. "On what?"

"Maybelle?"

"Nothing ever happened with Maybelle. We've barely even spoken since she joined the team."

Kenzie looked contemplative as she traced the neckline of Sutton's jersey with her fingertip. "Do you think you can handle being in a long-distance relationship during the season?"

"No." Sutton grabbed Kenzie's hand as soon as she started pulling away. "If you think I don't plan on talking to Diana about coming to Kansas City, you're crazy."

"You will?"

"I will."

"What if I'd ignored you when I came out of the locker room?"

"I guess I had really high hopes." She cupped Kenzie's cheek with her palm, reacquainting herself with how perfectly they fit together. "And I also figured if you turned me down, but I came to play on your team, I'd have an entire season to try to win you back."

Kenzie laughed loudly. "You would've been insufferable."

"Totally. Even during camp." Sutton followed the bow of Kenzie's upper lip with her thumb. "I love you so much."

"I love you, too. I missed you every single day."

"Hey, Shaw," Lucy called out from the bus. "This is a very cute display and all, but we have to get back to the hotel."

"I have to go," Kenzie said. "We're going to celebrate."

"Do you think they'd mind if I crashed the party?"

"I think they prefer to keep the guest list to just winners."

"Ouch."

"I'm moving home soon. We can get together and figure this all out."

"We'll talk before then?"

"A lot," Kenzie said, "but you'll have to call me because I deleted your number and all the messages you sent me after I called you last week."

Sutton let the amusement she felt overcome the pain. "That's pretty sad but an easy fix." She started to lean in.

Lucy interrupted them again. "Kenzie, come on."

"I'm sorry. I really have to go. To be continued?"

Sutton glared at the bus, and her imagination started to run wild. "You told me I ruined you for other people."

Kenzie groaned. "I don't want to talk about what I said. I want to forget that phone call ever happened."

"Was she one of those people?" She looked directly at Lucy.

"Who? Lucy? Oh God, no. She's the captain of my—" Kenzie pressed her lips together and shook her head.

Sutton smirked.

"Not my best argument."

"Nope."

Kenzie pointed to the bus. "I'm going to go."

"I'll see you soon, Chicken." Sutton felt Kenzie's broad smile in her heart. For what felt like the first time in months, Sutton took an easy breath.

She tried to turn and walk away, but Sutton couldn't bring herself to let Kenzie go. She had reconciled with Kenzie, her game was over, and she had plans to see Kenzie the moment they both landed at home. Then why did it feel like she was forgetting something?

She saw Kenzie waving to her from the window and started running toward the bus. Before the driver could pull away, she knocked on the door. As it swung open, she pushed her way in and climbed the few stairs. Kenzie stood in the aisle and looked at her like she was crazy, but Sutton didn't care. She walked up the aisle, ignoring the players asking questions or telling her they needed to go. Everyone could spare a minute for love.

"What are you doing?" Kenzie said.

"I, um…" Sutton looked around at the many sets of eyes staring at them. She reconsidered what she was actually doing. *Once you're in the box, you gotta take the shot.* "I couldn't let you go."

"I'll see you as soon as I'm back home."

"But I…" Sutton struggled with doing what was right and what was appropriate. She turned around to Diana. She needed the coach's permission. "Can I kiss her? Would that be okay? I don't want her to get in trouble or anything."

Diana put up her hand and started laughing. "You can kiss her."

"Can I kiss you?" Sutton said to Kenzie.

Kenzie looked at her with a goofy smile and nodded.

She stepped up to Kenzie, wrapped her arms around her waist, and drew her into her body. The moment she kissed Kenzie, Sutton truly began to heal. She was so lost in the way Kenzie ignited her every sense, that she almost didn't register the applause shaking the bus. They stepped apart and started to laugh.

Sutton licked her lips. "Now I can go."

"Like I'm going to just let you go after that," Kenzie said, running her hands along Sutton's shoulders. "I'm really happy right now."

"You have to. I have to go wallow with my team, and you have to celebrate with yours."

Kenzie wrapped her arms around Sutton and held her tight. She whispered in her ear, "You'll have to make it up to me."

"You can count on it."

"We'll just drive you back to the hotel, otherwise we'll be here all night," Diana said from her seat. "Driver, just go. I'll let Brett know."

Sutton held on to Kenzie while they swayed as the bus accelerated. She didn't care if she had to find her own way back to Jersey. All that mattered was already in her arms. They had a bright future ahead of them, and Sutton knew, without a doubt, that any day she spent by Kenzie's side would be a good one. With Kenzie, she knew that even on her worst days, she was still a winner.

EPILOGUE

I think we all knew this final was going to be between the United States and France. If you look back on the way these two teams played and developed over the past four years, the road led them to this moment."

"You say that with the kind of confidence many fans lacked after you retired last year."

Sutton smiled at the camera. "I believe in my team, Julie, and I never doubted they'd make it this far. With or without me."

"We still have a few minutes before the second half starts, and I'd like to ask you a little about your retirement."

Sutton chuckled at her fellow commentator. She had been given a heads-up that part of their halftime banter would be about her, but she didn't know exactly what direction Julie planned on going in. "There's more soccer involved than you're assuming, I'm sure."

Julie shuffled a few cards in her hands before looking back at the camera. "We started a conversation on Twitter before this World Cup started, and a lot of followers had one specific question for you."

"I'm not nervous at all."

Julie shot her a wink. "You retired one year before the World Cup, a mind-boggling decision to some."

"You included?"

Julie laughed. "Me included. You've said again and again that the timing was right, but a lot of people think it was very wrong. Tell us a little more about your decision."

"I think the game we're watching right now supports my decision completely. Professionally, I knew we had a solid roster and even more talented players waiting in the wings for their opportunity. I play with a lot of young players on my league team, Kansas City Smoke, that prove to me game after game that the future of the United States team is bright. And I was ready to focus on the next chapter of my life."

"I'm assuming you're talking about your recent nuptials to someone we've mentioned a time or two during the game."

"I married Kenzie Shaw last September, and every day with her has been better than the last." Sutton knew her smile was goofy and positively lovestruck, but she had given up trying to control herself when she talked about her wife. Off in the distance, she noticed a picture of them on a large monitor showing the live feed. Kenzie was stunning on their wedding day in her white dress. Her smile couldn't have been broader, and she looked absolutely angelic wearing a floral crown.

"How proud are you of her performance today?"

"Don't ask me that, Julie. I could go on all day, and halftime is almost over." They shared a knowing laugh. "I really couldn't be prouder. I was lucky enough to play by her side during one World Cup and an Olympic Games. Unfortunately, we didn't walk away from both victorious, but I am confident in predicting Kenzie will get her gold medal today."

"You're a newlywed, you also sat in on some coaching courses this year, and you've joined the ranks of commentators. What new roles can we expect from Sutton Flores in the next year or so?"

Sutton felt her face flush. She and Kenzie had recently discussed the way they wanted to handle sharing any big news. This particular scenario had come up. "Well, I'll be a mother by the end of the year, so that's a big title to add to the list."

Julie's mouth fell open in surprise. She practically squealed before congratulating Sutton.

"We're very excited, and so is our family. Especially my father-in-law who finally got over believing he was a bad luck charm and is in the crowd today. He's Kenzie's number one fan, and I know he'll feel the same about this baby." Sutton placed her hand on her small baby bump. "The future is bright, and it's all going to start with a win today."

Julie wiped a tear from under her eye. "Wow. Okay. Is there anything you want to say to Kenzie for when she inevitably goes back and watches this broadcast?"

Sutton looked directly at the camera lens. "We love you, Chicken," she said with a wink.

"We have five minutes before the teams take the field. What are your predictions for the second half?"

"I don't see many changes coming for the United States, which is smart. The starting eleven will come back out and play more. Tammy will want to hang on to those substitutes until later in this half if possible. France, on the other hand, being down by a point, will probably take a long look at their front line and consider putting in some fresh legs. If they're able to shake up their rhythm, they may be able to surprise the United States into giving up a point."

"I couldn't agree more. The second half of the World Cup final will kick off when we come back." Julie waited for the red light of the camera to shut off before turning to Sutton with wide eyes. "I'm so sorry for putting you on the spot like that."

Sutton waved her off. "Kenzie and I talked about the possibility of our personal life being brought up. We saw the Twitter conversation. What better way to announce we're having a baby than on national television during the World Cup?" She sat back for her makeup to be retouched quickly.

"For you two? I couldn't imagine anything better. Unless the United States takes home the trophy."

Sutton thanked the makeup artist before turning to look out on the field. The stadium was packed with cheering fans from all over the world. She could make out more than a few signs with Kenzie's name and number painted on them. The afternoon was warm by Australian standards, considering July was the heart of Melbourne's winter. The teams started to take the field. Sutton recognized Kenzie's hair immediately and she followed her wife with her eyes. Even though she was hundreds of feet away, she knew the moment Kenzie looked up to her booth and waved. Sutton waved back enthusiastically.

"Back on in thirty seconds," the camera operator said.

"Are you ready for what's next?" Julie said.

Sutton knew she was talking about the game, but she couldn't help but think beyond ninety minutes. At that moment, their baby moved. "More ready than I ever thought possible."

The whistle blew, and Sutton watched as Kenzie became a World Cup champion.

About the Author

M. Ullrich has always called New Jersey home and currently resides by the beach with her wife and boisterous feline children. After many years of regarding her writing as just a hobby, the gentle yet persistent words of encouragement from her wife pushed M. Ullrich to take a leap into the world of publishing. Much to her delight and amazement, that world embraced her back.

Although M. Ullrich may work full-time in the optical field, her favorite hours are the ones she spends writing and eating ridiculously large portions of breakfast foods for every meal. When her pen isn't furiously trying to capture her imagination (a rare occasion), she enjoys being a complete entertainer. Whether she's telling an elaborate story or a joke, or getting up in front of a crowd to sing and dance her way through her latest karaoke selection, M. Ullrich will do just about anything to make others smile. She also happens to be fluent in three languages: English, sarcasm, and TV/movie quotes.

Books Available From Bold Strokes Books

30 Dates in 30 Days by Elle Spencer. In this sophisticated contemporary romance, Veronica Welch is a busy lawyer who tries to find love the fast way—thirty dates in thirty days. (978-1-63555-498-4)

Finding Sky by Cass Sellars. Skylar Addison's search for a career intersects with her new boss's search for butterflies, but Skylar can't forgive Jess's intrusion into her life. Romance is the last thing they expect. (978-1-63555-521-9)

Hammers, Strings, and Beautiful Things by Morgan Lee Miller. While on tour with the biggest pop star in the world, rising musician Blair Bennett falls in love for the first time while coping with loss and depression. (978-1-63555-538-7)

Heart of a Killer by Yolanda Wallace. Contract killer Santana Masters's only interest is her next assignment—until a chance meeting with a beautiful stranger tempts her to change her ways. (978-1-63555-547-9)

Leading the Witness by Carsen Taite. When defense attorney Catherine Landauer reluctantly becomes the key witness in prosecutor Starr Rio's latest criminal trial, their hearts, careers, and lives may be at risk. (978-1-63555-512-7)

No Experience Required by Kimberly Cooper Griffin. Izzy Treadway has resigned herself to a life without romance because of her bipolar illness but wonders what she's gotten herself into when she agrees to write a book about love. (978-1-63555-561-5)

One Walk in Winter by Georgia Beers. Olivia Santini and Hayley Boyd Markham might be rivals at work, but they discover that lonely hearts often find company in the most unexpected of places. (978-1-63555-541-7)

The Inn at Netherfield Green by Aurora Rey. Advertising executive Lauren Montgomery and gin distiller Camden Crawley don't agree on anything except saving the Rose & Crown, the old English pub that's brought them together. (978-1-63555-445-8)

Top of Her Game by M. Ullrich. When it comes to life on the field and matters of the heart, losing isn't an option for pro athletes Kenzie Shaw and Sutton Flores. (978-1-63555-500-4)

Vanished by Eden Darry. First came the storm, and then the blinding white light that made everyone in town disappear. Another storm is coming, and Ellery and Loveday must find the chosen one or they won't survive. (978-1-63555-437-3)

All She Wants by Larkin Rose. Marci Jones and Tessa Dalton get more than they bargained for when their plans for a one-night stand turn into an opportunity for love. (978-1-63555-476-2)

Beautiful Accidents by Erin Zak. Stevie Adams doesn't believe in fate, not after losing her parents in a car crash. But she's about to discover that sometimes the best things in life happen purely by accident. (978-1-63555-497-7)

Before Now by Joy Argento. The instant Delaney Peyton and Jade Taylor meet, they sense a connection neither can explain. Can they overcome a betrayal that spans the centuries to reignite a love that can't be broken? (978-1-63555-525-7)

Breathe by Cari Hunter. Paramedic Jemima Pardon's chronic bad luck seems to be improving when she meets police officer Rosie Jones. But they face a battle to survive before they can find love. (978-1-63555-523-3)

Double-Crossed by Ali Vali. Hired thief and killer Reed Gable finds something in her scope that will change her life forever when she gets a contract to end casino accountant Brinley Myers's life. (978-1-63555-302-4)

False Horizons by CJ Birch. Jordan and Ash struggle with different views on the alien agenda and must find their way back to each other before they're swallowed up by a centuries-old war. Third in the New Horizons series. (978-1-63555-519-6)

Legacy by Charlotte Greene. In this paranormal mystery, five women hike to a remote cabin deep inside a national park—and unsettling events suggest that they should have stayed home. (978-1-63555-490-8)

Somewhere Along the Way by Kathleen Knowles. When Maxine Cooper moves to San Francisco during the summer of 1981, she learns that wherever you run, you cannot escape yourself. (978-1-63555-383-3)

Blood of the Pack by Jenny Frame. When Alpha of the Scottish pack Kenrick Wulver visits the Wolfgangs, she falls for Zaria Lupa, a wolf on the run. (978-1-63555-431-1)

Cause of Death by Sheri Lewis Wohl. Medical student Vi Akiak and K9 Search and Rescue officer Kate Renard must work together to find a killer before they end up the next targets. In the race for survival, they discover that love may be the biggest risk of all. (978-1-63555-441-0)

Chasing Sunset by Missouri Vaun. Hijinks and mishaps ensue as Iris and Finn set off on a road trip adventure, chasing the sunset, and falling in love along the way. (978-1-63555-454-0)

Double Down by MB Austin. When an unlikely friendship with Spanish pop star Erlea turns deeper, Celeste, in-house physician for the hotel hosting Erlea's show, has a choice to make—run or double down on love. (978-1-63555-423-6)

Party of Three by Sandy Lowe. Three friends are in for a wild night at billionaire heiress Eleanor McGregor's twenty-fifth birthday party. Love, lust, and doing the right thing, even when it hurts, turn the evening into one that will change their lives forever. (978-1-63555-246-1)

Sit. Stay. Love. by Karis Walsh. City girl Alana Brendt and country vet Tegan Evans both know they don't belong together. Only problem is, they're falling in love. (978-1-63555-439-7)

Where the Lies Hide by Renee Roman. As P.I. Camdyn Stark gets closer to solving the case, will her dark secrets and the lies she's buried jeopardize her future with the quietly beautiful Sarah Peters? (978-1-63555-371-0)

Beautiful Dreamer by Melissa Brayden. With love on the line, can Devyn Winters find it in her heart to stay in the small town of Dreamer's Bay, the one place she swore she'd never remain? (978-1-63555-305-5)

Create a Life to Love by Erin Zak. When sixteen-year-old Beth shows up at her birth mother's door, three lives will change forever. (978-1-63555-425-0)

Deadeye by Meredith Doench. Stranded while hunting the serial predator Deadeye, Special Agent Luce Hansen fights for survival while her lover, forensic pathologist Harper Bennett, hunts for clues to Hansen's disappearance along the killer's trail. (978-1-63555-253-9)

Endangered by Michelle Larkin. Shapeshifters Officer Aspen Wolfe and Dr. Tora Madigan fight their growing attraction as they work together to destroy a secret government agency that exterminates their kind. (978-1-63555-377-2)

Incognito by VK Powell. The only thing Evan Spears is focused on is capturing a fleeing murder suspect until wild card Frankie Strong is added to her team and causes chaos on and off the job. (978-1-63555-389-5)

Insult to Injury by Gun Brooke. After losing everything, Gail Owen withdraws to her old farmhouse and finds a destitute young woman, Romi Shepherd, living in a secret room. (978-1-63555-323-9)

Just One Moment by Dena Blake. If you were given the chance to have the love of your life back, could you ignore everything that went wrong and start over again? (978-1-63555-387-1)

Scene of the Crime by MJ Williamz. Cullen Mathew finds herself caught between the woman she thinks she loves but can no longer trust and a beautiful detective she can't stop thinking about who will stop at nothing to find the truth. (978-1-63555-405-2)

Fear of Falling by Georgia Beers. Singer Sophie James is ready to shake up her career, but her new manager, the gorgeous Dana Landon, has other ideas. (978-1-63555-443-4)

Daughter of No One by Sam Ledel. When their worlds are threatened, a princess and a village outcast must overcome their differences and embrace a budding attraction if they want to survive. (978-1-63555-427-4)